ROSE

Rami Ungar

To Shawn,
Happy reading &
pleasant nightmares.

[signature]

Rami Ungar
Visit me at www.castrumpress.com/authors/rami-ungar

Print Edition:
Printed in the United Kingdom

First Printing: June 2019
Castrum Press

ISBN-13 978-1-9123274-3-0

CONTENTS

ACKNOWLEDGMENTS 5

Chapter One 9

Chapter TWO...18

Chapter Three 25

Chapter Four 32

Chapter Five... 36

Chapter Six...44

Chapter Seven 49

Chapter Eight...55

Chapter Nine 60

Chapter Ten 69

Chapter Eleven...75

Chapter Twelve 80

Chapter Thirteen 89

Chapter Fourteen... 96

Chapter FiFteen 101

Chapter Sixteen 109

Chapter Seventeen 113

Chapter Eighteen..121

Chapter Nineteen 127

Chapter Twenty 132

About The Author..137

Books by Castrum Press 138

The Scalpel...139

1. Rig 141

One... 141

Two 157

Rami Ungar

ACKNOWLEDGMENTS

WHOEVER SAID WRITING IS A SOLITARY act needs a punch in the gut.

I say this because I've been in the game long enough to know that, while the actual writing of the story is done in front alone in front of a journal, typewriter or computer, getting the story to be halfway decent is the result of multiple hands.

Now, I can't possibly name all the people who helped me get to this point. I'm pretty sure that would be the length of a book in and of itself and you and I have no time for that. But I can give credit where credit is due to the most important people who, to use my pun from the Dedication, helped this novel grow from a seedling of an idea into a fully blossomed book.

Firstly, thanks to my old Science Fiction and Fantasy teacher at Ohio State, Maura Heaphy, in whose class I first came up with Rose Taggert and her unique, Kafka-esque predicament. A thank you as well to Manuel Luis Martinez, Paul Camper, Maura again, Dr. Douglas Back, Joleene Naylor and others for reading early drafts of the story and giving me pointers to separate bad ideas from good.

Thanks to Matt Williams, who introduced me to Paul and the team at Castrum Press. And thanks to Paul and the team at Castrum Press for giving me further guidance to fix up this book. Thanks to The Gilded Quill for the gorgeous artwork on the cover.

A merci beaucoup to Darrell Estes for helping me with French when the novel called for French translations and transliterations, a dank je to both Mau VanDuren and Lenore Hart Poyer with the Dutch for when I changed French to Dutch and an arigato to Yuko Kuwai for the Middle Late Japanese.

Thanks to my friends and family, who have always believed in me. Thanks to the Overarching Entity whom I identify as Hashem, who has answered my prayers for years. Thanks to the many writers and creators and readers who have encouraged my twisted ideas of what might make for fun literature.

And thank you, reader. Whether you be a long-time Follower of Fear or this is our first-time meeting, thanks for reading. This book would be some processed pieces of tree or a data file on a server without you and I'm glad you decided to check out Rose.

I look forward to meeting you all in the next story, whatever that may be. Until then, pleasant nightmares!

Rami Ungar

To the many people who helped this novel sprout from a seedling of an idea, cultivated it with enthusiasm and feedback, pruned out the many issues it had and helped it blossom it into a published book.
You guys are true gardeners of the imagination.

Rami Ungar

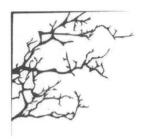

CHAPTER ONE

Okay, this is weird. Where the fuck am I?

I look around. I'm surrounded by a sea of vegetation: flowers and shrubs in hundreds of varieties, sitting in pots and trays atop a grid of workbenches. Surrounding the workbenches is a ring of trees that tower over everything, their upward growth halted by a glass ceiling. A literal glass ceiling, not the one taught in my classes. Past the trees I spy more glass, through which nothing can be glimpsed but total darkness.

I'm in a greenhouse. Why am I waking up in a greenhouse? I try to think back but I can't remember anything about how I fell asleep. In fact, I can't remember how I got to the greenhouse in the first place, or where this greenhouse is located. Am I supposed to be here? If so, why?

The questions make the pounding in head hurt worse. I force my thoughts to quiet long enough for the pain to subside to a dull throb. Able to think again, I try to remember what I was doing before I found myself here. Nothing comes to me.

Okay, no problem. What's the last thing I do remember?

Walking home. Yeah, I was heading home after meeting with my advisor. I had my textbooks and lesson plan for the coming semester in my bag. I crossed the street, turned the corner at Potbelly's and approached my— What kind of home do I live in? I strain but there's a gray fog obscuring my memories and the word for the kind of building I live in is missing.

I should know this. It's an everyday word! I push but the gray fog doesn't lift and the word doesn't come.

I skip forward to the inside of the building but that's also awash with gray.

Concerned, I rewind and get as far as the building where my department is housed but I can't remember the name of the building.

That can't be. I've been taking classes there for—I can't remember how long I've been taking classes there, at least four years, because I was accepted into the graduate program.

The exact number of years eludes me, as does the building's layout, the people in my program, my teachers and my advisor. It's all gone. I can't recall any of the classes or projects I've done past undergrad, though somehow, I do recall the information I've learned since.

My breathing quickens and I put a hand over my chest. Why can't I remember anything?

Okay, slow down. What do I remember? Let's see, my name is Rose Taggert. Last I checked I was twenty-one years old and I'm a...sociology grad. Yeah, I'm a sociology grad specializing in criminology. And I remember the stuff I've been learning in my classes; statistics, theories and social constructs, plus the work I was doing on gun violence. I'm a graduate at The Ohio State University, the second in my family to attend this university.

I also have two sisters, Hope and Madeleine and a brother, Brian. Brian and Hope are older than me and Maddy is younger. Hope is my other sibling to go to OSU, while Brian betrayed all that was holy and went up north to the University of Michigan. Maddy's in middle school. My parents are Roger and Barbara Taggert. My dad is a—

I can't remember what my parents do, which is insane because it's why I've had to work to attend college. Why can't I remember any of this? What's happened to me? I must find someone who can explain to me what's going on. A doctor preferably, or the greenhouse caretaker.

I slide off the table I'm lying on. As I do, two things come to my attention: I'm wearing a pink, strapless dress, which I can tell at a glance costs more than I'm used to spending on clothes. The other is the dress and table are covered in roses, red, pink and yellow ones with long, thorny stems, some of which fall to the ground as I swing my legs off the table. I bend to pick one up, careful not to prick myself on a thorn, rolling the blossom between my fingers, admiring the beautiful pink color and the soft velvet sensation of the petals. I normally don't care for roses—too many people have made jokes about my name for me to like them—but right now I'm curious. Who sees a sleeping woman in a dress and thinks, sure, let's put roses on her?

Abruptly, the rose dies in my hand: the pink fleshy petals turn black and crinkly, while the stalk becomes brown and brittle. I drop the rose and stand, alarmed. On the workbench and on the ground, roses wilt and die before my very eyes. What the hell?

As the flowers die, my eyes light on something lying at the foot of the workbench that's not a rose. I lean forward to take a closer look, only to jump back in horror. Lying in a pool of its own blood is a large brown cat, its stomach slit down the middle, its intestines hanging out like the contents of some grotesque piñata. The cat's face points in my direction, frozen in an eternal expression of surprise, as if it too can't understand what has happened to it.

My hands fly to my mouth, my heart pounds against my chest and my stomach heaves. I step back, tripping on the hem of my dress, falling onto my back. I cry out, my stomach gives another tremendous heave. Dead roses crackle underneath me as I heave myself onto all fours, my red hair tumbling past my shoulders. I wait, feeling something moving up my esophagus. Oh God, I'm going to be sick. I'm so going to be sick.

Something's wrong. It doesn't feel like normal nausea. It feels like...like snakes are moving through my chest and into my neck, around my esophagus rather than inside it.

This isn't vomit. It's...things...creatures, long, round and snakelike, dancing underneath my skin. Images of thin, black serpents moving around my trachea flash through my mind and panic rises. What if they bite and poison me with venom? Or strangle me from within?

My hands dart to my neck, though I'm not sure if I'm figuring out what's under my skin or trying to claw out whatever's moving around inside of me. The things in my neck zoom past my hands, twisting around my windpipe, cutting off the flow of oxygen to my lungs. I open my mouth to scream but nothing comes out except a reedy whisper. The things in my neck are pushing outwards at the skin of my neck, sharp tips boring through like tiny drills. There's eight in total, the points where they push form a ring around the circumference of my neck, like a deep-tissue choker of pain.

My chest burns. My brain screams. My strength is fading. Darkness creeps into my vision. I'm not going to make it; I'm not going to survive. I won't find out what's happened to me—

The things in my neck burst free, long and green and snakelike, each about two or three feet long. They swish whip-like through the air, blood flying off them, splattering plants and tables. The pressure on my windpipe vanishes and I suck in a deep breath before exhaling a pained scream. God, it feels like I've been stabbed eight times in the neck, only whatever stabbed me came from inside. Words like freaky and unreal don't begin to cover this situation.

The whips stop swishing and hang still in the air, furnishing me a moment to think of a real name for them. Tentacles, I decide. They are tentacles. Like an octopus or a squid. Though, why are they coming out of me?

Before I can find an answer, a pair of tentacles lash out and wrap around the leg of a workbench. Another pair wrap around the leg of the workbench opposite, the last two pairs grab the ground below and the top of the workbenches above. Then the first pair unwrap and lunge for the leg off the one in front of me, wrap around the leg and drag me forward. The second pair do the same with the workbenches on their side and pull me forward like a ragdoll.

I cry out as the tentacles work in unison, they crawl forward like a strange insect and carry me along on a frightening ride. I futilely grab at something, anything, to cling to but my frantic fingers repeatedly miss their purchase. My third attempt leaves my hands raw. I stop and allow myself to be carried, all the while, sobbing with pain and terror.

The tentacles clear the workbenches and climb a short stone wall onto the soil bed where the trees bask. The tentacles stop and I lay, half on, half off, the soil bed, while they hover, smelling the air like dogs. Before I can wonder what they hope to inhale, the tentacles crash into the soil, plunging deeply until only a few inches, close to my neck, remain visible. The tentacles begin to pulse. Spasms wracked them from deep within the earth, up their length and into me. I shudder and try to pull away but the tentacles reclaim me, burrow deeper and pin me against the dirt.

I can't escape.

Tears make rivers down my cheeks. I'm scared and bewildered. My neck thrums in agony. "What's happening to me?" I whisper aloud to the greenhouse.

"What the hell?" A voice replies. "Rose! What happened?"

I force my head up from the dirt and spot a figure standing in a doorway I hadn't noticed before. He wears a blue sweatshirt and brown jeans. An angular face regards me from underneath unkempt black hair and wire-rimmed glasses. The man is kind of handsome, with a gentle, boyish charm. There is something small, brown and rectangular tucked under his arm but I can't quite make out what it is.

He stares at me and I stare back. I open my mouth to ask who he is but I can't find my voice. The man puts whatever he's holding down on a workbench and rushes to my side. "Are you all right, Rose?" He crouches down beside me placing a hand on my shoulder.

I open and close my mouth several times before I'm able to get anything out. "What?" I croak.

"Rose," the man repeats, eyeing me with concern. "Can you move? Tell me what happened."

It takes a moment for my mind to process the obvious: this guy, whoever he is, knows me. I don't recognize him but considering how much trouble I'm having remembering, that probably doesn't mean much. Perhaps he can tell me what has happened to me, at least the bits that led to here and now.

"What the hell are these?" the man wonders aloud, touching one of the tentacles with the tip of his finger. It pulsates angrily, causing him to jerk his hand away. When nothing else happens, he gingerly touches the tentacle again. There's another angry pulse but that's all. The man then examines a few others, receiving the same reaction each time. He glances from the tentacles to me and then back to the tentacles. Looking at me once more before something draws his slowly widening eyes downward towards my hands. "What the—?"

I follow his gaze and a small, disbelieving gasp escapes me. My nails are turning a deep shade of pink as I watch them, while the skin around the nail slowly turns light green, the skin tingling as its color changes. The green color spreads steadily up my hand.

"What's happening?" I shriek, alarmed.

The man doesn't answer. He just watches with me as the green color spreads, crawling up my arms and onto my shoulders. My feet tingle and green moves out of my heels, up my ankles and under my dress. It feels like an army of ants is marching up my body. Soon everything below my shoulders feels abuzz with electricity until, inexorably, the green coloring ascends my neck, unfurling over my face. I blink, my eyes itching and I know, without seeing, that they have turned green too.

My hair tingles, and a moment later the tresses on my shoulders turn bright pink.

For a moment, nothing else happens. The tingling stops, leaving me numb. I wonder if whatever's going on is over. Seconds pass in which neither I nor the young man move or speak. I'm not even sure if we're breathing. Maybe he's just as scared as I am?

At least I'm not the only one who's lost in this insanity.

I exhale. Beside me, the young man lets out a sigh of relief. "Shit. Is that the end of it?"

"I don't know," I reply. "I—aaaah!"

I scream as pain flares beneath my scalp. Something presses against the top of my skull, expanding like a million tiny balloons under the skin. The young man jumps back, staring in horror as I writhe.

"What's wrong?" he shouts.

I open my mouth to answer but all that comes out is another scream. The skin on my scalp rips asunder. An image of thick tentacles flits through my mind and I reach for my head to see if anything is drilling out like before. Instead, six round spheres burst from my skull in a horizontal line on top of my head, forming a headband of pain in my hair. With a squelch they shift, as if settling into place and go still.

For what feels like an eternity, existence is pain. As the pain subsides to a thumping ache, my fingers examine the spheres tentatively, afraid that any disturbance may cause more suffering. Soft, fleshy, ovular. Six of them, all in a row. Blood dribbles and bubbles out, warm and sticky, from where they burst through. They feel like—

"Rosebuds," says the young man. "You grew little fucking rosebuds!"

Rosebuds? The word ricochets through my head. I have rosebuds on top of my head?

"What's happening to me?" I demand a fresh wave of tears slide out of my eyes.

"I-I don't know," the young man admits, scratching his own head. "I've never seen anything like...I mean, I didn't know...I just thought...it wasn't supposed to go like this."

It takes me a moment for what he said to register through the pain and then my eyes lock on his. "What?"

The young man realizes what he said and hurriedly averts his eyes. I frown. He's hiding something. A thousand questions rise in me, clamoring to be asked. How does he know me? Is this his greenhouse? Why am I here? I find my voice and ask the most prevalent question on my mind. "Who are you?"

The young man turns wide eyes to me, as if he can't believe I don't know who he is. "You don't recognize me?" When I shake my head, the young man continues to stare, until his eyebrows arch upward. "You seemed surprised when I said your name," he says slowly.

I nod my head, though I feel like he's talking more to himself than to me. The young man strokes his chin. "Rose, what do you remember before waking up?"

"I don't know." I say, slowly shaking my head. "Some things I can remember clearly but a lot of other stuff...it's like it's hiding in a grey fog. Especially stuff since I finished undergrad."

The man considers me, disappointment mixing with confusion. Then he slaps himself on the forehead. "Ah, Christ. I didn't think...fuck!" He sighs, muttering something in what sounds like another language. A minute of silence passes before he turns back to me. "I guess I should reintroduce myself, shouldn't I?"

I nod and he sits next to me on the stones surrounding the trees' soil beds. Extending a hand, he says calmly, "I'm Paris. Paris Kuyper."

Still feeling surreal and scared of further changes, I take his hand. His palm and the pads of his fingers are rough and his grip is firm. It's the hand of someone used to working hard. My father and brother have similar hands and that reassures me. "Rose Taggert," I reply, though I realize he already knows my name.

I let go of his hand. Hesitantly, I ask, "Paris, how do we know each other? I mean, are we friends?"

Paris gazes awkwardly at the ceiling. "Well—Hoo boy, this is awkward—How do I say this?" Paris blushes a deep red. "Rose—we're lovers."

"Lovers?" I repeat incredulously.

Paris nods scratching his head nervously. "Yeah. I mean, I guess boyfriend and girlfriend is the more exact term."

"Really?" I say, still suspicious. I hadn't pictured Paris and I as a couple when I first saw him. Yes, he's kind of good-looking but he's younger than me and I don't remember younger guys being my type. Then again, my tastes in men might've changed. We could have something going on.

Paris nods once more. "There's plenty of time to talk about that later, though," he picks up the object he had dropped earlier and now I see that it is a book, the spine looks battered and cracked. "We gotta figure out what went wrong here. This wasn't supposed to happen, not in a million years!" He flips through the book's pages as he sits back down, his eyes flicking over whatever's written inside as he skims through it.

"What wasn't supposed to happen?" I ask, though I already know what he's talking about.

Paris's eyes flick up from the book. An "uh-oh" sort of look crosses his face and he falls silent, avoiding my glare. He reminds me of a kid who got caught breaking a family heirloom by his parents and now expects a harsh punishment.

"Paris," I growl, feeling a little like a parent myself, "what did you do?"

He doesn't reply. I repeat my question more forcefully. Finally, he opens his mouth but what comes out is an unintelligible mumble.

"I'm sorry?" I still feeling like a parent with a naughty child.

"I saved your life."

I stare at him openmouthed. "What?" I no longer feel like a parent.

"I saved your life," he says again. Paris pauses before continuing, his eyes full of deep sadness. "You...you had a stalker. A guy you met at a party. You talked with him a little and he got fixated on you. At first all he did was follow you around and try not to get noticed but after we started going out and getting serious..."

He trails off for a moment before resuming. "I didn't know about him for months, not until you told me. You wanted to report him but you got scared of what might happen if you did. His family has connections in the university, I think his aunt and uncle are important professors in their departments and you didn't know how they'd react if you told the school what he'd been doing."

Paris shakes his head, as if clearing his thoughts. "Anyway, last night you and I were out at this club—you know, for dinner and dancing—and he showed up just as we were leaving. Things...got heated."

A haunted look covered Paris's face. "Your stalker knocked me down with one punch and tried to drag you into his car. You fought him hard. Harder than I ever could." A regretful air passes over his face and I feel sorry for him. How badly did he want to help me that night? Only for this stalker—a man I don't remember though now picture in my imagination has long, wild hair and a maniacal grin that would make the Joker jealous—to totally overpower him? I want to reach out and comfort Paris. After all, he said we were lovers, right? Even if I don't recollect him, would it be weird to pat him on the knee?

I lift my hand off the ground to reach for him only for it to falter in midair before dropping to the damp soil as I remember the reason that my skin is green and all these weird tentacles are coming out of my neck is because of something Paris did.

Instead I wait and listen as Paris talks.

"Your stalker was getting rough with you. People were staring and someone called 911. I tried to get to you but I was really rattled by that punch. I kept hoping someone from the crowd would intervene but nobody did. They just kept watching, gawking at us like a street performance. Why do people do that, instead of helping others out?"

The bystander effect. It's a well-documented phenomenon, one we've discussed more than once in my sociology classes, when people do not participate in a situation because they believe someone else will, inevitably leading to no one participating. I don't mention any of this though as I listen to Paris finish up.

"And then the stalker—God, he just got so scary! He smacked you hard in the head and you fell into his car's side mirror. You didn't get up. You just lay there twitching." Tears tumbled from his eyes and he put a hand to his mouth, trying and failing to suppress an anguished cry.

"Oh God." It slips out even as I still feel horror at what Paris has done to me. And then, "Oh Paris."

"Y-your stalker ran," Paris sobbed through the tears. "He's in hiding, nobody knows where he is. I took you to the hospital as fast as I could. A-and you...you were in some sort of coma." His voice cracks. "The doctors didn't think you would ever wake up. So, I snuck you out of the hospital. I was desperate. I just knew I had to try."

Paris holds up the book, not looking at it or me. "This is *the Shin Sekai no Shinki*," he explains. "It means *The Forest God's Record*. It's kind of a spell book, passed down through my family for generations. My family were Dutch traders, they bought it off some Japanese nobles back in the day. And I used it. I used it to save your life."

"And it worked. I mean, you're still alive. But your memories...oh God, you must've suffered some brain trauma when you hit your head. The spell, why didn't it fix...?"

Anguished cries came from deep within and tears streamed down his face. I ogle him in disbelief. *A spell book? He can't be serious.*

But then again, what other rational explanation was there for my green skin, my pink hair and nails, the rosebuds bursting out of my scalp and the tentacles drilling out of my neck?

Before Paris can stop me, I grab the book out of his hands and prop it up against my chest so that I can see what it says. The pages within are old, light brown and leathery with age, the edges of each page uneven and rough, yet the ink looks as if it was added yesterday. Most of the pages have only Japanese characters but every half dozen or so contain illustrations, garish and terrifying. One shows a woman in an open grave, rising from the earth with a hand outstretched. Another depicts two figures hoeing a field while leaves sprout from their ears. A third, very gory illustration, has shrubs and trees choking and tearing people in two with their branches.

An involuntary shiver runs down my spine, though not just because of the illustrations. Something about the book feels wrong to the touch, like finding decay and rot in a freshly built house.

"You can read this?" I ask.

"Somehow, yeah," Paris answers. "I can't read Japanese and apparently that book is written in Late Middle Japanese, which is a whole other animal but for some reason I can read it like it's plain English. It's crazy."

Crazy doesn't cover it. Feeling dirty for having touched the book I close the pages and place it down.

A spell book. *The Forest God's Record*, that's what Paris called it. Does it work? I've failed to uncover another explanation for what's happened to me so, I guess, maybe it does.

Paris looks at me like he's waiting for me to react but I'm not sure how I should. So much information rushes through my head—my changed body, Paris's story, the pictures in the book—I don't know what to make of it all. My head hurts thinking about it. Worse than it already does, anyway.

I take a deep breath. "You just went and cast a spell and hoped it would work?" The words sound harsher than I intend but I find I don't care.

Paris shakes his head. "I did a couple of spells before that," he explains. "Mostly to help with the greenhouse. Gardening is my hobby and the book is full of plant-based magic. You'd be amazed what sort of spells are in there. Of course, you kind of already know." He gives a soft, humorless laugh.

I'm still in shock. "Why? Why go through all this? Why make this happen?" I gesture at myself as I say this, especially at the tentacles in my neck and the rosebuds on top of my head.

This time Paris is the one who gives me a strange face. "Because I love you," he answers. "Isn't that obvious? I'd do anything for you."

He moves closer. His expression has changed, becoming fierce and determined. "I'm sorry about the side effects." He leans towards me. "I knew they might happen but I had to try. I couldn't let you go. You're too important to me, Rose. I know it feels like you've just met me and I know it's scary but I promised myself I was going to do this the moment I knew you were all right. So, please, forgive me."

Before I can blink, Paris's arms surround me, crushing me close to him. I smell earth and scented shampoo as he holds me, one hand cupped behind my head, the other on my side as his arm grips me close. Fresh tears fall from his eyes onto my face and between my lips.

"Paris." I say uncomfortably.

He responds by kissing me.

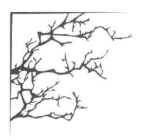

CHAPTER TWO

I'm so surprised I forget I'm in pain. A total stranger is kissing me. The stranger who has admitted kidnapping me from a hospital where I lay dying, admitted casting a magic spell on me, to save my life, only for said spell to change me into—I don't know what!

I want to throw him off, I want to unjoin our mouths and kick him for good measure.

Something stops me.

My attention focuses on Paris, on his handsome face, on his half-closed eyes and on his mouth on mine. His lips are firm but soft, his breath clean and minty, his touch strong and eager, like he's kissing me for the very first time. Compared to other kisses I've had, most of which I can remember, this is a good kiss, perhaps a touch above average in terms of ardor and taste and I'm not sure I want it to end.

My hand runs up his arm and grabs his sleeve while my other hand snakes to his shoulder. Paris whispers my name with exultation. I part my lips a little and lean in, covering his lips with mine. We break for a second to breathe then we're kissing again with twice the passion.

From somewhere outside the greenhouse I hear a doorbell chime.

Paris and I pull apart, breathing hard. His face is pink, I'm sure mine is too or at least it's hot. A moment passes before I notice Paris is angry. To be honest, I'm a little peeved too. That was a great kiss.

No, there is something else. Paris is...afraid. That makes me afraid as well.

Standing, Paris grabs something off a nearby workbench and unfolds it. It's a large black tarp, which he hurriedly lays over me so that I can't see a thing. "Hey!" I cry as the tarp's placed over my head. "Paris!"

"I'll be right back," he calls to me as the doorbell chimes once more. "Don't move. Don't make a sound." Before I can ask him where I'm supposed to go, I hear his sneakers scuff away. A moment later I hear a distant door open and Paris's voice floats back to me, barely loud enough for me to make out. "Dad, what are you doing here—?"

"You haven't called or returned my messages in days!" replies a deep, harsh voice. I shudder involuntary. The voice conjures up the image of a monster from a movie I saw years ago, eyes full of flame and mouth full of fangs. I curl into a tight ball under the tarp. "What have you been up to in that time that you can't call your own father?"

For a moment, there's silence. Then Paris replies in an annoyed tone, "Dad, I 've been busy with my classes. I'm taking six this semester, you know!"

Paris's dad? Curious, I cautiously pull down the tarp a little and strain my neck to see beyond the greenhouse but the tentacles in my neck restrict my movement and I can't see a thing. With a resigned sigh, I fall back against the ground and listen to the conversation floating through the open door.

"...have more than enough reasons to be suspicious of you! I know about your obsession with that girl from the university. Perhaps you've been setting up a shrine in your closet to her."

"That only happens in the movies, Dad."

"Don't talk back to me! Do you know how much I've invested in you and your education? Do you know what's expected of you? I wish you would stop acting like a child and grow up already."

"I'm not being childish! I'd just like to have some independence! I mean, what's the point of having my own apartment if I'm obliged to call home every day or you'll file a missing person's report?"

Apartment! That was the word for my home I forgot! Goddamn brain trauma. What else has it made me forget?

"What did I say about talking back to me!" Paris's father roars, smacking something that sounds like a wooden surface. "Don't think I don't notice. You want me to leave as soon as possible, I can tell by your face. You're up to something and I just know it's the kind of thing that's going to come back to haunt us! You never think beyond what you want and damn the consequences for everyone else." He paused, "I should've let you stew at that camp another month! Maybe then you'd act more like a man!"

A second, longer pause, before Paris starts speaking, his voice too low for me to hear. His father replies in the same pitch, their voices becoming a distant whisper. I stop listening, unable to follow the conversation. Still, I've heard enough to guess Paris's father doesn't seem like a very nice person. And he and Paris don't see eye-to-eye much. *What had Mr. Kuyper—that is Paris's last name, right? —said earlier? I know about your obsession with that girl from the university. Was he talking about me?*

The tentacles in my neck stop pulsing and become still. Slowly they slither out of the dirt and back into my neck, moving like snakes retreating into burrows. I feel them descend into my chest, thick cords lying on top of my diaphragm and wrapped around my rib cage. Halting only when the small, drill-like tips remain beyond my skin. I wait for a minute, sure something else will happen but to my relief nothing does.

Slowly, still a little nervous, I reach my hand up and examine the tips of the tentacles, pointed and sharp. Still nothing. Another wave of relief rolls over me. Whatever's going on with these things in my neck, it looks like it's over.

For now, anyway.

A minute passes. The conversation outside the greenhouse is still too quiet for me to hear. *What's going on in the other room?* I want to find out.

Lifting myself off the dirt I almost stand up, before deciding it's safer if I don't risk being seen by Paris's father, especially while I'm pink and green. Curiosity killed the cat, after all. Instead, I lower myself onto my hands and knees and crawl around the edges of the room, feeling a bit like an Army cadet in basic training. When I try to crawl faster however, my joints refuse. They're stiff, unwilling to move past a certain speed. I hear them grind against each other as I speed up and their protest becomes a loud, infuriated screech, like metal against rusted metal. Now I know how the Tin Man from *The Wizard of Oz* feels.

I take a deep breath. *Slow down Rose, your body's been magicked into something new. There are limits to what you can do. Just take it one step at a time and we'll figure it out.* Another breath and I begin crawling again at markedly reduced speed. This time my body moves with less difficulty and I my progress is faster than before.

I reach a glass sliding door and pause. Beyond, I can see a purple-black sky filled with dark grey clouds. I try the handle and it releases with a muted snick. The outside. Maybe I can look in on Paris and his father's conversation through a window without giving myself away.

I scramble to my feet pushing on the handle, praying the door doesn't make a noise or do anything else to let Paris's father know I'm here. The door slides open with barely a hiss. I check to see if anyone's watching and step into the night, closing the door behind me.

The first thing that hits me is how freezing cold it is. It's almost like an entity, moving around me with invisible arms and stealing the warmth from my body. I wrap my bare arms around my chest, shivering as I peer through the light snow that's drifting down all around me. My eyes widen as I realize where I am. Instead of a lawn or a garden or a sidewalk, as I had expected, there's a waist-high stone parapet surrounding a terrace balcony, with a glass table and chairs in the center. I run to the balcony and lean over the edge, gripping onto the metal bars that run the length of the parapet for support. The ground looms far below, at least twenty stories down. I lean back, dizzy and glance back at the greenhouse, which I now realize has been built on the balcony of a penthouse apartment. *A penthouse! What sort of person is Paris that he can afford a penthouse?*

Through the window I can make out two figures. Paris and his father. Crouching, I sneak closer to the window. Except for a set of glass double doors, the wall dividing the apartment from the balcony is made of the same stone material as the parapet, stopping at about waist height. Above the stone are glass windows, misted over in places from the snow and ice. Reaching the wall, I sink to my knees and peer through the windows.

The inside of the apartment's living room is warm and inviting, with cream-colored walls and brown leather furniture. Across from the living room, stainless steel countertops and dark, polished mahogany cabinets adorn the kitchen. A giant flat-screen television hangs above a crackling fireplace, while several posters of rock bands and what I assume are prints of famous paintings line the walls. Several potted plants cover tables and hang from the ceiling, giving the impression the greenhouse extends into the apartment. In the center of the room, standing a couple feet apart from each other, are Paris and his father. Both look more like wrestlers preparing for a match than a father and son having an argument.

I fix on the father. He's a tall man, a few inches taller than his son, with a thin angular face and light-brown hair combed back from this forehead. He's dressed in a crisp black suit with a red silk tie and shiny black shoes. A gold watch hangs from his wrist. He seems to tower over his son, like a giant over a small boy. From where I crouch, I can't see Paris's face but I can see his father's expression clearly and it's so severe it scares me.

I watch as Paris and his father continue speaking to each other, their postures and Paris's father's face radiating anger. Mr. Kuyper finishes saying something and purses his lips. Paris gesticulates wildly with his hands. I guess he's telling his father something he doesn't care for because his father's mouth thins until I can barely make it out.

Abruptly Mr. Kuyper rears a hand back and throws it forward, slapping his son full in the face. I gasp as Paris falls to the ground. From the floor, he glares at his father, rubbing his cheek.

There's a final exchange of words between them before Paris's father turns, striding down a hallway and out of sight. A moment later the windows shake in their frames, letting me know that Mr. Kuyper has left and leaving no doubt how angry he is.

Paris slowly stands, rubbing his cheek and turns toward the greenhouse. I stand also, moving as fast as I can towards the sliding door. I'm burning with questions, though I'm certain I'm not going to like some of the answers.

Opening the door, I step back inside. The warmth of the greenhouse greets me like an old friend. Paris stands in the center of the greenhouse, the left side of his face red. He looks surprised to see me but his face softens and he smiles. "Did you try hiding from my dad? It's okay. He's gone now."

I gape at him, unsure of what to say. I thought he'd be upset, embarrassed that I witnessed him being slapped by his father. Not this...nonchalance! My mouth opens and closes a few times before I'm able to find the words. "Your cheek! Are you all right? Your father—!"

Paris slowly shakes his head. "I've endured worse because of him," he admits, sauntering across to me. "This is a love tap compared to that. What about you? Are you all right? When did those tentacle things go back into your neck?"

"When you and your father got too quiet to hear, I think." I'm surprised by Paris shrugging off the slap. I would've gone off on his dad if I had been in the room. Then again, if I was in the room, I'm sure slapping Paris would've been the last thing on his father's mind. Speaking of which, that reminds me of something I've been wondering.

"It sounds like your father doesn't like me very much. I was the girl from the university he was talking about, right?"

"He doesn't like much of anything, to be honest," Paris replies, leaning against a workbench. "My family is old money and with old money comes expectations; attend the best schools, have the best jobs and, of course, marry someone from—" Paris makes air-quotes "the right background and pedigree." Paris rolls his eyes and continues, "whatever that means. He certainly wasn't happy when he found out that his son had fallen for a sociology grad with a butcher and a librarian for parents. I think I told you all this on one of our first dates. Hey, are you okay?"

While Paris talks, I'm rubbing my arms frantically. Why am I still so cold? It must be close to seventy degrees in the greenhouse but I feel like I'm still in the freezer outside. I want to ask Paris if there's a draft in the room but he's starting to slide in and out of focus.

"Rose? Rose! What's wrong?"

My strength gives out and I fall over. I'm shivering like mad, as cold as an icicle. Darkness swirls at the edges of my vision as Paris kneels beside me. He grabs my shoulder, only to let go just as fast. "My God, you're freezing!"

Panic flashes across his face but it's gone almost immediately, replaced by determination. Rolling me onto my back, Paris loops his arms under my armpits and drags me out of the greenhouse and into the living room, laying me next to the fireplace. The whole time he murmurs, "Get you warm, gotta get you warm," though I think he's talking to both me and himself again. I'm not sure. My brain feels fuzzy, my thoughts stuffed with cotton.

The heat from the fire kisses my skin and I immediately feel ten times warmer. Paris leaves me only to return a moment later with a thick, heavy blanket. He lays the edge of the blanket under me and then rolls it around me, leaving my head and neck still exposed. An image of a corpse in a rug rises unbidden to my mind and I push it away. That's not me, I'm not a corpse. Paris saved me, he brought me back to life. He said so.

Retrieving a pillow from the couch, Paris lays it underneath my head and brushes a lock of hair from my forehead. "There, you're warming up," he says. "You should be fine now."

"What happened to me?" I mumble, enjoying the warmth as it returns to my body. My brain is still fuzzy but at least I'm not cold.

"I'm not sure," Paris replies after a moment's thought. "But I think, based on the spell I cast...I think you are part plant now."

I stare at him. Did my muddled brain just mishear him? "I'm what?"

"Part plant," Paris repeats. "The spell I used said life had to be given for life to be saved. I sacrificed some roses from my garden. I thought you'd find that funny, you told me you hated roses." He forces a laugh. "Anyway, the book also said that there would be side effects. I didn't know what that meant, the text wasn't specific. I thought that you'd be sickly or couldn't eat meat after midnight or something. But I think the book meant this... this transformation. I mean, you've got roses coming out of your head and you've got those tentacle things in your neck—actually, I think those are roots. They went into the ground; I wouldn't be surprised if they were taking nutrients and moisture from the soil. I guess when it said, *life must be given for life to be saved*, whatever life was taken to save the person goes right into the person, changes them. It's the only thing that makes sense to me."

Paris looks towards the window, where snowflakes slide down and melt against the glass. "Roses don't do well in extreme cold or rapid temperature changes," he muses, looking back to me. "When you stepped outside, you got both and it nearly killed you. Anyway, you look okay now. Still transformed but basically okay."

"Well, that's good," I reply, feeling too tired to be angry. Besides, Paris did it to save my life. And then he saved me again after I came in from the cold. That's twice he's saved me and in less than an hour, too. I should be grateful.

"Thank you," I whisper. "For saving me, I mean."

A weak smile crosses Paris's lips. "I already told you. I'd do anything for you. Now get some rest. I'll watch over you while you sleep. Our new life starts tomorrow."

I start to close my eyes, then I remember something and open them again. "Paris, what about the cat?" I ask. "Why am I not turning into a cat?"

Paris blinks, confused. "A cat?"

"The cat in the greenhouse," I explain. "The dead one. Its belly..." I shudder as I remember it, the shocked look on its face.

"There's no dead cat," answers Paris. With a jolt something seems to occur to him. "Unless..." He dashes out to the greenhouse, a worried look on his face. A few seconds later comes the sound of an anguished scream. Moments later Paris stumbles back into the room, shell-shocked. "Marvin," he whispers, his eyes hollow. "Jesus Christ, Marvin."

Pity wells up in me. "Was it your cat?"

Paris nods his head mechanically. "I...I guess the spell needed more life, so it took Marvin's, because he was close by. He loved the greenhouse. And he liked you. You don't remember but he really liked you."

Several emotions sweep over me; sadness for Paris, pity for the cat and a vague annoyance that I can't remember any of this relationship I'm supposed to have had with him or the cat. I try to stand up and give Paris a consoling hug, however, Paris shakes his head, bends down and pushes me back against the pillow before I can even sit up.

"No, no, no. You rest." His eyes are still filled with sadness but there's concern there too. Concern for me. "I'll feel even worse if anything happens to you. Just sleep. I'll...I'll go mourn my cat."

I still want to help him, pat him on the back and tell him it'll be all right but right now I'm too tired. Odd. Just a little while ago I woke up after nobody thought I would ever wake up, according to Paris. You'd think I'd be unable to close my eyes. Instead I feel so sleepy. Maybe it's the transformation and my exposure to the cold taking its toll on me.

I just hope I don't turn into a cat later.

Shifting a little in the blankets, I close my eyes. Someone laughs in my ear. My eyes spring open, looking for whoever laughed. There's no one around but I'm terrified, certain there's something nearby that means to do me harm.

"What was that?" I ask Paris plaintively.

"What was what?"

"That laugh!"

"I didn't hear anything. Look, you're tired and you almost died a second ago. That's twice in one night! Get some rest. We can talk more tomorrow. Maybe we can reawaken your memories. Somehow, we'll make this work. And even if we can't reverse the side effects, I'll love you just as much as I always have. You'll see. Things will be better than they've ever been before."

I'm confused that Paris didn't hear the laugh but touched by his words. It's the kind of thing a prince might say to his princess, promising to save her from whatever trouble she's in and to always love her no matter what. Maybe Paris and I really are lovers.

Once more I close my eyes and exhaustion takes over. Gratefully, I slip into a deep sleep, hoping that tomorrow will be less terrifying than today.

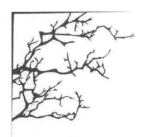

CHAPTER THREE

The smell of bacon frying rouses me from sleep. I keep my eyes closed and lie there, enjoying the warm blanket around my body and the smell of cooking meat. It soothes me after last night's terrifying dream. And it wasn't just terrifying but crazy. In the dream, a guy I was seeing named Paris Kuyper turned me into some sort of plant creature to save me from dying at the hands of a violent stalker.

Now I'm awake, I realize it was an insane dream, brought on by God only knows what. Still, as I was experiencing it, it felt terrifying and vivid.

Good thing it was only a dream. My transformation into a plant creature had been something out of a crazy horror movie, made worse by my inability to remember simple but important things. I couldn't remember the past two years, what my parents did for a living, or who Paris was to me. Which, now that I thought about it, was kind of sad. We were supposed to have this whole relationship that I didn't remember a thing about. Paris must've been shocked.

I give a small laugh, eyes still closed. Look at me, feeling sorry for a boy I made up in my head. I wonder if other people feel sorry for those they create in their dreams. I mean, I've heard of people feeling flustered and guilty if they have wet dreams of folks other than whomever they're dating, or even their crushes, but I've never heard of someone feeling sad for a dream person. But who knows? Maybe it's happened. I'll have to ask someone if they've ever had something similar happen to them.

Feeling better now, I sit up and open my eyes. I'm in a warm looking living room with a large flat screen hanging above a fireplace. The place is filled with potted plants and the walls are covered in posters for rock bands and prints of famous paintings. Sunlight shines through the windows to give the penthouse a warm, cozy feel. In the kitchen, Paris is hunched over the stovetop, a spatula in one hand and a frying pan in the other.

Oh my God! I'm in Paris's home. It wasn't a dream at all. No way. How is that possible?

I free my arms from the blanket and rub my eyes. No matter how hard I rub though, Paris is frying bacon and I'm in his living room. Heart pounding like a dance club track, I look down at my hands. The skin is light green and my nails are bright pink. I pinch my cheek but all that does is make my cheek throb. I slap myself but all that does is cause my other cheek to smart. The root things in my neck—oh my God, they are still there—give a menacing shiver.

Over in the kitchen, Paris takes the pan off the burner and scoops out several slices of bacon onto a plate. He catches me gaping at him and smiles. "Good morning, Sleeping Beauty." Then he registers the look on my face. "What's wrong?"

For a moment, I can't answer him. I'd just been thinking of him as a figment of my imagination. It's too surreal that he's talking to me now, asking me how I'm feeling.

I open and close my mouth soundlessly, my mind struggling to find a response. Finally, words manage to make it past the cloud in my head. "This is real," I whisper. "It's all real."

To his credit, Paris immediately understand what I'm talking about, because he doesn't ask me anything further. Instead, he sets the frying pan down, crosses to me and unwraps the blanket from around me. When my shoulders appear, he gently lays a hand on one of them and gives it a comforting squeeze. I'm grateful for his presence, even if I don't remember him, or anything about the relationship we have.

Freed from the blankets, I stand up and realize that I'm still wearing the same dirty dress I was wearing last night, the soil from the flower bed clinging to it. Only now half of said soil has rubbed onto the blanket. Paris examines the mess and sighs noncommittally, as if to say, what are you going to do? A question occurs to me I hadn't thought of before. "Paris, why am I still wearing this dress? I thought you said you sneaked me from the hospital."

"Hm? Oh!" Paris blinks rapidly at me. "Yeah, I did. The ritual required whatever you were wearing when you were, you know, injured or killed. Not sure why, that's just what the spell called for. I would've washed it before I put it back on you—it got dirty when you hit your head—but there wasn't time. Anyway, if you want me to, I can get rid of it. Get you something clean to wear."

I open my mouth to tell him I would love new clothes but then there's a crawling sensation under my skin. With a rattling hiss, the roots in my neck slither out, waving around and pointing towards the greenhouse. At the same time, I'm overcome by an urge to lay myself down on the soil and let the roots do whatever they do in the dirt. I can't explain it but it's a feeling I can't question or ignore.

Leaving Paris hanging, I run to the greenhouse, my limbs still heavy and stiff. It's bright and warm as I burst inside, the sight so beautiful that my head long rush is brought to a halt as I take in the splendor of the room. There are flowers of every variety and the air is fragrant with over a hundred smells. All of it blends together in a wild tableau of sight and scents, yet none of it is overwhelming or off-putting. In the back of my mind, I wonder if this is what Heaven looks like.

The roots remind me of why I came here and I'm drawn over to a pair of trees. I lay myself face-up on the ground between them, the roots plunge into the soil, digging in until only a few inches remain above the ground. They pulse and the urgency that brought me here scatters.

A minute passes. The tranquility of the greenhouse and the pulsing roots ease me allowing the shocks of last night and this morning to dissipate. However, I can't get rid of the deep, terrible sadness in my gut. Somehow, I know that this strange new existence, a part-plant part-woman thing, is now my new normal. Paris said it himself, he might not be able to reverse the side effects. I could be green and pink forever.

At least the guy who made me this way says he loves me no matter what and he's going to take care of me from now on. That's a plus.

A twig snaps behind my head. I open my eyes and look up at the trees I'm lying between. Two people stand over me, twisted and screaming silently in pain and terror.

I gasp, blink twice in rapid succession. The two figures disappear and the trees return: a yew tree and an orange tree, buds growing on the latter. I stare, confused. Why did I think they were people screaming in pain? I glance from one tree to the other. Was that some sort of hallucination?

Then that I notice...no way...yes, there are faces in the wood of the trees! Not real faces, obviously. There are rises and depressions and knots in the woods, clustered together in the right way to look like faces. It must've been a trick of the light, making the faces look real and the branches resemble bodies twisted in pain.

Still, it's interesting that there are two trees in Paris's greenhouse that look like they have faces in them and right next to each other too. Did Paris grow them that way on purpose? If so, why? From somewhere in the back of my head, I remember that faces in trees is part of Game of Thrones, a show I've yet to watch, despite everyone telling me I should. Maybe Paris's a fan.

The sound of muttering drags my eyes away from the trees. As if summoned by my thoughts, Paris stands in the entrance to the greenhouse, holding the old book from last night and reading something from it out loud. I remember the book's name, Shin Sekai no Shinki. *The Forest God's Record*. Paris said it had magic spells inside it, one of which saved me from death. I wonder if he would show me those spells, even teach them to me, if I asked? It might be useful to know magic, especially now that I'm part plant.

Now that I think about it, there's one more thing I'm curious about. "Hey Paris."

Paris's head shoots up from the book. "Yes?"

"Who is the Forest God? The one in the book's title, I mean. Is it the god of all forests or something?"

A ponderous look comes over Paris's face. "Tough question. Truth be told, I don't have all the details. Just what's been passed down through family lore and what I've been able to find out through research. But you must understand what the Japanese mean by the word *kami*, or god, first. They don't think of gods like Christians do, or like the Greek and Romans did. You see, in Japanese beliefs, everything is inhabited by a god. Animals, plants, stones, tools, even humans contain a spirit that can be considered a kami."

"So, everything's a god?"

"Kinda, yeah. I mean, there are some kami that are more god-like than your average god: Amaterasu the sun-goddess, Susanoo the storm-god, Izanagi and Izanami, who created Japan and many of the gods. But there are also demons, ghosts, ancestor spirits, they can be gods too and some of those could become so awesome, worship was the only way to keep them from laying waste to the world. But yeah, everything's technically a god.

"The one the book's named after, however, was supposed to have ruled a forest not too far from some noble family's ancestral lands centuries ago. I think it gave the noble family the book as a gift or a keepsake. At some point, the book was sold to my family, who were Dutch traders and merchants. Back then, the Dutch were the only nationality allowed to do business with the Japanese."

"Why did the god give them the book? And why did they sell it to your ancestors?"

Paris shrugs, closing the book with a deep sigh. Walking over he sits down sits next to me and lays his head in his hand. "I can't find anything in this damn book about your side effects," he complains. "I've searched it up and down but there's nothing about the side effects or how to reverse them." Another large sigh. "Dammit. I didn't want this to happen to you."

"It's not your fault," I say, mostly meaning it.

"But it is my fault," Paris responds, his eyes full of sadness. I think of last night, his father slapping him like that and Paris passing it off as no big deal. I've endured worse because of him, was what he had said. His life must be so full of hardship and my transformation is the latest kick in the pants for him.

We sit in silence for a while. I want to reach out to him but what do I say? The sadness in his eyes is so deep, it makes my chest ache. And from the way Paris glances at me before peering down into his lap, I think he might want to reach out to me as well. Not in the same way I do but I can feel it. He wants to make the situation better, though he's not sure how.

A couple more minutes pass by before the roots pull themselves out from the dirt and slide back into my neck and chest. Relieved, I stand up and walk back to the living room, eager to escape the awkwardness of the greenhouse. Paris walks with me, turning right to enter the kitchen. The bacon is waiting for him on a ceramic plate. "You hungry?" he asks.

I open my mouth to say, "Yes, I'm starving," before noticing that I'm not. In fact, I don't think I've been hungry since I woke up last night. Does that have something to do with being part plant now? Maybe I don't need to eat anymore. But how do I get sustenance? How will I live?

Paris asks me again if I'm hungry, pulling me out of my thoughts. I shake my head.

"Well, you should take a shower." He eyes my dress, now even more grubby from its most recent encounter with the soil in the greenhouse. "Go upstairs and take a shower. Leave the dress outside, I've got some of your clothes here." Indicating behind me, towards the back of the room. I follow his pointing finger and spy a recess in the wall I hadn't realized was there before. I go to it and find the stairs Paris mentioned hidden behind what I thought was the back wall.

"Thanks," I say, walking upstairs.

"No problem," he calls. "Just don't turn the water too hot. Plants don't do well when the water's hot enough to boil."

"I won't," I call back, glad for the information. Now that I'm a plant, I'm much more fragile than before. I'll have to pay more attention to what can help or hurt me, at least until Paris can find some other way to return me to the way I was.

At the top of the stairs, I find two rooms: a bathroom on the left and a bedroom on the right, with a linen closet between them. I turn to the left and close the door behind me. The lights flicker on and I'm almost blinded by how bright everything is. When my eyes adjust, I find myself gawking at how huge the bathroom is, big enough for several people to stand inside with plenty of personal space. Not to mention how sparkly and opulent it is: everything is tiled in white and looks like it was cleaned that very morning. At the far end of the room is a bathtub where three people could soak in comfortably, as well as a shower stall with multiple shower heads set into the walls at different angles, along with some sort of touchscreen.

Once more, I wonder what sort of people Paris and his family are that he can afford to live in luxury like this. My childhood home's bathroom was small and narrow and had one old shower fixture. I had to share it with five other people, two of which used to spend hours just looking for pimples to pop while everyone else waited to use it. As a kid, I would've killed to have a few hours alone in a bathroom like this.

About a minute passes before I remember why I'm here and I begin to strip. When I'm free of the dress and underwear, I feel lighter, like shackles I didn't know I was wearing have fallen off. Even so, when I look at myself in the mirror, I feel those shackles return in the form of my new body. Every inch of my skin, as well as my irises, are a shade of sickly pale green. The only variation in my new green texture is my abdomen, which is a lighter green than everything else, probably because those parts are usually covered by clothes. And on top of all that, my hair and nails are cotton-candy pink, the root tips protrude from my neck and the six rosebuds that burst out of my scalp last night adorn my head like an organic tiara. I'm a total freak, someone who could only be at home at one of those old-timey traveling freak shows.

I recall the woman I used to be, the woman who, in my last clear memory, is wearing a black graduation gown and hat with a white tassel, beaming with her family in front of the Ohio Stadium as a friend takes pictures of us together. In that memory, I have pale skin, red hair and blue eyes, which numerous biology teachers throughout the years have commented as the rarest hair and eye combo of all in our species. But beyond that, I'm perfectly normal and happy.

This woman staring back at me from the mirror is completely different from her and I loathe her for it. It's only with a great effort of will that I'm able to turn away and step into the shower.

After a few fumbling attempts I discover the touchscreen controls the shower jets but only after I get sprayed with freezing cold water from behind and then scalding hot water from above, I get the thing working take a relaxing shower. Warm water rushes over my body, making me feel not just physically clean but mentally, in a way the greenhouse couldn't. For the first time since I woke up last night, I'm a regular girl again, just concerned with getting clean after a very long ordeal.

At some point, there's a knock at the door. Instinctively, I step further back into the shower stall, even though the glass is so misted over I can't see beyond it. The door opens with a soft creak and Paris says, "Here are your clothes." His arm slips into the room, a blurred streak moving beyond the misted glass. He lays something down on the sink by the door before his arm reaches for the pile of soiled clothes on the ground. When he's gathered those up, his arm retreats, leaving me alone once more.

I stay in the shower a little while longer before I turn it off and step out. As I dry off, I look through the clothes Paris has found me. On the sink, I find a white bra and underwear; a flowery purple dress made from some soft material; a dark gray button-up sweater with black buttons; and black, high-heeled strapped sandals; and several different ribbons, clips and tiny scrunchies in a variety of colors. The clothes fit me perfectly. I guess that makes sense. After all, Paris and I are dating. It's not inconceivable I stay over some nights and keep clothes here.

After tying my hair back with a black bow, I hasten downstairs to find Paris waiting for me in the living room, his legs crossed as he sits on the couch. "Well, don't you look nice," he says, standing up.

"Thanks." I'm pleased, even though I know he probably grabbed these clothes because he knows they flatter me. I notice the *Forest God's Record* on the coffee table and my earlier desire to learn from the book returns. Maybe I can work through it with Paris? I clear my throat and say, "By the way, Paris, I wanted to ask you about that spell—"

"You know," Paris interrupts as he stands and moves close to me, putting his hands on my arms. He pushes me against the wall, his body leaning in close to mine. "You wore this dress on our first date. I remember thinking how sexy you were." He caresses my cheek with the back of his hand, his eyes roving from my dress to my face. "How sexy you are now." He presses his lips against mine.

His kiss is just as hungry, just as ardent as it was last night. Even more so, because he's pressing me tight to him and he's almost hurting me as he holds me but I barely notice, because this is also a nice kiss and Paris's is so nice, kind, concerned and—

Beyond his issues with his dad, I barely know anything about him.

Something my mother would say to my sister Hope when she was a teenager and which she started saying to me and my sister Maddy when we became interested in boys, echoes through my head. "Never kiss a boy you barely know, no matter how nice or good-looking he is," she instructed.

"Why not?" We'd ask, embarrassed by the topic.

"Because it makes boys think you're easy," Hope explained. "To them, a girl who kisses a boy she only just met is a girl who will get in bed with a boy on the first night. You don't want people to think that, do you?"

We didn't and so we didn't kiss boys we barely knew, even if at that age we thought we knew better than our parents. Later we'd come to realize that not all guys would think this and Mom was just trying to make sure we didn't do something we'd regret later in life but we still followed that bit of advice. After all, we got more respect when we waited at least a couple of dates to take that first step.

Mom's voice is chiding me in my head now and I recognize the wisdom in her words. We may be boyfriend and girlfriend but I don't remember Paris. And kissing him while knowing that makes me uncomfortable.

I push Paris away, my cheeks hot. Paris glowers at me with confusion and hurt and what I think might be anger. "What's wrong?" He demands in the voice of a petulant child.

I take a deep breath, trying to figure out how best to phrase this. "Paris, you're nice. And I like that about you. And I know we're supposed to be in a relationship and all but I still don't remember you. I've only known you for a day. Barely even that." I take another deep breath, steeling myself with my mother's advice. "Can we slow down a bit? Get to know each other again? Please? I'd appreciate it if we could."

I wait for Paris to respond. He stares at me at disbelief for a few moments before mumbling. "Yeah, sure. That's fine."

He glares at me with a strange look on his face, a look so full of anger and menace that I recoil. "Rose," Paris rumbles, "how about we take a step outside? Huh?"

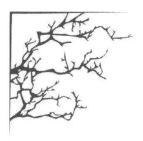

CHAPTER FOUR

I stare at Paris; certain that I've misheard him. "What?" I ask.

"I said," Paris hisses, "let's step outside."

"But I thought you said…" I shiver, trying to avoid Paris's glare. It's like an entirely different person is standing in front of me, another Paris who's the opposite of the one I was talking to a moment ago. What happened to the man who saved my life because he loved me? Where did this other guy come from? "I thought you said that it was dangerous for me to go outside."

"Well, I'm sure a little bit of cold won't hurt you," he reasons. "Besides, we need to test your limits. You never know when it'll be important to know how much time you can spend outdoors before your body shuts down."

"But last night—!"

"I wasn't timing it," he points out, his voice a low growl. I flinch back, as if slapped. "Were you timing it? No? Then let's experiment."

Paris grabs my arm and pulls me towards the door, squeezing so hard I cry out in pain. From my neck, there's a rattle and the roots slide out of my neck. They hover, swaying like snakes trying to get a bead on a target. Paris side-eyes the roots, especially their sharp tips and relaxes his grip a little, though his hold is still too tight.

Paris slides open the balcony door and leads me outside. He glances at his watch and announces, "Experiment beginning… Now!"

Our feet crunch as we trudge through the snow towards the parapet. In the light of day, I see skyscrapers all around, majestic buildings with logos running across their tops, parks crisscrossed by concrete lanes and the Scioto River spanned by bridges in the distance. I'm in downtown Columbus, probably in one of the luxury residential buildings near the Ohio Statehouse. I've never beheld the city from this height before. A part of me wants to take a moment to enjoy the view but the cold makes it impossible to enjoy anything. The entity with many tendrils is already taking away my body heat, leaving me slower and weaker, dulling my brain. Even the roots in my neck are slowing down, moving lazily from side to side.

"Paris," I whimper, nervous.

He refuses to look at me, his eyes fixed on the cityscape, his expression blank and unaffected by the cold. "Isn't it beautiful?" he muses, though he doesn't seem to care one way or another. We reach the parapet and he puts a hand on top of the metal railing. "One of the best parts of downtown to live in. Expensive too but I can afford it. In fact, I can afford just about anything. All that I'll ever need, I can get. All that you'll ever need, I can get."

"Paris, please!" I plead. How is he not freezing to death in this cold? Even Paris, with his normal body, wearing only sneakers and jeans and a sweater, should be shivering violently right now but he acts like it's a mild summer's day. Meanwhile, I'm about to faint from the chill penetrating all the way to my bones. I pull on my arm, desperate for release but Paris's grip is as unmovable as stone. Is he normally this strong or am I just too weak while I'm outside in the cold? Probably both.

"Before your stalker attacked you," he continues, ignoring my struggles, "I made sure you had someone by your side when you needed someone. You loved me for that. You could depend on me; unlike all the other men you've ever had in your life." He finally looks at me and I'm startled to see a soft smile on his face. "No matter what happens, Rose, I'll make sure you're all right. But you must take care of me too, okay? This can't be a one-sided thing, where I give and give and you take and take. You've gotta give me something back. Got it?"

I want to look away from that soft smile, because I don't trust or believe it. There's malicious intent behind it, intent to hurt and control. Survival instincts tell me to keep eye contact, though, to let him know I'm listening. Just keep him calm, I think, not daring to look away. Don't upset him further. If you do, you have no idea how he might react. My voice trembles as I say, "Okay. I mean, yes, I'll give back."

The smile on Paris's face grows wider. "Good," he says. "I'm glad we see eye to eye on that." He kisses me and I kiss him back, putting my free hand on his arm. Tears fill my eyes but I dare not let them roll down my cheeks. If Paris sees me crying, I'm sure he'll be furious. When he draws away, his hateful smile reminds me of a cat with the yellow bird whose name I couldn't remember either in its mouth.

I wait for him to turn around and guide me back inside but he doesn't. Instead he smiles wider and I realize he means to continue with this punishment masquerading as an experiment, whether or not I agree to his terms. I wonder if he will keep me out here till I die?

An eternity of cold goes by with Paris maintaining a tight grip on my arm. My roots grow sick of the cold and, like stop-motion figures from an old movie, retreat into my neck. I begin to grow woozy as my vision blurs and I moan softly. Paris hears it and flashes me that cruel, bird-eating grin.

I fall against the parapet, on the verge of passing out. "Time!" Paris calls and takes me back inside, leading me to the couch before draping a thick, fuzzy blanket over me.

"Twenty minutes," he announces, speaking directly into my ear. The violent shiver that wracks my body has nothing to do with the cold. Humming a rock tune to himself, Paris strolls over and closes the balcony door before striding to the kitchen. "You can survive out in the cold for at least twenty minutes. Well, now we know for the future."

Twenty minutes? It felt like hours. At least it's over now.

Warmth returns to me in small doses. I draw my knees up to my chest, wanting to cry, but I don't, in fear of setting Paris off.

Again, as if thinking of him had the power to summon him, Paris appears behind me and places a hand on my shoulder. I jump and Paris makes shushing noises at me, slipping his free hand onto the opposite shoulder.

"It's all right," he assures me, his voice low and soft. He walks around the couch and bends down till we're at eye level, his face warm and full of kindness. It's the Paris from before, the one who saved my life and said he loved me. "I won't make you go out into the cold again. That's over. We know your limits now." He strokes my cheek gently. "Not unless we have to, anyway." He laughs as if telling the punchline of a funny joke. "We're going to be happy here. You'll see."

I nod my head vigorously. "Yes. Yes, we will. Be happy, I mean."

Paris smiles. He believes me.

Which is good, because I don't believe in this nice Paris anymore. This is just an act. The Paris who snapped because I wouldn't kiss him and took me outside to punish me, that's the real Paris. And if the real Paris considers it rational to threaten my life over a kiss, I'm terrified to find out what happens if I deny him anything else.

What kind of man did I get myself involved with?

I catch movement out of the corner of my eye and I look towards the greenhouse. Through the glass looking out onto the balcony, I can see the shadow of a figure moving through the greenhouse, the opaque glass obscuring any features. Someone else is here.

I leap off the couch, dart past a surprised Paris and through the greenhouse door, blanket still wrapped around, searching around for the unknown houseguest. To my surprise, though, I find the greenhouse empty, not a person in sight. I blink and jerk my head in every conceivable direction but the number of people in the room doesn't change. I'm all alone.

The disappointment is like heavy weights on my shoulders.

"Rose? Is everything all right?"

Paris stood in the doorway, looking confused and annoyed all at once. "Maybe you should rest a bit," he suggests. "I think the cold did a bigger number on you than I gave it credit. You're acting funny."

It takes me a moment to recover. "I'm sorry. You're right, the cold's messing with my head." I make a gesture with my hand to indicate just how much my brain's been addled. "Please, could you help me back inside, Paris?"

His face relaxes and he offers me his arm before leading me back inside and towards the kitchen. I sit in one of the chairs in front of the island, while Paris goes to the fridge and pulls out some bread. He starts on about another experiment for us to try, to see if I can eat anything, or if I even need to eat. I nod my head, barely paying attention; I'm thinking of the shadow I saw in the greenhouse. I could have sworn I saw someone in there. But if there was someone, where did they go? And why didn't they save me when Paris took me outside?

As Paris places a plate with bread in front of me, I decide it doesn't matter. Before I get too deep into this—this thing I have with him, I'm going to get out of here.

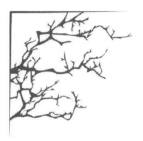

CHAPTER FIVE

Paris tries to feed me toast, bacon, eggs, milk, orange juice and yogurt. I end up puking each one in his sink. To my relief, Paris doesn't get angry with me. Instead, he gives me water—something that I can stomach—and rubs my back before leading me back to the couch and draping the blanket over me again. "You did well," he assures me. "That's enough experiments for today. We know a bit more now about your body. So, you just rest, okay? You just rest."

I will, thanks, I think, full of disdain. After all, you're the one who forced those experiments on me. I don't dare say it out loud, though.

The rest of the day is like a dream. Paris eagerly waits on me hand and foot, making sure I'm comfortable, showing me how to bring up streaming services on his TV, building up a fire when he notices my hands are still cool to the touch. Later in the day, he makes us both herbal tea and I find I can drink that as well. It's a little much, to be honest but I go with it. After all, it's not every day you get the experience of a princess with an attentive prince. Or is a princess with her attentive footman more accurate?

Whatever it is, it's better than the alternative.

Keeping that in mind, I don't allow myself to relax around Paris. Not now that I know what kind of person he is and the kind of things he'll do if he gets mad at me. The best thing for me would be to get out from under Paris's thumb and put as much distance between us as possible. After the "experiment" on the balcony, there's no doubt in my mind I want to do just that.

But how do I get away from him when going outside will kill me? And do I dare even try, knowing what he'll do if he captures me?

The following day, Paris gathers his things to leave for a full day of classes, promising to be back by six. He hesitates when it comes time to leave though, fussing over my blanket and wanting to check every limb and digit to make sure I'm okay. Only when I tell him that I'll be fine and it'll come back to haunt him around exam time if he doesn't show up for classes does he leave, kissing me on the forehead before he goes. When he's gone, I attempt to relax, though remaining vigilant. After all, Paris could come back and decide to stay with me rather than go to classes.

I stay on the couch, watching and listening. After a few minutes, the furnace switches on, filling the air with warmth and noise. After a few more minutes have passed by, I relax a little more and retreat into my thoughts.

When I was in junior high, I was very involved in school theater and during my last year, I got the female leads in both the winter and spring productions. Both times, I starred opposite Andy Claycraft, who was cute and at age fourteen had a great tenor's voice. We started dating a couple of weeks before opening night in April, which no doubt helped our on-stage chemistry. But after the last curtain fell and it started to get warm, Andy changed. He didn't want me to hang out with my friends, to talk to other guys and got grouchy every time I couldn't see him. I began to get the impression that if he could, he'd keep me locked away from the rest of the world. That scared me but I tried to ignore it. After all, Andy was a decent guy, despite his hot-headed moments. What was the worst he could do?

However, our relationship and any pretense that my fears were baseless, went up in smoke when I stayed late after class one Friday to talk to my history teacher. As soon as I stepped out the front doors of the school, Andy started shouting at me, accusing me of flirting with Mr. Lauterbach. I was shocked and stammering from embarrassment, told him I was just going over some points for my final essay so I could ensure an A grade. Andy called me a liar I called him a jerk and threatened to break up with him if he didn't stop acting out. He responded by slapping me hard enough to leave a bruise.

Out of nowhere, my brother Brian, who was home from school early and had come by to pick me up, appeared and tackled Andy to the ground, putting him in a headlock. When the teachers finally arrived to break up the commotion, Brian and I explained what Andy had done to me. The teachers led Andy away to the Principal's Office. Brian led me to his car while I cried and held my cheek, ignoring the stares of everyone who'd watched but hadn't bothered to intervene.

I don't know what happened to Andy after that, beyond that his parents were called to the school and he wasn't around for the last few weeks of junior high or at the high school most of my class went to in the fall. I do remember that my parents sat my sisters and I in the living room soon after the slap and gave us a long talk about how romantic partners were supposed to treat each other and what to watch out for in someone we were dating. I felt the conversation was redundant; after all, I'd experienced it firsthand. I knew what to look for now and I swore I'd never date a guy who hit girls again.

Guys like Andy and Paris don't believe women are equals. They believe women should be controlled so they themselves can perceive themselves as masculine and formidable and will do whatever they can to ensure that control is never questioned.

Degrading comments about their partner's bodies and minds, isolating them from so-called loser friends and even violence. All of them are on the table to guys like Andy and Paris. Afterwards, they'll tell you they love you and they didn't mean it and it'll never happen again. All lies, because the girls they tell it to want to believe their partners love them and will believe all sorts of lies to keep that belief alive. Even if it kills them, by which time it's too late for them to realize what was glaringly obvious: that these guys are scum and they can't be changed by love, no matter how much we desire them to.

And somehow, I'm in this situation again, only this time it's worse: unlike when I was dating Andy, Paris and I are both adults and there's no Brian or school administration or parents to keep him from hurting me again. How am I supposed to get away from him under these circumstances?

What had changed for me? How did I enter another relationship with an abusive guy when I know better? If I could remember how I ended up with Paris in the first place, I'm sure that would help. But nothing has come back since I woke up in the greenhouse. I still can't remember any of the last couple of years and in addition to whatever Paris's home is called, which I forgot again, I can't remember a lot of other random stuff: the name for the places where people go to worship or the buildings where trains go to pick up and drop off people, what a sailboat or a stop sign is supposed to look like, the names of landmarks I've known since childhood, or even things like how to use an oven or how to boot up and use a computer. All of it's hidden behind a wall of grey mist, keeping me from feeling whole and to some extent normal again.

Some of that I can live with, I can't see how it would be helpful in my current situation, like using an oven. But what if some of the useful knowledge, like how to use a computer or the place-names I can't remember, doesn't ever come back? How will I ever get away from Paris when my brain can't tell me how to do something as basic as an online search?

I wish I was at home. Not the home on campus but my home in Marion. I wish I was in our living room, reading a book while Maddy practices ballet, Mom and Hope unload about annoying kids and parents at their respective jobs from the kitchen and Dad and Brian fiddle with machines in the garage while discussing whatever men discuss while alone. A typical Saturday at my happy place. What I wouldn't give to be there now.

I shake my head, tired of pondering my situation. I need to occupy myself with something else for a little while.

I free myself from the blanket, turn on the TV and start flipping through the channels. For a while I watch a news channel but the stories they report are depressing and do nothing for my mood. A shooting in another state, a murder in a nearby city, speculation on which unlikeable politician might run for President next year. It gets to be a bit much, so I switch it off and watch a comedy series on a streaming service until Paris gets home.

We have dinner; or rather he has dinner while I sit and nod half listening as he tells me about his day. Some of the places and a few of the people he mentions sound familiar to me but none of it clears the fog over my memories away.

Around nine, I yawn and mention to Paris I'd like to sleep. Hopping to my side like an eager footman again, he walks me upstairs to his room. "I'll take the couch," he assures me over my protests. "Taking it slow, remember? 'Sides, I got a ton of homework." He smiles and I fake one in return.

Paris heads back downstairs and I change into some pajamas I find in the drawer Paris stores my clothes in. Dressed for bed, I slip into the king-sized bed, pulling the satin blankets over me. The bed and sheets are soft and I burrow deep into them, contented. The sound of a stereo comes from downstairs, rock music floating softly through the floor. I let out another yawn and fall asleep as a man sings about life on the road and how he and his girl were made for it.

***

I wake with a start and find myself lying on my knees while my upper abdomen hangs over the edge of the bed. For a hazy, dream-influenced moment, I wonder if a monster has come out of the bed and is pulling me into the mattress but then I see that the roots in my neck have slithered out and are searching for a surface to wrap around or push off from. I roll my eyes even as I'm overcome by the hunger to let them down into the earth. Well, better get this over with.

As I traipse downstairs I catch sight of Paris is cooking in the kitchen. He turns and calls out to me but I ignore him and sprint the last couple of feet to the greenhouse, flopping onto my back on the nearest bed of dirt. At once, my roots burrow deep and start pulsing. I breathe heavily, like I've run a marathon in the short distance between the bedroom and the greenhouse.

For a while, there's nothing but me, the greenhouse and the roots pulsing. The great need that compelled me downstairs to the greenhouse ebbs away and I fall into a meditative silence.

After a time Paris appears, holding a box in his arms. He clears his throat. "Um, Rose? Can I discuss something with you?"

I lift my head lazily. "You know, this greenhouse is absolutely beautiful."

He blinks, surprised. "Really? You think so?"

I see the eager look on his face and realize I'm so at ease, I forgot to keep my guard up. "Yeah," I say quickly. "It's really calm and pretty in here. It shows how much work you put into it."

Paris blushes at the compliment. "Thanks," he says. "I got into gardening when I was a kid. My mother used to have a sunroom when she was alive and she let me help her tend the garden with her. She always made gardening a lot of fun: we used to sing songs together while we worked and she would tell me about how amazing plants are and what they can do for people."

A sad look crosses his face. "When she died, I kept gardening in the sunroom until my bitch of a stepmom tore it down and turned it into an indoor pool. Gardening kept my mother's memory alive for me. Now I do it because I like it. It's like you're in control and able to create something beautiful, isn't it? Besides, plants are amazing. They can make their own food and some of the most powerful medicines out there can be synthesized from plants. It's mind-blowing to work with something so potent. Don't you agree, Rose?"

I nod, not out of agreement but to keep him in a good mood. Paris smiles at me before hitting his forehead with the tips of his fingers as he suddenly remembers what he wanted to say before I distracted him. "Oh, I almost forgot. There's something I wanted to ask you."

"Sure. What's up?"

"Um, do you mind if I take some blood samples?"

I do a double take, sure I misheard him. "Say that again?"

"I've been thinking," Paris explains, striding over to me. "You're still a mystery to the both of us and *the Record* doesn't have any answers. So, I thought I'd take some of your blood, see if I can't find anything out about you. I have access to a highly advanced biology lab, the benefit of having a father who is the CEO of a pharmaceutical company, so I'll run some tests and see if I can find anything useful. Are you okay with that?"

"Um...?"

But Paris was already prepping, setting the box down on the stone embankment and pulling out vials, alcohol swabs, a blue strip of rubber and a syringe. I eye the silver needle, my heart hammering against my chest, sweat breaking out on my forehead and on my palms. I have the worst phobia around needles. Trips to the pediatrician as a kid used to require one parent and two nurses to hold me down so the doctor could give me my vaccination. To this day, I still don't do well with them.

I squirm as Paris pulls a couple of cotton balls from the bag, scooting away from him and that sharp little needle. Paris notices my reaction and offers me a sympathetic smile.

"Scared of needles?" he asks. I nod my head. Paris sighs in understanding.

"Don't worry." He pats my hand reassuringly. "I've got a bit of experience with this. It won't hurt much, I promise."

Paris gives me another heartwarming smile and soaks a cotton ball with rubbing alcohol. Feeling along my arm for a vein before selecting a spot and dabbing it. Throwing the used cotton ball behind him, Paris ties the blue rubber strip around my arm and grabs the vials and needle. The whole time he hums a rock tune, like he's putting together a cabinet on a Sunday afternoon.

I'm still scared and I struggle harder as Paris raises the needle. A whimper escapes my throat and tears prickle the corners of my eyes. In the dirt, the pulsing roots slow, as if sensing my distress. Paris only smiles again, holds down my arm with his free hand and says, "Here we go." Before I can close my eyes, he inserts the needle.

There's a sharp tugging sensation and something slides underneath my skin. I hiss in pain and the roots shift nervously in the ground. Dark red fluid flecked with neon green flows into a tube attached to the syringe. God, that's weird. It's so weird, it takes my mind off my fear and pain. Everything about me is so weird. I see my green skin or pink hair and must remind myself that's my green skin and my pink hair. When I look at the rosebuds on my head—which I've learned can't be crushed no matter how hard I press something into them—it takes me a moment to remember they're attached to my scalp and not some girly headband. Now my blood has neon green bits in it. What's next? Asexual reproduction?

Still humming, Paris screws in one of the vials. Blood sloshes in and he proceeds to fill each of the vials until they resemble red glow sticks.

"All right, I'm taking the needle out." He gives me another reassuring smile before adding, "You did well. I'm very proud of you." He draws the needle from my arm and a little blood dribbles out of the hole in my skin. Applying a cotton ball to the wound, Paris grabs a small box and pulls out a wide bandage, which he places over the cotton ball.

"Be right back." He stands and takes the vials out of the greenhouse. A moment later he reappears minus the vials.

"I'll take those to get examined," he tells me, sitting back down. "It won't take me long to get some results." A shadow passes over his face and his hands ball into fists. "It's one of the few benefits of being his son," Paris snarls, his voice as angry and as predatory as when he took me out onto the balcony. "The bastard's a controlling egomaniac. He expects me to do whatever he says and I can't say no to him without getting my head bitten off. But then he does things he calls presents or favors, like letting me use my trust fund a year early, buying me my own apartment, access to his company's lab. He doesn't do it because he loves me, though. It's all to remind me that he's my father and I'm supposed to be grateful to him. Grateful, for Christ's sake! But I've nothing to be grateful for. I could get by fine without any of the shit he gives me. I don't need any of it, not from him. I hate him. He makes me so mad. All those damned shitheads make me so mad!"

Abruptly Paris stands and sweeps everything off the nearest workbench, sending it crashing to the floor. Picking up an empty flowerpot he launches it at the wall, followed by the bottle of rubbing alcohol. I watch in terror, curling up into a ball and trembling. *The mask is off, the monster's out of the closet*, I think wildly.

Paris spins around and scrutinizes me, his eyes wide with unfathomable rage. I close my eyes, waiting for him to charge me, grab me and hurt me.

But nothing happens. Nothing at all.

I open my eyes with trepidation, confusion mixed with apprehension. Paris is studying me like a raging bull about to strike. The greenhouse is so quiet, I can hear his every inhale and exhale. Our eyes connect and a look of horror passes over his face.

Without warning, Paris rolls up the sleeve of his shirt, screams at the top of his voice and bites his forearm. Blood trickles out from between his teeth, falling to the floor with little plops. I cover my mouth with my hands, muffling a horrified scream.

An eternity passes by in two seconds. Finally, Paris lets go of his arm and runs out of the greenhouse, leaving me behind still wondering what the hell I had just witnessed.

Another minute goes by before my roots slide out of the dirt and once more retract inside me, freeing me to walk around. As I enter the living room, there are footsteps on the stairs and Paris emerges with his shirt sleeve still rolled up and his elbow wrapped in gauze. He looks away from me, abashed.

"Um," I begin, not sure what I should say, or of what will happen if I say anything.

"Sorry you had to see that," says Paris, refusing to look at me. "I've had it rough and I don't always know how to deal with it. Nobody ever taught me how to deal with my anger and I...I'll go clean up the mess in the greenhouse." He shuffles past me, moving like a man who has lost all hope of happiness.

An idea pops into my head. "I'll clean it up," I announce. Paris turns and surveys me with surprise.

"No, you don't have to do that. After all, it's all my fault—!"

"It's fine." I stride over to him and then, to his amazement and to mine as well, hug him. "Look, I'm living in your home. We're a couple, right? So, let me help you and...maybe things won't be so rough anymore. 'Kay?"

Paris looks on the verge of crying. Instead he throws his arms around me and pulls me close. "Thanks, Rose," he whispers.

"No problem," I reply, even though my heart is knocking a jackhammer against my ribcage. "I'm happy to."

I want to say something more but then I spot something sticking out of Paris's pocket. Another idea comes to me and I reach down and pluck his phone out, quickly pushing it up into my sleeve before he can notice. Paris lets go of me, looking much better than he did before. "I'm going to go run these samples over to the lab." He walks over to the kitchen and picks a cooler up from the island. "I'll be back later today, okay?"

"Okay," I reply, flashing him my best fake grin. "Take your time, all right?"

I watch as Paris goes to the front hallway, puts his shoes on, grabs his keys from a hook on the wall and then leaves. A moment later the locks slide into place and there's silence. I wait a minute, then look down at my hand and the phone I pulled from Paris's back pocket while we were hugging. It's nothing special or high-tech, just a simple flip phone to call and text people.

Perfect for getting me out of Paris's home and out of his grasp.

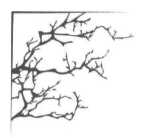

CHAPTER SIX

I speed-walk to the far end of the greenhouse, holding onto the phone so tight the plastic casing digs into my skin. I have his phone. I have his phone! Now I can get out of here and away from Paris before he does something permanent to me. More permanent than what he's already done to me, anyway.

I stop and sit at the edge of the soil bed at the back of the greenhouse. I don't know what's happened to me these past couple of years to push me into the arms of someone like Paris but I know I'm not going to let it keep me in this relationship. Especially when I don't remember it. Nope, I'm getting out of here and I'm getting out of here quick.

As I consider all of this, I glance over at the yew and orange tree with their odd pained faces, reminding me of my own pain and terror since I woke up in this greenhouse. And that's when I observe the bulges and twists in the trunks. If I look at them in a certain way, they do kind of look like human limbs. The yew tree looks like it has an arm on either side of its trunk held rigidly against its side, like a soldier at attention. The orange tree looks like someone crossed their arms in front of their chest, hugging themselves. And that's not all, I can make out what look likes rudimentary breasts on the orange tree, just far enough below the pseudo-face to be anatomically correct.

No wonder I thought they were people at first. They look like how I feel living here and I was seeing all that subconsciously or something.

How they got in the exact shape to mirror my mood, I don't know but that's not important. Escaping is.

I return my full attention to the phone and flip it open. Only three little numbers and I'll be on my way out of here. What happens after that, I don't know. Perhaps I'll end up in a government lab, where I'll be poked and prodded and dissected for the advancement of knowledge and the US military. Or maybe the cops who find me will take pity on me and spirit me and that magic book away to my family, where they can take care of me until we can figure out how to fix what Paris did to me. After all, was he unable to reverse the side effects? Or was that just his way of controlling me? With a guy like that, you can never be too sure.

A loud squawk echoes above my head. I look in that direction and a black form swoops down from the ceiling towards me. I shriek, throwing up my arms over my face. There's another squawk and the sensation of warm plastic disappears from my hand.

I drop my arms, confused. The phone is no longer in my hand. I stare at my empty palm. "What the—?" I wonder aloud.

From behind me I hear a series of short, throaty barks, one after the other, like a laugh. I spin around and see a large black bird with a long thin beak staring at me from one of the shrubs. It's a crow and it has Paris's phone in its talons.

I rush at the bird, reaching for the phone. The crow only squawks in irritation and hops to another shrub. I jerk a hard right and follow it. "Give that back!" I shout.

But the bird doesn't give me the phone. Instead it hops along the bushes and trees, dodging and pecking at my outstretched hands every time I get too close. One of its strikes succeeds in piercing my skin and I bleed a little. The roots in my neck give a warning rattle as I examine the wound. To my astonishment though, the wound closes almost immediately, as if it never existed.

I have super healing powers. Neat.

Before I can marvel at my healed hand a bit more, the crow takes flight again, this time alighting on the top of the palm tree, Paris's phone still tucked safely between its talons. The bird glares down at me and I glower back. For some reason, I feel like it's testing me, judging me on my attempts to get the phone back. We regard each other for what feels like an eternity. Finally, it flaps its wings and takes flight, at the same time dropping the phone over my head. I shriek as the device hurtles towards me but I reach up anyway to catch it. The phone hits one hand bounces off the palm and then falls into my other hand. My fingers wrap around it before I can lose it again.

"Yes!" I cry. I turn around, looking for the crow to gloat at it but it's not in the greenhouse anymore.

My eyes narrow as I hunt for the bird. Where did it go? I turn around a couple of times, sure I'm just overlooking it but it's nowhere, not even underneath the workbenches or resting on a leafy branch. I'm all alone again. I go to the balcony door and test it. Locked tight, so there's no way the crow could have gotten in or out through there. More puzzled than before, I step out of the greenhouse and back into Paris's home however, it's not in the kitchen nor the living room. I check upstairs for good measure. No sign of the bird. I come back to the greenhouse almost expecting it to be there, haughtily contemplating me as if to say, *I've been here this whole time, silly girl. Didn't you see me?*

But the crow's still not there. I really am all alone.

"How?" I ask aloud. The question hangs in the air for a moment before I remember what I came here to do. I flip it open and input the numbers.

One ring. Two rings. "911, what is your emergency?"

My heart hammers in my chest and my breath hitches. That's the police on the other end. What am I supposed to do now?

"911, is anyone there?"

That's right, I'm supposed to speak. What do I say?

"I'm being held here against my will by my boyfriend."

A pause. Then, "Ma'am, do you know where you're located?"

I shake my head, even though I know the dispatcher can't see me. "I'm not sure," I explain. What's Paris's home called? Dammit, I forgot it again! I can't even remember the word that describes that it's on the roof! "It's big, expensive and it has a balcony."

"Stay on the line, ma'am. We're tracing your call. Can you find any mail with an address on it?"

Before I can say, "Let me check," I hear a familiar squawk and the phone's pulled from my hands. Up above, the crow is flying close to the ceiling, the phone in its talons. I can hear the dispatcher asking in a tinny whisper if I'm still there.

I chase the crow around the greenhouse, hands outstretched in case it drops the phone like it did last time. My legs are too stiff and slow, though, and I lag further behind it at every turn. "Goddammit!" I shout in frustration. Above me, the crow lets out another chorus of barking laughter.

After what feels like an age of playing ring-around-the-greenhouse, the crow drops the phone. I dive and somehow manage to catch it before it hits the ground. I allow myself a moment of relief before checking the phone. The call's been disconnected. The crow's talons must've hit the End button or something.

"Goddammit!" I repeat, searching for the crow so I can throttle it. But again, it's vanished. I check the kitchen and living room, then upstairs and finally back into the greenhouse. The crow is nowhere to be found. How the hell is it doing that? Is it Houdini reincarnated?

I shake my head. I'll bother about the crow later. For now, though, I have another phone call to make. Hopefully this one lasts long enough to send help.

From the front door, a voice calls. "Rose? I'm back!"

My stomach lurches into my throat. Paris is back. What will he do to me if he finds out I used his phone to call the police?

"Rose!" Paris calls. "I forgot my phone. Do you see it anywhere?"

"No!" I yell, hoping I don't sound guilty or untruthful. I run towards the storage cabinet as fast as my limbs will let me, an idea popping into my head. "Where do you keep the broom and dustpan? I can't find them." I call while frantically searching for a place to hide the phone. I spot a broom and dustpan between the storage cabinet and the workbench next to it. I bend down, place the phone by the cabinet's base and pull the broom and dustpan out. When I turn around, Paris is leaning in the doorway.

My heart is doing a jackhammer against my ribcage again. Sweat breaks out on my forehead. Oh God, please let those be the only signs of fear I'm showing right now. "Never mind, I found them. And I found your phone, too." I bend down to retrieve it. "See? It's right here." I smile.

Paris crosses the distance between the door and the storage cabinet, grabs my wrist and squeezes. I cry out and the roots in my neck slide out with a rattle.

"I never lose my phone," Paris growls with a suspicious frown. "Especially not that phone. My dad monitors my normal cell phone to make sure I'm on the up-and-up. I use that one to make calls that I don't want him knowing about. How odd that you're around the first time I lose track of it." He takes the phone from me but doesn't place it back in its pocket.

"That is a weird coincidence," I agree, struggling to keep this fake-cheery façade up. "Paris, could you let go of my wrist? You're hurting me."

"Did anything happen while I was gone?" Paris interjects, squeezing harder. The roots slide out further, swaying angrily. "Anything at all?"

My voice becomes a whimper as I speak. "Nothing," I tell him. "Paris, please!"

"Nothing?" His grip tightens and the bones in my arm protest. Fresh tears well in my eyes and my roots slide out more, rearing their tips up like cobras preparing to strike. If he doesn't let me go soon, my wrist will break and I don't want to test how strong my healing abilities are. Oh God, what can I say to make him stop—

For the third time that day, an idea pops into my head. "A crow got in here," I manage, gesturing with my free hand to the greenhouse. Paris blinks and the grip on my wrist eases. The roots hover, waiting to see what happens next. Encouraged, I add, "Yeah, it just appeared and tried to attack me. I tried to chase it out but it got out on its own."

Paris scrutinizes me. "That's odd," he remarks. "I've never noticed any crows around this building before." He lets go of my wrist and proceeds to investigate the greenhouse. I watch as he searches, hoping against hope that he doesn't decide I'm trying to fool him and turns on me. After a couple of circuits around the workbenches he says, "Well, there's definitely no crow here now."

"It was here," I insist. The moment it's out I wish I could take it back. Even to myself, I sound desperate to be believed. Paris glares at me suspiciously, then looks at the phone he took from me. It's buzzing in his hand, the little screen on the top flashing a number at him. While I have no way of knowing who it really is, in the back of my mind I'm sure it's the 911 dispatcher trying to reach me.

Without a word, Paris drops the device to the ground. He lifts his foot up and brings it down with a crunch. I gasp as he stomps on the phone, over and over and over, like he's trying to kill a massive, tough-shelled beetle. When the phone resembles little more than a pile of glass and metal, he looks at me and says, "I've been wanting a new phone anyway. This model's just a piece of trash," before stalking out of the greenhouse.

I stand there in shock, staring at the broken remains of my shattered hope. From the living room Paris shouts, "I'm leaving again. See you later," before the front door opens and closes. The sound of the door reminds me that I'm holding a broom and dustpan and I decide I better start cleaning like I said I would. If Paris comes back again, it won't look good if there's still a mess in here.

As I throw the pieces of broken pots and phone into the trash my roots slide back into me, I realize something: that crow prevented me from getting away from Paris. I could've found the address to this place, or even given the dispatcher time to triangulate my position like in the cop shows, if that crow hadn't cut my call short.

It was almost as if it wanted to make sure I couldn't be rescued from Paris. But that's ridiculous. Crows are smart but not that smart! They don't have malicious intentions!

But if that's true, why did it try to keep the phone away from me? And why did it only appear when I was trying to make a call?

I stop sweeping and consider it. If that crow did want to keep me here, then why? What possible reason could a crow have for wanting me to stay in Paris's home and at his mercy?

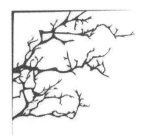

CHAPTER SEVEN

I don't know where I am. It looks like a forest but the plants are all strange and otherworldly. Some are made of wood, others of light or smoke and one tree's bark is made from human skin. Many have features I never imagined on plants: tentacles, insect legs, animal faces, human faces, human limbs, mouths, snouts, eyes, horns, claws and things I can't name. It's Salvador Dali on nightmare fuel but more vivid than any paintbrush could paint.

Weaving in and among the strange plants are animals even stranger still: rabbits with sharp spines and long tails; white and purple and green foxes with multiple tails walking on two legs; odd, ape-like beasts with several arms and eyes like cats. There's even a woman whose body appears to be half-spider, with long hairy legs and fangs dripping poison.

Everything's staring at me. Those with limbs point at me and those with mouths whisper, though I'm not sure if they're whispering to me, to themselves, or to each other. I'm not even sure what they're saying, only that it's in another language and the sound of it makes my skin crawl.

Among the creatures, I spot one with a form I can't quite make out, humanoid at times but at other times it's something much bigger and terrifying—And it's laughing. Laughing and pointing. Pointing at me.

It's making fun of me.

I want to ask what's so funny but a hand grabs my shoulder and spins me around. Paris faces me, mutated and monstrous, fingers transformed into claws, mouth full of fangs and eyes alive with manic glee. I shrink into a seven-year-old girl, the last age I was when I believed in monsters in the closet and shiver in terror as he considers me. I'm in a fairy tale, except it's a Grimm fairy tale with a dark ending.

Paris licks his lips hungrily, his tongue long and snakelike. "You're mine," he growls, leaning towards me. I stare into his mouth, rows of curved, serrated teeth lining his throat, going back into eternity.

* * *

My eyes fly open and dart around Paris's bedroom. Windows set between the wall behind me and the ceiling let in wan moonlight and illuminate the sparse bedroom. There aren't many places to hide but I check each one anyway. Besides the bed I'm sleeping in, there's only a long row of drawers set along one wall, a bookshelf and closet dominating the other. An alarm clock on one set of drawers marks the time as a little past one in the morning. I slip out of bed and, like the seven-year-old I'd been a moment ago, check the drawers and the closet. There's no one here but me. No Paris, monstrous or otherwise. No strange plants or animals. Nothing that looks humanoid but isn't. I'm alone.

I sigh with relief. It was only a dream. God, that was a scary one. I know what inspired it, too: that book Paris gave me yesterday, the one with all the stories of kami gods and yurei ghosts and yokai spirits in it. He'd said it was a gift to give me a better understanding of the Forest God who had created *the Record*. And yeah, I'd found the book absorbing when I read it. I didn't realize it had gotten so deep under my skin, though.

I know where Paris's monster form came from, as well. For the past couple of nights, I've been sleeping alone in this room while Paris takes the couch. He said he's being a gentleman while we wait for my memories to come back but I'm scared. Every night, I've gone to bed expecting to wake up and find Paris in here, commanding me to undress for him. And I know that even if I don't want to, even if I'm not ready yet, I'll do it anyway, because the alternative is too terrifying to consider.

But thank God I'm alone, so I shrug my shoulders and slip under the covers once more. *It was just a stress nightmare. People have them all the time.* I'm worried Paris is going to blow up again like he did the other day, so of course it ends up in my dreams. I must stop worrying and be careful, at least until I get out of here. Then everything will be better.

Sleep drifts back over me as I close my eyes. Tomorrow I'll decide what to do about Paris, neatly overlooking the fact that I've promised myself that every night since the phone incident in the greenhouse, only to break it the very next day. But tomorrow I'll stick to it. I'm sure I will.

A loud thump on the floor outside the bedroom. My eyes open and I sit up, wide awake again. What the hell was that?

I gulp and clear my throat. "P-Paris?" I call. No response.

I slip out from beneath the sheets, grab my bathrobe from the foot of the bed and step out of the bedroom. To my surprise the hallway is empty. I tiptoe towards the stairs. "Paris!" I hiss. "Was that you?" Once more no reply, which worries me more than it reassures me.

Suddenly, from the bathroom, comes the sound of skittering on the tiles. I freeze for a second before forcing myself to slowly turn towards the bathroom door. "Paris, are you in there?" I whisper. There's no answer. I open the door, walk in and turn on the light. When my eyes adjust, I see the bathroom is as empty as the bedroom. I raise an eyebrow. What the hell is going on?

I turn off the lights and turn to go. The hairs on the back of my neck stand on end. Someone is here with me.

I spin around and turn the lights back on... nobody! A cold sweat breaks on my forehead. I switch the lights off again, this time I back out of the bathroom and check every direction.

I can't explain it, I know someone was there with me, if only for a second.

A part of my brain tries to convince me that paranoia is setting in after my nightmare but another part is certain that I'm a plant creature saved from death by magic, so I might as well be on the safe side.

I walk down the stairs, my eyes dart and search for my unseen guest or Paris or both. When I reach the first floor, I find it empty, except for Paris sleeping on the couch. I raise an eyebrow, uneasy. Was it my imagination after all?

I glance around the living room and spot Paris's wallet, keys and a few other items on the coffee table. I tiptoe over and bend down to examine them but his smartphone isn't among them. I deliberate for a moment before sneaking around the coffee table, watching Paris in case he wakes up. Slowly, monitoring every inhalation and exhalation, I lift Paris's blanket. Even in the dim light, I can see he's wearing a T-shirt and a pair of grey, pocketless sweatpants. The phone is nowhere in sight. I lay the blanket back down and investigate the rest of the couch but the phone isn't there either.

Inwardly, I groan. *Where did Paris hide his damn phone?*

"Rose."

I jump, head whipping in Paris's direction but he's fast asleep and his lips closed. Panting, I place a hand over my chest with relief, for a moment I thought I was dead.

Now I think about it, the voice hadn't sounded like Paris's. *Then who—?*

"Rose." I jump again but this time I know where the voice is coming from. I make my way to the greenhouse, arms crossed defensively over my chest.

"Who's there?" I murmur.

"Rose," the voice whispers, reminding me of leaves scraping against concrete. "Over here."

I follow the voice into the greenhouse. The moonlight gives the entire room an enigmatic, ethereal aura, like the bizarre forest from my dream. I look around but nothing seems amiss.

"I'm here," I reply, wondering why I came by myself. I should wake up Paris, tell him someone's in the greenhouse. It could be the stalker Paris warned me about, come to kill his rival and get me back, for all I know. Or maybe it's a burglar, someone who's been casing Paris's home and wants to steal everything valuable. Or—

Or maybe it's something from my dream.

A minute passes, though nothing happens. I wait another minute, still nothing happens. I calm down and instead become impatient. Finally, I sigh, annoyed and decide to go back to bed. It must be my imagination playing tricks on me. Maybe in the morning I'll bring it up with Paris, tell him that I thought someone was here last night. How will he react to that? He could show concern, check to make sure that I'm not coming down with an illness or going crazy. Or he might get mad and shout at me for not waking him. I never know how he might react to something. And if I set him off by accident—

A shadow falls over me from above. I look up. Something hangs from the glass ceiling like a giant spider, its features hidden in darkness. The thing jumps to the ground and lands right in front of me, shaking the greenhouse with its impact. I scream and stare at it in horror, taking in the creature's form illuminated in the moonlight.

At least eight feet tall, milky-white skin wrapped around bulging muscles, a blocky head with green flowing hair and a mouth full of sharp, curved incisors. Two pointed horns curve out of its temples and a tiger-print loincloth encircles its waist. The beast looks down at me, the whites of its eyes the size of saucers. "Rose," it says, its voice the same one I heard earlier.

I run. The monster makes a grab for me but I'm already through the greenhouse door. Forcing my legs to move faster than they've ever moved before, I run up the stairs and into the bathroom, turning on the lights and slamming the door behind me, locking it for good measure. The beast runs up the stairs, the walls trembling with each step. I jump into the bathtub as if it were an oasis of safety, peeking over the edge in terror. The roots in my neck slide out, waving and striking every nearby surface in a rhythmic pattern, like a tribal drumbeat of warning to enemies. I doubt it will scare the monster away.

There's a knock at the door and I shriek, ducking below the tub's edge. It's found me! It's going to kill me!

"Rose!" Paris's voice calls. "Rose! What's wrong? Talk to me! Rose!"

Paris? Where's the monster?

I peek out over the edge again and the roots stop their drumming, though they don't slide back into me. My voice quavers as I respond. "Paris, is it just you out there?"

There's a pause before I receive an answer. "Yeah, it's just me. Listen, why don't you open the door and—"

"No!" I shout. "Paris, there's a monster out there! It called me into the greenhouse and chased me up here!"

"Rose, you were just dreaming," replies Paris gently. "You just had a bad dream and—"

"Paris, I wasn't dreaming!" I shout back. "I was awake! I saw a monster! It's out there!"

"Rose, there are no such things as monsters!" Paris replies.

"And dying women can't be brought back to life and turned into plant creatures!" I point out.

Paris doesn't respond for a moment. Then, "I'll check the apartment." I hear him walk around the second floor before descending back down the stairs. After what feels like an eternity, he ascends the stairs again. "Rose?" He knocks on the door, as if making sure I'm still in here. "I checked the whole apartment. Even checked the greenhouse and the balcony. There's no one here but you and me."

For a second, I'm not sure how to reply. A monster of that size couldn't just disappear! But why would Paris lie to me about that? So how did it—?

Paris interrupts my thoughts by pounding hard on the bathroom door. "You going to come out of there, or do I have to break the door down and come get you?" The tone of his voice lets me know I don't want to make him do the latter. I lift myself out of the tub and unlock the door. At the same time, the roots slide back into my neck and grow still. They've decided the danger's passed. Out in the hallway, Paris looks very grumpy at having been woken up.

"You sure you weren't dreaming?" he asks, his eyebrow raised.

Despite how afraid I am, both of Paris and of the monster, I say, "Paris, I know what I saw. It was a big monster, with horns and a tiger loincloth and teeth and all this hair—"

"Sounds like you dreamed of an Oni," Paris yawns dismissively.

"A what?"

"Never mind, I'll tell you in the morning. Hey, if you want me to, I can spend the night with you. Make sure you don't have any bad dreams."

"No, that's all right," I reply a little too quickly. Paris's frown deepens. I think quickly, kiss him on the cheek. This placates him and his frown lessens. "I appreciate the gesture, though," I add. "You know, maybe I was dreaming. That's probably what it was."

"You sure you are all right?"

"Positive," I answer, turning off the bathroom lights before heading back to the bedroom. "Good night," I say closing the door.

"Good night," Paris repeats. The steps groan as he heads backs downstairs.

When I'm finally alone, I let out a small sigh and crawl back into the bed. Despite what I told Paris; I know what just occurred. There was a monster in the greenhouse and it chased me upstairs. I didn't dream that.

What's more, Paris seems to know what it is, too. He called it an Oni, whatever that is. Too bad I must wait till morning to find out.

I shiver, a hundred thoughts buzzing through my head like wasps. I push them away and pull the covers over my head, feeling again like a seven-year-old girl, sure a monster was living in her closet, waiting for her to go to sleep so it could eat her in one big gulp. Only this time the monster is real.

And something tells me I haven't seen the last of it, either.

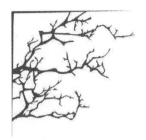

CHAPTER EIGHT

KNOCK! KNOCK! KNOCK!

I groan. My head is pounding this morning, like someone is taking a hammer to an anvil. Only the anvil is my fucking temples and the pain is bad enough to make me say fucking.

KNOCK! KNOCK! KNOCK!

I groan again and open my eyes. I realize that while I do have a headache, the pounding isn't in my head, it's someone on the door. I check the clock and see it's just past seven-thirty.

"Rose?" Paris calls. "Are you awake?"

Before I can reply, "I'm up," Paris lets himself in. He's already wide awake as he wishes me good morning and selects clothes out of the drawers. When he's pulled out a sweatshirt, an undershirt, jeans, boxers and socks, he sits down on the bed and asks me if I had any more dreams last night.

"No, I didn't," I grumble with a little more irritation than I intended, rubbing my temples. Paris frowns and his brow furrows. A second later the back of his hand strikes my cheek with a clap like thunder, sending me back down into my pillow. My tentacles rattle and slide out, pointed in Paris's direction. I moan and press a hand to my throbbing cheek. I flash back to the afternoon with Andy Claycraft on the quad outside school and experience the same sense of rage and humiliation I had that day, along with an underlying fear of the beast before me. God, why did I let myself sound so upset around him? I know what he does when he gets upset!

"You should watch the way you speak to me," Paris snarls. "After all, you woke me up in the middle of the night because you had a dream about an Oni in the apartment. Shenanigans like that makes me kind of cranky, you know."

"Paris, there really was an Oni!" I know he's already in a bad mood but I must make him understand that that Oni thing was real and it meant to hurt me! Even if he's psycho, he does care about me and want me to be okay, doesn't he? "I didn't dream that, I—!"

"You dreamed last night. I looked through the whole house. There was no Oni. You didn't see one. You dreamed it. End of story."

"Paris!" I'm disgusted to hear myself pleading with him but his denials are upsetting me. Why does he insist that it can't be real, when we both know magic and gods exist in the world? Is it because he always wants to be right or some macho bullshit like that? I don't need that right now! "I'm telling you; I didn't dream—"

The rest is cut off as Paris throws his bundle of clothes away, jumps on top of me and wrestles me onto my stomach. My tentacles slap and cut his face but he grabs them out of the air and holds them down. Terrified, I burst into tears. "Paris—" Paris drives his nails into my arm, drawing blood. I whimper as his mouth presses close to my ear.

"You dreamed it!" he snaps. "You dreamed it and if I hear another word about it being real, you're gonna regret it. Got it?"

I'm too terrified to speak, so I nod my head instead. Paris whispers "Good," and pulls his nails out of my skin. "Because I really don't like doing this stuff to you." He kisses the top of my head, then a little below my ear and then on my cheek. "But sometimes people have to do things they don't like doing. I've been doing things I hate all my life just to satisfy other people and I do them every time you make a mistake. But I only do it because I love you. I hope you can understand that."

He turns my head and kisses my mouth and I kiss him back, scared of what he'll do if I don't. As we kiss, Paris gets more excited, kissing me harder, running his free hand down my side and onto my butt. A bit of tongue slips into my mouth.

I pull my mouth away from his, panting. "Can we stop?"

I expect him to say no, instead he nods and says, "You're right. We're wasting time. I gotta get ready for class."

He climbs off me, tugging on my roots so that I'm forced into a sitting position. When he releases them, they whirl madly around me, searching for the enemy that held them down. When no enemy appears, they slow and retreat, though I still sense them shifting inside me, ready in case of trouble.

I furtively glance at Paris trying to gauge his mood. The back of his hand flies into my cheek again, hitting me so hard that I fall out of the bed. My roots zoom out but Paris is already out of range. "I decide when we stop," he says, gathering up his clothes and heading to the door. "Get dressed and be downstairs in ten minutes. Don't keep me waiting."

The door slams shut and I'm left alone, my roots still hunting for Paris. When I sit up, the tears return in full force. I swore I would never be in another relationship like this, not after Andy Claycraft. Perhaps because my life took an awful turn and I looked for comfort anywhere—even from the arms of a monster, or because he charmed me and hadn't revealed his true nature until I was too deeply attached, and dependent, on him. Somehow, I had allowed myself to get stuck in one again. Trapped until I find a way out, from Paris, and not die of cold or lack of nutritious soil *or something.* Until then, how do I make sure I don't die in this relationship? How do I deal with daily torture and terror?

My roots are still whipping around looking for enemies. They're going to make getting dressed difficult. I wish they would go back into my neck already.

Suddenly, the roots stop moving and I watch in amazement as they then slither back into me before becoming still.

I sniff and dry my eyes. I was able to make them stop and go back inside me before they realized there was no enemy to fight. I didn't know I could do that. Somehow, despite my situation, that makes me feel a little better.

I sit up and check the clock. The LEDs read seven-thirty-seven. My heart jumps into my throat and I lose the good feeling I just gained. Paris said I had ten minutes to get dressed. How much time has passed? I hurry and grab my clothes from the dresser, sure Paris will come up to check on how I'm doing any second now.

I head downstairs wearing a loose long-sleeved blouse and black jeans. Paris is waiting for me in the kitchen, digging into waffles with syrup and drinking a cup of coffee. He looks up from his meal and smiles. "You look nice."

"Thanks," I reply stiffly. I guess he's already forgotten he had to get rough with me this morning.

I remain guarded as I pull out a chair and sit across from him at the island. As I do, Paris passes me his tablet. "Check it out," is all he says. I take the tablet from him and feel my eyes go wide as I see the image on the screen. It's an illustration like the ones in *the Record*, though instead of disturbing brush-stroke images involving people coming out of graves or being mauled by trees, I'm staring at a familiar monster. Although this one has a rounder head, white hair and red skin, it's the same monster I saw last night, right down to the tiger-print loincloth.

"You asked me what an Oni is," Paris explains nonchalantly, cutting up another slice of waffle. "Well, there's an Oni. It's kind of like an ogre in Japanese mythology. Some punish sinners in hell, others go around causing sickness and death. There's a whole gallery of them on that thing if you care to look."

I glance at Paris, who's already lost interest in the matter and return to the tablet, scrolling through the pictures and the different artist renderings of Oni. There's one of a blue-skinned Oni with four arms from some anime; a statue of one that resembles an old man; and another one depicted tearing up a village and scooping up helpless townspeople into its mouth. Each Oni is a little different from the others but they're all the same beast.

"Where did I hear of them?" I ask Paris, putting the tablet down. "I don't remember ever seeing one before and there weren't any in that book you gave me."

"You probably saw one in an anime or something." He downs a gulp of coffee and continues, "You definitely didn't hear it from me. I don't like Oni." His face twitches as he speaks.

"Why do you hate Oni?" I ask before I can stop myself.

His face twitches again and he glares at me. "I just don't like them," he answers, a note of bitterness in his voice. Paris goes back to cutting up pieces of waffle with gusto and I return to the tablet. I won't ask him anymore or tell him I've never been an anime fan at any time of my life that I can remember. He's still in a bad mood and if it gets worse, I don't want to know what I'll be forced to do to put him in a better one.

"Calling someone the child of an Oni is implying they're illegitimate!" Paris shouts suddenly, throwing his mug at the wall. It shatters into a million pieces and stains the wall brown.

I scream and drop the tablet as Paris slams his palms on the countertop, his nostrils flared. "You know what some parents in Japan do if their child misbehaves or doesn't live up to their standards? They call them the child of an Oni! Do you know what that means? In Japan, calling a kid the child of an Oni is one of the worse things you can say to him! It's like saying they're nothing but a nuisance, that they're not worth the trouble of existing! It's like saying they're not even their father's child! Do you know how many times my dad has implied I'm not his son based on how I act? Do you? DO YOU?!"

I cringe as Paris walks around the island towards me and I close my eyes, expecting the beating of the century.

I feel a pair of arms encircle me and a head falls onto my shoulder. I open my eyes and see Paris hugging me and crying, his tears staining my blouse. I stay still, terrified a single move could set him off again.

When nothing happens, I pat his back gently, like a mother with a small child. Paris hugs me tighter and gazes up at me, his face the portrait of anguish. He kisses my cheek and then lays his head in the crevice between my neck and shoulder, sniffling.

After a minute or so, he lets go of me and returns to finish his waffle with a morose look on his face. I watch him silently as he devours the last of his breakfast and places the dish and silverware in the dishwasher. Gathering up his stuff for school he surprises me with another kiss on the cheek. "Thanks," he murmurs. "See you later." And then he leaves.

I sit there for a minute after the door shuts, awestruck. What the hell just happened? My mind floats back to when he was hugging me and crying on my shoulder. It was a 180-degree shift from his mood a moment before and completely unexpected. I think again of a small child, moving from one emotional extreme to another at the drop of a hat. It's the perfect comparison and it makes me feel a little sorry for him. If Paris is what happens when a father questions if his son is his son more times than the son can count, it's no wonder Paris is the way he is. A part of me even wants to give him a hug the next time I see him and tell him it'll be alright, because I'm sure nobody in his life ever did.

That doesn't mean I will, though. Or I won't try to find a way to keep him from ever hurting me again.

A few minutes later, as I'm cleaning up the mess made by the coffee mug, a thought occurs to me. I'm in Paris's home. Even better, I'm alone in Paris's home. He's gone and he won't be back for several hours. My heart soars. Now's the perfect time to find out something, a weapon, a piece of blackmail, anything to get me out of here and keep me from getting hurt by him ever again.

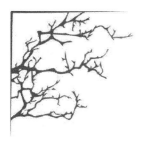

CHAPTER NINE

After my roots have done their daily dig for nutrients, I make my way upstairs and turn right into the bedroom to start my search. I look around the room, taking in everything afresh, including my pajamas on the still-unmade bed. I start with the drawers. Nothing useful reveals itself: T-shirts, dress shirts, sweats, underwear and socks. There are some pornographic magazines and a DVD below a layer of denim jeans that look like Paris might have had these when he was in high school. Not what I'd call a weapon or blackmail material.

I look through the closet and all I find are two suit jackets and a couple of pairs of expensive shoes. The bookshelf also proves fruitless, populated with textbooks, biographies and a couple of novels. I even check under the bed and mattress, as well as by the windowsill, before moving onto the bathroom. Nothing.

I almost head downstairs to continue my hunt when I remember one more place to search. There's a third room on this floor, the door painted the same color as the walls around it, blending into the point that I forget it's there. The linen closet. A light bulb goes off in my head. Of course! It would be the perfect hiding place.

I open the door. Inside are four shelves piled high with sheets, pillowcases and ten different colored hand and bath towels. I search, careful not to move anything out of place in case Paris is the type to notice when things have been shifted around. The bottom shelves yield nothing and neither do the middle-bottom or middle-top shelf. As I start on the top shelf, about four inches above the top of my head, I start thinking of other places Paris might hide something he didn't want found. Perhaps he has a hiding place in the kitchen, knowing I don't eat human food, let alone cook. Or behind one of the posters on the walls. Or—

My finger taps something hard underneath a bedspread. My hand hovers in place. I blink. That doesn't feel like part of the shelf, more like leather.

I slip my hand underneath the bedspread and unearth two books. One of them is an ancient-looking tome with a leather jacket bound in an old ribbon. I recognize it as *the Shin Sekai no Shinki*, *The Forest God's Record*, the book Paris used to save me from death. The other is a small thin book with the word JOURNAL written in big gold letters.

I open *the Shin Sekai no Shinki* and let my fingers roam across the pages. The paper feels weird beneath my fingertips. It reminded me of parchment but was stiff and strangely warm.

Like human skin.

I flip through the pages, lingering over the flowing script and the garish illustrations. One of those illustrations makes me pause and do a double take: it depicts two people standing side by side, their legs becoming tree trunks that sink deep into the ground, while their arms reach above their heads, turning into leafy branches. It reminds me of something but I can't remember what.

The book is starting to creep me out, so I close it, redo the ribbon around the cover and hide it back underneath the bedspread. I then turn to the other book, the one with JOURNAL stamped on the cover. I open to the first page and discover English lettering, although the words are not English. I scrutinize the first line to decipher its meaning.

Ik denk dat ik verliefd ben op mijn criminology lerares.

My eyes grow wide in their sockets. I know that language, I took classes in it during my high school and undergrad years and passed every single one with flying colors. It's Dutch. *Why is Paris's journal in Dutch?*

My thoughts drift back to what Paris had told me the night I first met him, about his ancestors being Dutch traders, which was how they acquired *the Record*. Maybe Paris learned Dutch to get close to his heritage, to read his family's old papers about *the Record*, or because it's a family tradition.

Or maybe he just didn't want other people to read his journal and Dutch is a fitting language to conceal whatever he was writing. Considering the likelihood of running into someone who speaks and reads Dutch, in a country whose people are notorious for not speaking more than one language, I can believe that.

Still, it's a crazy coincidence that the language Paris chose to hide his writings in happens to be the same one I had chosen—I hadn't want to continue with Spanish and French had been too close to Spanish to be a challenge, Dutch sounded exotic enough to appeal to me—I mean, what are the odds?

And what are the odds that those two trees in the greenhouse look like people in pain and terror? Or that your boyfriend has a magic book to save your life just when you need it? A lot of crazy coincidences in one whatever-this-place-is-called.

I look back at the first line of *the Journal*, my mind seamlessly translating the entries into English.

Ik denk dat ik verliefd ben op mijn criminology lerares.
I think I'm in love with my criminology teacher.

My breath catches in my throat, is this Paris's journal? Is he talking about me? I scan the first entry and spot my name in the third sentence. Too curious to stop now, I read from the beginning.

I think I'm in love with my criminology teacher.

I took the criminology class for the credits, then I saw my teacher. Her name is Rose Taggert, she's got red hair and blue eyes and such a sweet, sweet smile. From the moment I saw her walk into the classroom, wearing a green T-shirt and a long black skirt, her high heels clicking on the classroom floor, I think I was attracted to her. Who'd have thought love at first sight was a real thing?

Well, you know me, if I'm even a little interested in someone, I'm not sure how to act around them. And when I try to interact with them

The sentence breaks off, leaving the rest of the line blank. The next couple of lines are filled with sentences that have been started and then scratched out with a pen. I can only make out one of these sentences between the scratch marks. It says

When I tried to flirt with Chrissy.

Chrissy. An old crush? I check the next couple pages but she's not mentioned again. I guess whoever she was, she wasn't worth mentioning beyond that one scratched-out sentence.

I shrug and continue where Paris picks up the story again.

I was so nervous when she started going around the class, having us introduce ourselves. Somehow, I managed to keep myself from stuttering as I said my name, my year and my major. And she smiled. She smiled at me. At me! Not since Ariel has anyone smiled at me, at least not with sincerity like she did. The world is usually full of people who ignore me or find ways to shit on me or both but she smiled at me. And the look in her eyes as she looked at me. She was checking me out, no doubt about it.

I don't know if I've ever been checked out before in my life. It's weird and also kind of flattering.

Like I said before, you hear of love at first sight, though, I always thought that was the talk of shitheads and the people who laugh at me. This world is full of them, people looking to put me down or to hurt me. They were at the camp, everyone at that camp was a shithead and they all did their dirty business on me. And my dad's a shithead too, though he says he does things for my own good. They're all a bunch of shitheads and they fall in love with other shitheads and they fuck the brains out of other shitheads and they have shithead babies and they all want to gang up on me and shit on me.

But not her. Rose Taggert. "Call me Rose," she said. I want to call her Rose so bad—in private and without all my classmates around. I would've come up after class and talked to her but there were so many shitheads who were ahead of me in line. Were they in line because they had questions about the material, we'd be covering this semester, or were they trying to get her into bed with them to have their shithead babies? Probably the latter, knowing the people I deal with in an average day. And that includes the shithead bitches. Shithead bitches will fuck anyone that looks pretty and they can have pretty shithead babies with and these days that can mean other shithead bitches.

Next time I'll sit in the front so that I can talk to her first. Rose isn't a shithead. She's an angel. A real angel. And I know she likes me, she said so when she checked me out after I introduced myself.

I want to find out more about her. I want to know more about Rose.

And we like each other, so I should know more about her. I will know more about her.

I look up from *the Journal*. There's so much to go through, my head hurts trying to figure out where to start. Or is that my brain having trouble remembering all this? Probably a combination of both.

I start with the first revelation: I was Paris's criminology teacher. And while I can believe that was how we met, is that how our relationship began? I re-read the first entry but it strikes me as off. For one thing, if I was Paris's teacher, that would mean I had a relationship with one of my students. I don't think I'm the sort of teacher interested in romantic relationships with my students. It just doesn't seem like me, at least the me I was before.

There are other things that feel wrong, like Paris's writing style: the way he describes things is odd, like how he describes our connection and how he describes other people. It's not just angry, it's antagonistic, as if Paris expects everyone to hate him. Everyone except for me, that is. Somehow, I'm separate from other people and I'm also attracted to Paris, the only other person in this narrative who isn't a shithead.

If this is Paris's recollection of how our relationship started, it's a skewed one.

I move on to the next several entries, my eyes scanning the words and my brain translating them. And as I read, I spot a pattern: Paris describes the classes I teach, the things he's learning, what I'm wearing, including the accessories I put in my hair and the exact shade of lipstick I put on and our growing attraction, expressed in secret winks towards one another, light touches on arms and shoulders when everyone else's attention is diverted. After-class conversations laced with seduction. The Rose Taggert in these entries is aware of the rules against students and teachers dating but nonetheless finds herself unable to resist the strong attraction she feels for Paris. In fact, she revels in the forbidden thrill of it.

None of this is familiar to me and it doesn't clear any of the fog over my memories either. In fact, the more I read, the less the Rose in the book resembles me. Or did I change that much between my last memory and whenever this takes place?

Eventually Paris and I go on a secret first date, which leads to meeting outside of classes, at places where students and teachers won't be seen, let alone seen together. We drive to parts of the city most students don't go out of their way to eat or see movies at. The romance blossoms accelerated by the thrill of doing something we shouldn't. Eventually our love blooms into passion and we sleep together regularly, either at my small one-bedroom place or at his massive one.

Now parts of these entries and our dates feel familiar to me, though not in the way they should. Some of the dates we go on feel like they happened to a pair of total strangers, while others...I feel like I had them but I had them with someone else. And while there's plenty of conversation about school, current events, celebrities and even some comments about Paris's past, mentions of my past and hobbies are non-existent. Nothing about my family, my school days, my love of theater or my dislike of video games. The only discussion of interests outside of criminology is that I like nature parks and flower gardens, which is something I might mention in one of my classes if it came up. Did we never have a conversation about my life?

Also, of note, there's no reference at all to Paris's rage and violence towards me. Does it never happen during these dates, or does he think they're not important enough to write down?

As I keep reading, Paris's anger at the world becomes apparent; his hatred of shitheads, his father and others he blames for his supposedly crappy life, keeps appearing and reappearing. And with each entry, the way he expresses his anger grows a little darker, a little more explicit. Threats of violence against people he claims are interfering in his relationship with me—other teachers, other students, a waiter with a too-neat smile, a librarian making a joke about an author I'm reading, a homeless man on High Street who asks me for change—appear with increasing frequency. I grow queasy as I read the things he wants to do to them, some of which involves barbed wire wrapped around baseball bats, ropes used as nooses and restraints and things involving urine and feces I didn't think people could do to other people.

Paris is not normal.

I finish an entry dated from December and my head gives a nasty throb. Dammit, this headache just won't go away. I must be trying to remember too much at once.

Perhaps I should stop reading and put this horror-journal away for today. Maybe even for forever.

I turn the page and my mouth falls open and I gape at the entry there. Prior to this point, Paris's handwriting has been neat and orderly cursive. But here, Paris has switched print, everything from the size of the letters to the spaces between pen marks are all over the place, some letters more resembling squiggles than the Roman alphabet. It was like Paris's hand was shaking uncontrollably as he wrote it.

I stare at the entry, the words filled with anger and rage.. Pure, unfiltered fury, radiating off the page like heat from a space heater, hot enough to burn.

Rose vertelde me vandaag dat ze een stalker heft.

Rose told me today she has a stalker.

I stare at those nine words. Rose told me today she has a stalker. My stalker. Was this what led to the incident outside the club? Was this the beginning of how I became a plant-creature? I continue reading.

Rose told me today she has a stalker.

We went to get a bite to eat at an Italian restaurant downtown but Rose wasn't eating that much. I thought she might not be feeling well, or that maybe juggling school, teaching and homework was getting to her. She just started to cry when they brought out the veal marsala and I knew then that this was something more.

I comforted her, pulled out a couple twenties and took her out of the restaurant before more people began staring. Bastards can't leave well enough alone, they love other people's misery! Wouldn't I love to hit them with a shovel! Wouldn't I love to stick my ass over their mouths and shit in them! Wouldn't I love to stick a champagne bottle up their assholes and ask them through the shit in their mouth how the bubbles feel! Fucking shitheads deserve everything I dish out to them!

Once we were out of the restaurant, Rose and I walked around until we hit the riverfront. Somehow, the flowing water and the moonlight reflecting off the Scioto had a calming effect on Rose.. She filled me in about the guy who'd been following her.

She had met him back in spring semester at some sort of function at school. I'll call him ME, because this shithead does not deserve to be named in a book dedicated to our love. Rose said he seemed nice

65

enough to talk to but she hadn't expected to see him after the function. He's not in the same department as her and we all know how tough grad students have it. If you're not in the same department, you jump through hoops just to meet each other outside of classes. It's nuts!

Anyway, ME decided he was going to jump through hoops to see Rose without consulting her first. In fact, based on a conversation lasting a couple minutes at most, he believed Rose was his one and only true love. And he wouldn't take no for an answer.

At first, she thought seeing him all over the place was simply a coincidence. After all, a lot of grads spend time in Thompson Library; classes are held all over campus, no matter the major; and, of course, everyone likes to hang out on the more scenic places on campus like the Oval when the weather gets nice.

But then she started seeing him when she left Townshend Hall to go home. Every time she left Townshend Hall to go home. Even if it was dark and cold as hell out. He would act like it was just a big coincidence but after the second or third time, Rose started getting creeped out. Especially considering that this guy's department is in another building on the furthest edges of campus and the sociology department is in the center. You can't chalk all those meetings up to coincidences like that.

Rose began finding excuses to leave early and other ways to get out of the building so she wouldn't have to run into ME but that only made him escalate. He found out where she lived and moved into a building nearby when an apartment opened. He went to her front door and asked if she'd like to grab coffee. She told him she was too busy for dating but he kept insisting. After we became official, she told him she already had a boyfriend.

Rose's methods of avoiding him at school only made him act more like a psychopath. He cussed at her and tried to break into her apartment. Only when she told him she'd call the police did ME scram. Still, he didn't let up: he sent her angry letters, showed up at all of Rose's favorite places. He even followed her to Marion when she went to visit her family over Thanksgiving break! I mean, how fucked up can you get?

His family is hooked up with the university—I think she said his folks are important professors in their respective departments and are even on friendly terms with the president—he says if she tries complaining to the school or the police, his folks will make life difficult for her. She doesn't know what to do. ME could ruin her entire academic and professional career! And all because she's not interested!

I have no idea how she was able to keep all this from me. I mean, I can understand not saying anything but I thought I would've noticed she feared something. We've been spending so much time together and I'm usually good at spotting shitheads. How did I not notice this mega-shithead was menacing her?

Rose started crying again after she finished telling me about ME. I took her in my arms and told her I'd take care of it. And I will take care of it. I'll find ME. I'll find out everything I can about him. His class schedule, where he lives, what he likes to do on the weekends. Everything and anything I can use against him.

And then I'll teach him a lesson about how his behavior isn't acceptable. I'll beat him with bats studded with nails till he's black and blue and wrap his dick in barbed wire so he'll know the pain he caused Rose. I'll make him drink my piss and let him snack on Rose's shit, because that's the only thing of hers he deserves to get near. I'll turn his back into a chessboard with a knife and peel off the skin with piano wire. I'll waterboard him in ice water until he feels like he's dying. And when his agony is at its worst, I'll gut him like a fish, slash him open from throat to cock. It'll be a fitting end for him.

And it won't be hard for me to do. After all, I've killed before. And it was easy.

I slam the book shut and throw it across the hallway. It strikes the wall and falls to the floor, the golden letters spelling JOURNAL flashing up at me. Journal? More like a horror novel! Paris's telling anyone unlucky enough to find this journal and read Dutch that he's killed people and that he'll do it again to anyone who so much as looks at me funny! I knew he could get violent when he's in a bad mood but this is more than just self-harm and beating your girlfriend. This is a whole other level of monstrous.

"I don't even know him," I say aloud. It slips out, a random thought that somehow made its way to my mouth instead of my brain but I realize it's true. I thought I knew Paris, I thought he was nice and caring. Then he showed his nasty side and I realized he was the kind of person you should actively avoid. Naively, I thought that was all there was to him, that I'd seen every one of his layers. I was so wrong. There's an angry, disturbed creature underneath his human skin, one not afraid to admit that he's killed before, found it easy and probably even had fun doing it. Whether or not it's true, the fact he wrote it in a journal is serious enough.

I must get out of here. Cold or no cold, I must leave before he finds out I know his secrets. Before he wants to do all those vile acts he mentioned in *the Journal* to me and kill me so I can't tell anyone.

I stand up to grab *the Journal* off the floor and replace it where I found it. As I rise, my head pounds ten times worse than before. I cry out and sway on my feet, my legs like jelly. I totter to the linen closet, reaching for the topmost shelf to steady myself. Instead I grab a fistful of bedspread and fall to the ground, taking several blankets and *the Forest God's Record* down with me. They fall over my body, bathing me in darkness.

And then I'm gone.

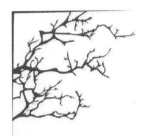

CHAPTER TEN

"Oh God," says a voice from far away. "Oh God-fucking-dammit."

I stir and notice my headache is gone. The sweet relief I feel vanishes, however, as I remember what I was doing right before I fainted. Oh God, Paris has killed people and threatened to kill others, especially anyone whom he doesn't like interacting with me. He's more disturbed than I thought. I must let someone know, before he kills again—

The floorboards creak beside me. Someone is up here with me, standing right over me. I freeze, my eyes still closed so they don't know I'm awake. Is it Paris? If it is, then he'll know I found his journal. He might ask if I read it. It's in Dutch, though. I can convince him I wasn't able to read it. He'll think that his secrets are safe. But what if I can't fool him? Or what if he gets upset because I was rooting around in his linen closet and found things he didn't want found? What if he gets upset about the sheets I pulled off the shelf? What if—?

"Paris, what did you do now?" The voice from earlier. It belongs to the person who's standing over me. And it's not Paris.

I open my eyes. Mr. Kuyper, Paris's father, stands over me with a moue of distaste on his face. He sees I'm awake and his frown becomes more pronounced. I only stare. What's he doing here?

For a moment, neither of us say anything. We just regard each other, as if our mutual confusion can be cleared up just by staring. After a few moments of mutual staring he coughs and asks, "Are you Rose Taggert?"

I'm surprised by the fact he knows my name but I don't trust myself to speak yet so I only nod my head by way of acknowledgment. Mr. Kuyper looks to something on the floor. I follow his gaze and spot *the Forest God's Record* on the floor, sitting next to where I dropped Paris's journal. I glance from the books to Mr. Kuyper and register fear in his expression. Not a lot, his face still looks mostly angry and disgusted but there's enough fear to be noticeable. I look back at the books. Is he afraid of *the Journal*? Does he suspect what Paris has written in there?

"Did Paris—did my son use that book on you?" Mr. Kuyper asks. "Did he make you...green?" He says it like it's a curse word.

So that's what he's afraid of. The Record. He knows it's real and what it can do. I nod my head again and manage to croak, "He said he was saving me from dying. He said my stalker tried to kill me."

Mr. Kuyper groans, "Perfect," before turning away from me to face the wall. "That's just great." Raising a leg, he kicks the wall. I look on as he swings his foot back and forth smashing into the wall all the while cursing under his breath. When he's kicked the wall about twenty times without doing any major damage, he stops but remains facing the wall. His half whisper reaches my ears. "Goddammit Paris, what the hell have you done now?"

Like father, like son, I muse.

As if sensing my thoughts Mr. Kuyper spins to face me, sprawled out on the ground. "This is all your fault," he spits.

Before I can so much as say, "What?" Mr. Kuyper kicks me in the stomach. The breath is knocked out of me and I curl into a ball with a pained wheeze. Instantly, my roots fly out of my neck and wrap themselves around Mr. Kuyper's leg.

"What the hell?" He pulls his leg free of my roots and backs out of range before they can stab his leg. My roots reach for him, rattling like snakes. The look of distaste on his face doubles.

Definitely Paris's father, I think as the pain in my stomach dulls to a throbbing ache I know will stick around for a while. I force myself off the floor and into a kneeling position. To my surprise, my roots stop trying to attack Mr. Kuyper and help me up, latching onto door handles and walls and using their impossible strength to help me stand. I forgot they could obey my thoughts.

When I'm standing, I fix Mr. Kuyper with a dagger stare and, for added measure, will my roots to wave menacingly at him. It has the intended effect because Mr. Kuyper takes another couple of steps back. I allow myself a small, satisfied smile.

An uncomfortable silence descends upon us. Finally, Mr. Kuyper looks at his feet and mutters, "Sorry I kicked you. And that I blamed you for..." He gestures at me with a wave of his hand. I get his meaning. "It was in the heat of the moment, it wasn't fair to you and I apologize."

Well, that's the first time any man from this twisted family has apologized to me for anything. I don't know whether to be grateful or stunned. I mutter something about him being forgiven. And then I ask the question I've been wondering since I realized it was Mr. Kuyper here with me. "What the heck are you doing here?"

Mr. Kuyper has an expression like I just asked the most obvious question in the world. "Well, I was looking for you."

My eyes go wide with surprise. Me? Why was he looking for me? And how did he know I was here?

Downstairs a door opens and closes. "Rose, I'm home!"

My breath chills in my lungs and a mien of terror rises on Mr. Kuyper's face. We're both thinking the same thing: Mr. Kuyper knows I'm here and what Paris has done to me. And now Paris, who has proven how dangerous he can be, is home. And the last thing Paris would want is for his father to know about me.

Only I don't think Mr. Kuyper knows his son has killed people, or claimed to, anyway. He knows about *the Record*, so maybe he knows about some terrible spells in it that could really hurt or kill a person. But if that's all he knows, then if he goes downstairs and confronts his son—

I grab Mr. Kuyper's sleeve as he turns towards the stairs. "Don't," I whisper harshly, my voice still hoarse. "He'll kill you. He said he's killed before."

"I believe you," says Mr. Kuyper without hesitation. Does he know about *the Journal* or does he have information I don't?

"Rose?" Paris calls. "Where are you?"

I will my roots to slide back into my neck, marveling at how easy it is to control them with just a thought. "I'll distract him," I whisper to Mr. Kuyper. "You get out and call the police."

For a moment I expect him to say no. But then he nods his head and I sigh with relief. Walking down the stairs, ignoring the pain in my belly, I clear my throat and call out, "I'm here!"

Paris is standing by the couch, laying his schoolbag on one of the cushions. He smiles as he sees me and I smile back. "There you are," he says. "I missed you today. By the way, I have something for you. You won't believe what I found in your blood tests—hey!"

I throw my arms around Paris and kiss him. Paris's eyes grow wide before he closes them and wraps his arms around me. When I pull away from him, he has a dreamy, satisfied expression on his face. "Wow," he says. "Where did all this come from? I thought we were taking it slow."

"Well," I say in my most seductive voice, "I just realized how much I missed you while you were out today."

"Did you?"

"Mm-hm. I mean, you're so kind and thoughtful. You've taken such good care of me since my stalker hurt me. All on top of taking care of the greenhouse, your home going to school full-time and dealing with all the nasty people in your life. It's a lot to take on but you do it so well."

Paris's face lights up brighter than a Christmas tree. "I am pretty awesome, aren't I?"

"You are. And it made me realize how much I love you."

"It did?"

"Yeah and that made me miss you. It made me miss you a lot!"

Before Paris can say another word, I kiss him again and lead him into the greenhouse with my front and Paris's back facing the living room. Paris, hungry like a starved dog, follows me without breaking contact from my mouth. My hands travel across his back, while his hands travel lower and lower on my mine. I allow him to go there, unable to believe how well this is going. He's like putty in my hands.

Paris kisses my neck as we step into the greenhouse. We stand there necking for a moment, when he pushes me lightly into a workbench. I grunt but do not otherwise protest, continuing with the charade as he embraces me again and sucks on my shoulder. From my vantage point, I can see into the recess where Mr. Kuyper is hunched like a gargoyle with *the Record* and *the Journal* tucked under his arm, watching his son giving me a hickey. I have no idea if he's as amazed as me that this is going so well, or if he might be enjoying the view but I don't care. I signal for him to get out with a gesture of my hand, he starts sneaking to the door and walking on the tips of his fancy black shoes.

Good. If he gets out...well, I don't know if he'll call the police. He may be the kind of guy who would run over his own mother to avoid a scandal that could ruin his reputation and calling the police on his psychotic son qualifies as a scandal. Regardless, I'm sure he'll do something. He knows I'm here. He knows his son has been using *the Record*. We both agree Paris might have meant it when he said he killed someone. I'm sure he'll read *the Journal*, or at least have it translated and see how twisted Paris really is. He won't be able to leave Paris and by consequence, me, alone.

In the meantime, I must keep up this act for as long as possible. "Oh Paris!" I say, trying to sound breathy and ecstatic. "I've been waiting for this all day!"

"I've been waiting for this even longer," Paris breathes, lifting his head off my neck and gazing into my eyes with an excited but blissful look. I force myself to focus on him and ignore Mr. Kuyper as he passes the couch. "It's all I've wanted, for someone to love me."

And then the happy expression on Paris's face morphs into a rage-filled scowl. "Too bad you don't mean a goddamn word of it."

Before I can move, Paris grabs an empty flowerpot off the workbench, turns around and flings the pot like a baseball at his father. The pot hits Mr. Kuyper in the side of the head, shattering into a hundred pieces. Mr. Kuyper shouts, sways and collapses to the floor, the books dropping from under his arm and sliding across the floor.

I scream, my eyes flicking between Mr. Kuyper and Paris, who looks like he's about to burst into flames from anger. Paris glances at me, nostrils flared, eyes ablaze and I flinch under the heat of his glare. "I'll deal with you in a moment," he hisses leaping into the living room and clambering over his father's prone body, turning him over and swinging his fists. Mr. Kuyper looks up dazedly at his son, struggling to full awareness as his son punches him first in the face, then in the stomach and then again in the face.

"Paris—oof!" Mr. Kuyper tries, only to get punched in the stomach again.

"You bastard!" Paris's voice is a deadly roar full of venom and rage. Every word is punctuated by the dull thud of fists striking Mr. Kuyper's body. "You finally fucked up! You crossed the uncrossable line! You just had to go sticking your nose in where it doesn't belong! Well, guess what? This time, I'm the one handing out the punishments! This time, you're the one who's going to get fucked up!"

I watch, frozen like a statue, as Mr. Kuyper's face becomes a purple and swollen mess. After what feels like an eternity, Paris's punches slow and his breathing grows ragged. I look at his hands, the knuckles bruised and bloody, though not as badly as Mr. Kuyper's whole body seems to be.

"Now that you know about Rose and *the Record*, I have no choice," Paris pants. "I'm going to have to kill you."

From his waistband Paris pulls a sleek, shiny handgun. My eyes grow wide and my mouth forms a small o of shock and terror. I didn't even feel that gun on him when I was making out with him. How long has he had that on him?

Paris points the gun at Mr. Kuyper's head with both hands and flicks the safety off. "I wish I could say it was nice knowing you," he comments, a terrible, gleeful grin on his face. "But it hasn't been nice knowing you. So, I'll just say, I'm glad you're finally going to be out of my life."

The paralysis that has kept me in the greenhouse from the beginning of Paris's assault breaks. God, he's really going to kill his own father! I rush to his side as fast as my body will let me and grab his wrists. "Paris, please!" I cry. "Don't do this! You don't want to kill your father!"

"Shut up!" Paris takes a hand off the gun and grabs a fistful of my hair. I cry out and my roots twist out with a rattle. Before they can defend me, Paris throws me down beside Mr. Kuyper. He glowers down at us, his face a mask of wrath. The gun in his hand alternating from my head to Mr. Kuyper's like a deadly pendulum. Although Paris isn't speaking, I can hear his voice in my head, hateful and elated: *You or him? You or him? Who deserves it more?*

"Paris," I beg, tears welling in the corners of my eyes. "Please don't do this."

Paris stops the gun at my head. I flinch and close my eyes, sure I'm about to die.

"Did you two enjoy fooling me?" Paris asks, his voice low and dangerous. "Did you two have a good laugh about it?"

My eyes fly open. "What?"

"Did you two laugh while you were fucking your brains out?" Paris's voice rises to a shriek, the gun shaking in his grip. "You told me you wanted to wait, to take it slow. But you two were together the whole time, fooling me!"

Oh God. It's Andy Claycraft all over again.

"Paris," Mr. Kuyper coughs, surprising the both of us. I don't think either of us thought he would be able to speak after the beating he took. "We haven't been sleeping together. I didn't even know she was here till a few minutes ago. Besides, you two were never dating in the first place—Aagh!"

Paris rears back a leg and delivers a kick to his father's groin. Mr. Kuyper grunts and curls onto his side, clutching himself as if his penis is in danger of falling off. The whole time, the gun hasn't moved from my head.

Terrified tears spill from my eyes. "Paris, please don't do this to us. Please, don't kill us. You don't want to do this. Please. I...I really care about you." I gulp, sure he's going to see through my lie. I would've said I loved him but after being accused of sleeping with his father, I'm positive he wouldn't buy that one. My only chance is to get him to think I care about him. It'll at least buy us a few seconds more of life.

I hold my breath, watching as Paris frowns down at me. The whole world appears to slow down and go still in that moment.

A twisted slash of a grin crosses Paris's face. "Yeah," he says meditatively, his eyes bright. "Yeah. Yeah. Okay, I won't kill you. Not yet, anyway."

I let out my breath, relief flowing through me. He's not going to kill us. We've been given a reprieve, time to figure out how to get away from Paris and get help.

Paris makes a spinning motion with the gun. "Lie on your backs," he commands. "Both of you. Don't move a muscle. If you do, I'll kill the both of you here and now."

We obey, Mr. Kuyper grunting and moaning with every movement. From our new perspective, we watch Paris, gun still trained on us, pick up *the Record* and journal, disappear out of eye range into the greenhouse, returning a few seconds later and moving behind us.

"Put your wrists together behind your back." Paris barks. We put our wrists together. "Closer!" We move them closer together. Paris puts something tiny on the side of my hand and then does the same thing to Mr. Kuyper. I hear a flapping noise behind me and Paris says something that sounds like Japanese.

Whatever he put on my wrists felt like rubber wire as they wrapped around and secured my wrists together. I glance at Mr. Kuyper and see what look like vines encircling his wrists, invisible hands tying the vines together like bonds around his wrists.

Bonds...

Paris is tying us up. He wants to make sure we can't get away. But why?

When the plant-ropes have finished wrapping around my wrists and go still, I test them. They're strong, so strong I can't even adjust the position of my wrists in them. My heart thuds in my chest as fear overtakes me once more. *What's Paris planning for us?*

"Get up." Paris gestures at the door with his gun. "Both of you. We're going on a little trip."

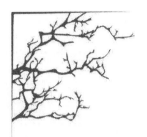

CHAPTER ELEVEN

Paris gestures for us to stand up. We clamber to our feet, Mr. Kuyper grunting with every movement. I can only imagine what sort of torment he's going through. It's a wonder Paris didn't break any of his bones. Though there's always a chance he caused some internal bleeding. Would I even know if he had? Oh God, if there is internal bleeding, Mr. Kuyper's as good as dead now.

"Take a last look around, Rose," Paris instructs. "This was the safest place in the world you could be. You'll never see it again."

I take a final look around Paris's home, taking it all in. I don't feel any loss over leaving. Even though it was bigger and nicer than anywhere I've lived before, since the moment I woke up in the greenhouse this place has brought me nothing but fear and pain, all caused by a single, terrible jailer. The only thing I'll miss about this place is the greenhouse, because it was a source of both nourishment and comfort when I was in there.

Speaking of which, I wonder where and when I'll lay down my roots again. I look towards the greenhouse one last time and notice something odd. From where I'm standing, I can see the far corner of the greenhouse where the yew and orange trees are. Only they're no longer there. Instead there's a giant palm tree I've never seen before. Where did that come from? It wasn't there when I lay my roots down this morning. And if that's there, then what happened to the yew and orange trees?

Before I can wonder any further about it, Paris tells us it's time to go. We march towards the front door and my heartbeat speeds up. I'm about to leave this place. I'm about to go outside! On any other occasion I'd be happy about that, as it would mean leaving Paris and finding safety. However, under these circumstances, I'm dreading what's to come.

Through the door is a small, narrow hallway tiled in marble and with fancy, gold-framed paintings on the wall. In front of me and to my right are doors to other homes, nameplates next to the doors announcing their occupants' surnames. On my left is an elevator and a door with a nameplate proclaiming STAIRWELL in capital letters.

A hand pushes me forward and I nearly stumble into the door opposite Paris's. Paris locks his own door behind him before gesturing with the gun to the stairwell. Mr. Kuyper and I shuffle towards the door next to the elevator. Silently, I pray one of the neighbors would step out of their homes or off the elevator and rescue us. When we start making our way down the stairs, I pray someone else is using the stairwell, a Bruce Willis type who can save us from the gun-toting madman. But not a soul appears, we make it past the ground floor and to the underground parking garage uninterrupted.

Once inside the parking garage, Paris points to a car, a large Mercedes with tinted windows, four spaces from the door. "That one over there."

Beside me, Mr. Kuyper curses. I glance behind me and see Paris grinning wickedly. "Yeah Dad. You let me know you were here the moment I got home. You really should be more careful where you park if you're going to go snooping around other people's homes. Now where are your keys?"

Paris roots around in his dad's pants pockets until he pulls out a set of keys, unlocks the Mercedes and has us scoot into the second row. When we've sat down, Paris reaches over and buckles us in, keeping the gun pointed at our foreheads as he works. With our arms tied behind our backs, we can barely move, let alone escape from our seats.

Finally, Paris slides into the driver's seat, adjusts the seat and mirrors and turns the engine over. The car roars to life and a screen in the center of the dashboard lights up. Paris examines the screen and clicks his tongue loudly as a disco song comes on over the car's stereo. "Jeez Dad, you're still listening to that crap?" he complains. "I keep telling you, disco's dead and should stay that way." He switches the radio to a rock station slipping the car into reverse.

As we roll out the garage exit, I'm blinded for a second by the bright light of the sun. When my vision adjusts, downtown Columbus is busy with cars and people walking in and out of businesses. I stare at it all as if I'm seeing it for the first time. How long has it been since I was on these streets? I can't remember, it's all in the gray area of my memories.

"Don't try getting anyone's attention outside," Paris says from the front seat. I look at him as he merges the car into traffic. "If you do, I'll shoot you both and then drive the car into the Scioto."

Mr. Kuyper and I look at each other. That didn't even occur to me. Did it occur to him to try that? I'd ask but any sort of talking could be dangerous. Instead, we sit in silence as Paris drives towards the highway.

Sometime later, we get off the highway and enter a neighborhood that is vaguely familiar to me. It's not until I see a field filled with rows and rows of concrete sculptures of corn that I realize that we're in Dublin, one of Columbus's suburbs. That field of corn, or *Cornhenge*, as the locals call it, is one of Dublin's unique features, a quintessentially Ohioan art piece meant to honor the inventor of several hybrid corn species and remind people of the city's agricultural heritage. I haven't been back to this neighborhood since I came to the annual Dublin Irish Festival with Hope, Maddy and our parents the summer before my senior year of undergrad, so it's no wonder I didn't recognize it until I saw the corn. Why is Paris taking us here now, though? I give Mr. Kuyper a questioning look but he only shrugs his shoulders. He's as clueless as I am.

Paris's head is diagonal to me from where I'm sitting. I can see part of his face in the rearview mirror but his face is inscrutable. I glance at Mr. Kuyper, he's staring ahead at Paris and probably wondering the same thing. After the beating he took, back in Paris's home, I doubt he'll dare to ask.

I debate with myself for a minute before clearing my throat. "Paris, what're we doing here?"

"Making a quick stop," is the only response I get. He doesn't volunteer anything more.

I raise an eyebrow in Mr. Kuyper's direction. He returns the raised eyebrow as best he can with half his face swollen and purple.

Finally, we turn off a busy street onto a road surrounded on either side by a thick blanket of trees. A sign nailed to one of the trees contains five numbers on it. An address.

The car rolls down the road until it curves around a bend and reveals a large house with a brick front. Paris parks the car and turns off the ignition. "We're here," he announces, sliding out of the driver's seat, *the Record* and his journal once more tucked underneath his arm.

Paris comes around the back and unbuckles us. We step out and I shiver at the cold air. I have six minutes before the cold makes me faint and then kills me. Is that why we're here? So I can shiver to death in an unfamiliar place?

Mr. Kuyper studies the house with suspicion. "Paris," he rasps, the first time he's spoken since his son kicked him in the balls earlier, "what is this place?"

Paris glances up at the house, disappointment and regret cross his face. "It's mine," he says. "I bought it with my trust fund. I was hoping when Rose and I were..."

He doesn't finish his sentence but I don't need him to. I already know what he was going to say. This was going to be our home, if I had fallen in love with him as he wanted me to. I don't know if I should be touched by him buying me a house or weirded out that he planned this far ahead in our relationship.

Assuming we even had a relationship, a voice in my head reminds me. I remember what Mr. Kuyper blurted out earlier, about how Paris and I weren't dating at all. Was that the talk of a man who refused to admit that his son was dating someone from a different social class? Or was he about to reveal an uncomfortable truth?

As if sensing my thoughts, Paris's face grows angry and he scowls at us. "But now you two have ruined it all for me!" he shouts. "You two conspired against me and made it impossible for Rose and me to live here together! So now I'll have to find some other use for it. In the meantime, though, it's time we should be going."

Paris throws the car keys into the woods surrounding the house. I get a sinking feeling in my gut. He doesn't expect to come back here. Or at least, he doesn't expect to ever need the Mercedes ever again.

We're commanded to walk around the back of the house. When we turn the second corner on the building, we're confronted with something I hadn't been expecting: a forty-five-foot long green vehicle that stands nearly as tall as the house's garage. An RV. Paris walks up to the RV's door and inputs a combination on the keypad beside it. The door hisses open and lights inside the RV flicker on.

"Get in," Paris orders, gesturing again with the gun. We step inside.

I pause at the threshold stunned by the opulence in front of me: the inside of the RV looks like the inside of a three-star hotel! The main living area is comprised of two couches, three wall-mounted televisions, a kitchenette with stainless-steel appliances, lamps attached to chrome fixtures, tiled walls and hardwood floors. Through a door in the back, I can make out a bed on a platform, piled high with a velvety-looking comforter and pillows. For the umpteenth time since I woke in the greenhouse, I'm amazed at how different Paris's life has been from mine.

Someone pushes me in the small of the back and I stumble forward. I glance behind me and Mr. Kuyper almost falls into me, while Paris holds his hand out like a traffic cop telling a driver to stop. "Both of you in the back," he orders.

When we're in the back bedroom, which is just as sumptuous as the main living room, Paris has us sit at opposite ends of the room. I sit by the door to the bathroom, while Mr. Kuyper sits underneath a square window. Paris stands in the doorway, surveying us like I imagine a museum curator might survey a new exhibit, making sure everything is in its place.

"And now," Paris says dramatically as he reaches into his sweatshirt pocket with the arm holding the books and pulls something out. His fingers unfurl and I see what resembles little brown beads. Then he intones something in the language he spoke back when he had us on the floor. The little beads in his hand shiver, rise in the air and shoot towards Mr. Kuyper and me. We watch in amazement as the beads burst open, tendrils reach out and grow several feet long. I realize with a start that the beads aren't beads at all but plant seeds, magically manipulated by one of the spells in *the Record*.

The tendrils—roots, I understand, with a flash, like the ones in my neck—wrap around us and draw our limbs together. Mr. Kuyper and I try to break them but the roots refuse to budge. We're wrapped up tighter than a pair of mummies. Paris smirks and tucks the gun back into his waistband.

"Don't even try screaming," he taunts. "I had this room customized to be soundproof. You can't even hear a gun go off in this room. Believe me, I tested." Paris pulls up the blind over the window above his father and reveals a small hole by the window's right edge. Mr. Kuyper and I stare in horror at what is quite clearly a bullet hole.

Paris pulls the blind down again and heads to the door. Before he leaves, he cocks his head back to the bedroom, "Sit tight. We're going back to where it all began." He closes the door with a laugh. I wait for a lock to slide into place but all I hear is Paris's receding footsteps. He's so confident that we can't get away, he's leaving the bedroom door unlocked.

A moment later, the motor turns over and the RV's frame vibrates. The wheels turn and the RV rolls around the house and down the road towards the busy street we turned off earlier.

We're on our way. To where, God only knows. God and Paris Kuyper.

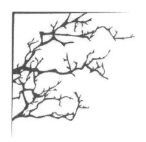

CHAPTER TWELVE

Twenty minutes pass before either of us dares to move. I wanted to start moving and break out of these plant-ropes the moment Paris began driving but I don't know what sort of magic he's employed right now. For all we know, he has invisible eyes watching us in here, making sure we don't get up to anything while he drives. So, when Mr. Kuyper starts struggling against his bonds and attempts to stand up despite his legs being tied together in three different places, it takes me by surprise. Isn't he worried Paris will see us?

Mr. Kuyper doesn't manage to get to his feet but he does manage to scoot towards me, his legs resembling an inchworm I saw once in a cartoon when I was a kid. He fixes me with a glare and says, "Well? Are you going to try to help me or what?"

I hesitate while listening intently. When I don't sense any change in the RV's speed or hear angry footsteps coming our way, I scoot across to Mr. Kuyper. It's rough and slow-going, throwing out my bound legs in front of me and then using them to pull the rest of me forward. After a few feet, my butt burns from the friction. I persevere, however and we manage to meet each other by the foot of the bed.

"Spin around so your back's facing mine," Mr. Kuyper orders. I groan, tired of that commanding tone of his, the same one his son uses when he's in a bad mood. I obey anyway and spin around on my rear, irritating it further before feeling Mr. Kuyper's fingers against the roots around my wrist.

"Now try breaking the ropes around my wrists," he says. "And hurry it up before Paris decides to check on us."

I want to snap at him "I'll get it done as fast as I can, stop bossing me around," but decide to keep my mouth shut. We're both stressed, scared, tired and neither of our bodies are in the shape they're supposed to be. Better to get ourselves untied and deal with Paris rather than pick a fight with each other that will lead to nothing in the end.

My fingers trace up Mr. Kuyper's hands and find his bonds. I grab a small length of root between my fingers and pull on it. When it doesn't budge, I try picking through it with my fingernails instead. Slowly, the root's tough skin gives and tears and I feel something damp touch my fingers. Sap from the roots.

For the first time in I don't know how long, I grin. Finally, something good is happening.

I work my nail through the root like an old-fashioned saw, dragging it back and forth, getting a little deeper every time. After a couple of minutes, I finally slice through the root and a long length of it falls to the ground. Smiling wider now, I turn my head around to look at the back of Mr. Kuyper's.

"I got through!" I announce triumphantly. "Try moving your wrists now."

Mr. Kuyper grunts and I hear the fabric of his suit jacket slide against each other. "I can't move!" he says, sounding like he's complaining to customer service about a faulty product.

I glance down at his wrists. One length of root dangles from Mr. Kuyper's wrists, while the others are still wrapped tightly around them. It's then I recall noting that each seed had several roots sprout out of it when Paris cast his spell back in the living room. I must cut through all the roots to free our wrists.

When I inform Mr. Kuypers of this, his response is less than amicable. "Well then, get to it!" he snaps. "Before Paris decides to take a bathroom break or something!"

"Alright!" I huff. I start on another root, sawing my fingernail through the root as fast as I can.

For a few minutes, an uncomfortable silence falls between us. When I can't stand it anymore, I clear my throat. "Um, what did you mean, Paris and I weren't dating?"

From behind me, I hear Mr. Kuyper's clothes rustle as he turns to look at the back of my head. "What?"

"Back at the...at Paris's place," I explain. "You said Paris and I weren't dating. What did you mean by that? I thought Paris and I were supposed to be a couple."

I can almost hear Mr. Kuyper raising his eyebrows. "Don't you know the answer to that?" he asks. "I mean, you should know better than I."

I shake my head. "No, I don't. I woke up in the greenhouse a couple nights ago and I couldn't remember anything for at least the past two years. I can't remember the names for places or things and a bunch of other stuff. I can't even remember how to boot up a computer or what Paris's home is called."

"Amnesia? What are you, a soap opera character?"

"Yeah, I know, I know," I sigh. "But the point is, I don't remember anything past undergrad and I only have Paris's word to go on."

"And that's not something you can trust anymore, is it?" he deduces. "Fine, I'll tell you. Truth is, you two weren't together. You were his sociology teacher but that was it. You two barely spoke to each other."

"How do you know that?" I ask. "Us barely speaking, I mean. Did you come to my classes or something?"

There's a moment of silence before Mr. Kuyper answers. "I came to check on Paris one evening after work last semester. I must check on him occasionally. He's...always needed a bit more guidance than his peers."

Is that what you call it? I wonder. *Needing more guidance? I think he needs a more than a bit.*

Out loud, I reply, "If he's always needed more guidance, why didn't you keep him at home?" *Or maybe put him in an institution*, I silently add. *Where he belongs.*

Mr. Kuyper laughs humorlessly. "Look, my family has a certain image to keep up. That image, in part, keeps our business growing and our influence with the right people intact. The slightest rumor could ruin years of financial and political influence. Keeping Paris at home when he should be off at college and living on his own, at his age, would've made certain tongues wag and I couldn't have that. So, I had no choice but to let him move out."

I remember what Paris said the first night I met him, about how his family being from old money came with certain expectations. Just how much are those expectations to blame for the mess we're in now? A large percent, most likely.

"Anyway," Mr. Kuyper continues, "I came to check on him one evening after work and I found him lying on the floor, drunk, in that greenhouse of his. He started telling me all about how he was in love with Rose Taggert, his sociology teacher, that she and him were a couple and some other guy was trying to steal her away from him. Only the way he phrased it made him sound a lot more possessive. He talked like someone had tried to steal his property instead of the girl he loved. And he said some things that I found strange, like how he was always with her, even when she didn't know it."

I pause in sawing another root. Something about being followed sounds vaguely familiar.

"Well, I got him to bed before he could get any drunker. The next day I went to find out a bit more about Paris's sociology teacher."

"And you found me," I finish.

"Yeah, but you weren't...green and pink," he says, pausing midway through the sentence. "And you know what I found out? That you didn't even know Paris. He never said anything in class or came by office hours. The relationship he had spent so much time telling me the night before was all in his head."

"Furthermore, I learned that you had just gotten engaged to your boyfriend, Mark Eskin. You showed off your ring to me and—"

I stop sawing again and whip my head around. "What was that name you said?"

Mr. Kuyper looks behind him. "Mark Eskin," he repeats. "Your fiancé. I think he was an environmental studies grad student or something useless like that."

I don't respond. A thousand sensations are racing through my body, many of them I don't have names for. Some of them I can name though: warmth; comfort; safety; laughter; happiness; and a strange, uncomfortable feeling I recognize as lust. I feel like someone's filling me with gas and stardust and pure, white light. It's like I'm experiencing a high, like some of my more party-minded classmates and students might describe after a night out on the town. *What is this I'm experiencing right now?*

The answer comes to me almost as soon as I ask the question: Love. As cliched as it might seem, this is what love feels like. And even though in my conscious mind I don't remember this Mark Eskin at all, even though I don't have an image of what he looks like, a part of me does remember him and knows I love him, that he is that one true love everyone speaks of and dreams of finding.

"What does he look like?" I ask hurriedly..

"What?"

"What does he look like?" I demand. "I don't remember."

There's a pause. "Um...blonde? Kind of looks like he needs a haircut? Brown eyes? Thin build? I don't know, I only just saw a photo of him on the news today."

What he says after the part about Mark's build flies through my head without making an impression. For the first time since I woke up in the greenhouse, some of the grey fog over my memories is shifting away to reveal something. From its depths emerges something like a short movie in my head. In it, I'm wearing the pink dress I woke up in and my hair is done up in an elaborate bun. I'm dancing with a man, about my age, with blonde hair that normally frames his face past the ears but tonight has been slicked back, making him look very dashing and even noble. His brown eyes stare at me from an aquiline face full of love and adoration. Music surrounds us and I'm happy, so happy. We're engaged, everyone is happy for us and we have our whole lives ahead of us. And although I know that there will be plenty of happy moments, right here and right now is the greatest night of my life.

The memory ends, leaving me with a nostalgic glow. That was our engagement party. I wish I could remember more than just that one snippet but I'm glad I finally got that back. It feels like a hole in my soul I hadn't known was there has been filled. For the first time since I woke up in the greenhouse, I know true happiness.

From behind me, Mr. Kuyper murmurs, "I'm sorry for your loss."

His words drag me from my happy thoughts. "What loss?"

Mr. Kuyper doesn't answer for a moment and I can almost hear the gears in his head clicking as he thinks. Finally, he says, "Earlier today, I was in the break room at work getting more coffee. The TV was tuned to the news, the story was about you and your fiancé."

"About Mark and me?" Something cold drops into my stomach.

"Yes." Mr. Kuyper clears his throat. "Well, more about you. You disappeared the night of your engagement party. According to the report, both you and Mark Eskin were leaving the venue together for his apartment and someone attacked you in the parking lot."

I'm sure I already know who that someone is. Even so, I ask, "Did anyone see who it was?"

"The report said the suspect is still on the loose," Mr. Kuyper replies. "But it did say you haven't been seen since that night. And..." A deep sigh. "And it said your fiancé's funeral took place this morning."

My soul fills with ice. "Mark's dead?" I say, my voice cracking. Tears form in the corners of my eyes.

"I'm sorry," says Mr. Kuyper. "By the time anyone found him, there was nothing they could do. He'd been unconscious for several hours in below-freezing weather." Then, as if he couldn't think of anything else to say, he repeats, "I'm sorry."

Something inside me breaks and I burst into tears. Mark. Oh God, Mark. No! How could this have happened? I just found you again! I just remembered who you were, what you meant to me! How can you be dead? How can you have been taken from me like this?

The world around me becomes distant. I can't feel the bonds around my body, nor can I feel the vibrations of the RV. Silence fills my world and I close my eyes to envelop myself even further in isolation. I am alone in my grief and I let it out. My wails echo through the darkness, reminding me Mark is gone from this world and that he is nothing more than a pile of meat in a coffin in the ground somewhere. Even if I do remember him and all the happy times we had together, I'll never be able to see him, or hold him, or tell him how much I love him ever again.

I'll never love again. I know this to be true. Mark and I were soulmates, meant to be together. And now that he's gone, there's no way I'll love anyone like I loved him. Even if I do somehow manage to escape Paris and return my body back to normal, I won't be able to find the love I enjoyed with Mark, a love I could remember without remembering the person whom the love was for.

Perhaps it would be better if I joined him in death, rather than continue this miserable existence without him. Is life right now even worth living? Based on what's happened to me, I'd say no.

I cry for a while, my sobs and wails eventually turning to hiccups and sniffles. I wallow in my darkness and grief, not thinking, only feeling. Feeling empty. Numb. Maybe even dead inside. Oh, what I wouldn't give to be taken from this world right now. That would be a blessing.

From outside my darkness a voice drifts in, at first only faint, then growing stronger and louder. The words worm their way into my brain, disturbing me in my grief. My mind tries to shake them off but they pull on me and force me to pay attention.

I open my eyes and the world returns. Behind me, Mr. Kuyper is speaking. It was his voice that pulled me out of my darkness.

"When I saw the news report, I remembered Paris was obsessed with you," he is saying. "And I wondered if he had something to do with your disappearance and your fiancé's death. Maybe he even had you tied up in his place, like something out of those novels my wife likes to read. Anyway, it's why I believed you when you said he might've killed someone. I already suspected Paris of killing your fiancé." There's a pause, followed by a third "I'm sorry."

My body starts to shake with rage. What right does he have to tell me he's sorry? After all—

"This is all your fault." The accusation spills out of me.

Mr. Kuyper's head whips around to look at me. "I'm sorry?" he repeats. This time he isn't wishing me condolences.

"You heard me." My voice is low and dripping with venom. I hate him and his monster son. I hate what they've made me into. "This is your fault. I saw how you slapped Paris the last time you visited him at home. I can only imagine how much worse the beatings were when he was growing up. It's no wonder he's such a psycho." My body shakes from rage. I'm so angry, I can't control what I say next, though I doubt I would hold back if I was in control. "And because of your son, the son you raised, I'm a plant-woman, we're tied up in the back of an RV heading to God knows where and Mark is dead! He's dead! And I hold you just as responsible for that as I do Paris!"

"Don't you dare blame me for Paris's crimes!" Mr. Kuyper snarls. Craning my neck, I can see his face. It looks just like Paris's had earlier, angry enough to burst into flames. "This is a hard world and it doesn't forgive softness or weakness! Paris was weak as a child, my job as his father was to prepare him for his place in the world and make him more of a man! You hear me? I was helping him! I was making sure he didn't turn into a little bitch who lets everyone walk all over him. I even sent him to a tough-love camp just to make him stronger."

"Yeah and how did that work out?" I shoot back. "Huh? How the fuck did that work out?"

Mr. Kuyper gapes at me, speechless. I smirk with satisfaction. "You tried to help your son? No, you just tried to make him how you think a man should be. And now he's going to kill us when we get to wherever we're going. I hope all that toughening up was worth it."

Mr. Kuyper's hard eyes shoot daggers at me. I don't flinch. I stare daggers right back. So many lives have been destroyed because he tried to mold his son into his definition of an alpha male. After a minute, Mr. Kuyper looks away from me. I smirk, again, although my satisfaction is temporary, leaving only my rage and a new sense of hopelessness. What did I just accomplish? Nothing at all, beyond making my only ally in this horror show angry. And we're still tied up in the back of Paris's RV.

As much as father and son have fucked up lives, I may have fucked up ours even worse just to prove a point. And I regret it.

A tense silence fills the small room. It's several minutes before Mr. Kuyper breaks it by clearing his throat.

"Look, we can assign all the blame we want later," he says in his best conciliatory tone. "But right now, our priority should be getting off this goddamn RV and finding some help. So how about we call it a truce for now and work together? Alright?"

I agree without hesitation and go back to sawing through his bonds. I don't think I'll ever forgive this man and, like he said, getting out of here is more important than finding someone to blame. So, for now, I'll work with him but the moment we've stopped Paris, I'm going to make sure the whole Kuyper family pays for all their awful acts.

I finally manage to saw my way through the bonds on his wrist with my nail. The last piece of cord comes apart with a snap, Mr. Kuyper sighs with relief as he swings his arms in front of him and rubs the circulation back into his wrists. A few minutes later, he's managed to pull and tear his way out of the rest of the plant-roots binding him, a few minutes after that and I'm able to move too. The roots Paris used to tie us litter the floor, like the remains of a jungle plant that was hacked to death.

Mr. Kuyper and I glance at the door to the RV's main living quarters and then at each other. "You ready?" he asks.

I nod. "Let's get him."

Mr. Kuyper slides open the door a fraction of an inch. Beyond is only darkness. Mr. Kuyper puts his face to the crack and squints his eyes. "I can't see anything. All the lights must be off."

He lets me peek through the crack. Like he said, it's completely dark. I make out some vague shapes in the darkness but I can't tell what they are. The RV's engine is still running, so that means Paris hasn't stopped for the night yet. Unless—

"Can *the Record* make the RV drive while Paris sleeps?" I whisper.

Mr. Kuyper's face blanches. "I hadn't thought of that," he admits. "I don't know." His face then relaxes. "But it might be easier to take Paris if it does. If he's sleeping, we can get him while he's in bed and drive the RV back to Columbus."

I consider Mr. Kuyper's plan and decide it makes sense. When I nod my head, he grabs the light switch. "In case he's still driving," he says in way of explanation. A moment later, the bedroom goes dark and Mr. Kuyper slides the door fully open. When our eyes adjust, we sneak through the main living area, Mr. Kuyper following just a couple of steps behind me, both of us careful to avoid knocking into the countertops and the furniture. Nowhere do we find Paris: not at the dining table; not on the couch; not even in the bathroom. That means he's still driving the RV. So much for subduing him easily.

A few more paces and we spot his outline in the driver's seat. Mr. Kuyper and I stop, observing him from our vantage point in the shadows. His hands are on the wheel, adjusting it with every movement of the RV. His eyes in the window reflection seem lost, off in their own world, like he's on autopilot.

There's a tap on my shoulder. Mr. Kuyper points at the dashboard. Paris's gun is in one of the cup holders, the grip sticking out like a lopsided cell phone.

Mr. Kuyper and I look at each other. How are we going to get that away from him? he mouths.

I look back to the gun. It's too risky to reach. Even if I crawled on my belly, the moment my arm got a certain distance above the floor—

I look back at Mr. Kuyper and mouth, I got this.

Lowering myself to the ground I crawl forward on my belly. I'm an Army cadet again, only this time one with another trick up her sleeve. I can almost feel Mr. Kuyper staring at me and wondering what I'm up to but I ignore it. When I'm behind Paris's chair, I close my eyes, concentrate on the gun and imagine my roots reaching out to grab it from the cup holder

The roots shift in my chest, one slithers out of my neck across the floor toward the cup holders and avoids the lights from passing cars and streetlights that spill through the RV windows. I feel a rush of excitement as it glides up the side of the console. As if making sure it has what it is looking for, it taps the gun's grip before wrapping itself around it.

Behind me, I hear Mr. Kuyper inhale.

My root lifts the gun out of the cupholder with a slight clatter. The noise alerts Paris, who takes his eyes off the road. "What the hell?" he shouts.

I pull back my root fast as lightning and grab the gun before it slips back into my body. Before Paris can turn his head around, I jump to my feet and point the gun at him like I've seen cops in the movies do. "Turn this thing around, Paris," I command, flicking off the safety. "We're going back to Columbus."

For a moment, Paris says nothing. He just keeps driving, looking at both the road and at my reflection in the windshield. I feel my intense hatred for him grow.

"Didn't you hear me, Paris? Turn this thing around!"

"You better do as she says, Paris." Mr. Kuyper's reflection appears beside mine in the windshield. "I told her what you did to her fiancé. She's really upset with you now."

If Paris is perturbed by this news, he doesn't show it. "I'd rather die than let you take me back there."

I smile. "That's fine with me. Either way, we're going back to Columbus."

"You going to let her do that to me, Dad?"

Mr. Kuyper doesn't say anything for a moment. Then he says, "Honestly son, you've crossed too big a line this time. Perhaps it would be better if she shot you."

Paris is still driving in the same direction. I'm getting sick of all this talk. "Paris, turn back to Columbus right now, or I'll—"

My voice catches in my throat as I see something in the road sprinting straight towards us. Something white and green-haired, wearing a tiger-skin loincloth. It's the Oni. And Paris is still driving towards as if it's not even there. Mr. Kuyper should've noticed it by now. It's running right towards us! Why don't they see it?

Twenty feet away, the Oni leaps into the air. It's going to collide with the RV's windshield. I scream and pull the trigger, aiming at the Oni's head.

Several things happen in quick succession; a loud bang and a fist-sized white spot appears in the glass with an almost inaudible tinkle, Paris cries out and makes a sharp turn to the right and Mr. Kuyper and me are sent flying with the RV's momentum.

I watch the gun fly from my hand as my head smacks into the wall.

A flash. A burst of pain. And then nothing at all.

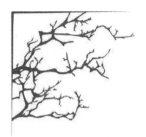

CHAPTER THIRTEEN

My head aches. I groan. This is the second time I've blacked out, as well as the second time I've woken up with a headache, all within the course of a day. At least I think it's been a day. I have no idea how long I've been out.

Once I can think past the headache, I notice there's movement both inside and outside my body. Confused, I open my eyes. Green lines, blurry and uncertain, flit across my vision. I blink several times and realize as things come into focus that my roots are out, searching for dirt to lay themselves in while I'm sitting on my butt, tied up in more of Paris's root-bonds. Why aren't they just dragging me to the nearest source of fertile soil? They've done that before.

"Finally awake, you bitch?"

I look up and see I'm back in the bedroom. Paris is standing a few feet away, holding a hammer. But it's not him or the hammer that grabs my attention but the platform where the bed is supposed to be. The mattress, comforter and pillows are gone. Instead there's a rectangular wooden frame, boards nailed to two sides of it and some going up on a third.

"Paris." My voice quavers. "What are you doing?"

I try to push myself off the ground but find myself tied up with new plant-ropes and every time my roots throw themselves toward the open bedroom door, they bounce off something I can't see, like bouncy balls against a window. One root bounces toward my feet, after hitting the invisible window, in that second I glance downwards to follow its path and I see a ring of dirt has been placed all around me. Just above the dirt, there's a strange, shimmering light, like pictures of the aurora borealis that I've seen in books.

"You like my invisible wall?" Paris asks, drawing my attention back to him. "I needed to keep you put, while I work on your new bed."

"Bed?" I repeat, an edge creeping into my voice. I really need to put my roots down. Like, right now.

"Well, I'm not taking you outside to get your nutrients," says Paris, as if explaining something obvious to someone stupid. "It's cold enough to kill you. And I want to keep you alive for a little while longer."

I look back at the wooden frame on the platform. Then I notice three large, white bags against the opposite wall. I can't see the brand on the bags but their contents are spelled out in large capital letters: ALL-PURPOSE NUTRIENT-RICH GARDEN SOIL.

Paris is making me a personal flower bed, so I can get my nutrients. For a moment, I think he's doing this as a gesture of kindness, before I remember what he said about keeping me alive a bit longer and my heart sinks.

Paris grabs a long wooden board from outside the bedroom door, he places it along the third side of the frame, retrieves a nail from his sweatshirt and starts hammering it in. His movements are slow, as if to test how long he can take to construct the flower bed.

"Um...Paris?" I interject. I can't keep the edge out of my voice. I feel like there's an electric blanket under my skin, sending crazy signals to my brain, giving me grade-A anxiety. My roots start hitting the invisible wall harder and faster. I really need to put them down and soon.

"Just stay put," Paris tells me, not looking up from what he's doing. "I'm taking my time to make sure I do this right."

No, he's not, he's doing this to punish me, to let me know I'm back in his power and he plans to use his power as much as he can.

Paris finishes with the first nail and lifts a second which he proceeds to hammer in, moving even slower than he was before. My breathing becomes rapid and shallow and I see a grin flit across Paris's face.

"Paris, please!" I don't care that I'm begging. My heart is beating like mad, my chest feels tight and tears are forming in my eyes. I really must put my roots down. "Paris, please hurry up!"

Paris makes no effort to increase his work pace. Instead he goes even slower than I thought possible, nailing in the second board and then a third. All this takes an age to do. By the time he's finished with the fourth side, I'm in hysterics, tears forming rivers down my cheeks and my roots pounding frantically against the invisible wall like rain as I beg for Paris to finish.

Finally, he goes to the bags of soil, rips one open with his bare hands and pours the dirt into the newly built structure. It crashes with a *thump!* against the box's sides and the bottom of the bed. Then the second bag, which makes a softer impact and then the third. After patting down the dirt to make it flat and even, Paris walks over to me and breaks the ring around me with the tip of his sneakers. The shimmer above the ring vanishes and my roots strike nothing but empty air.

For a second, the roots hover in the air, as if comprehending the barrier's gone before springing to life, heaving me out of my sitting position and onto my stomach, across the bedroom and up into the soil bed. Despite being tied up like a girl on train tracks in an old movie, I manage to turn myself onto my back before my roots plunge into the soil and make further movement impossible. Instantly my breathing returns to normal and the panic that has consumed me dissipates. When I cry this time, it's tears of relief.

From the door, I hear a laugh. I lift my head and see Paris smirking. He crosses from where I'd been sitting to the foot of the bed, placing his hands on the edge of the bed's wall. "Look at you," he sneers. "So pathetic. Begging me to hurry up so your freaky body can get its nutrition." His smile widens. "You think that's bad? You have no idea what's coming. When it does though, you'll think of me depriving you and see this as me being merciful. Then you'll wish you hadn't betrayed me. You ugly little sow."

Now that I've calmed down a bit, I feel my anger from last night return. I glower at him. "What happened to loving me no matter what? You said I was beautiful, even if I had green skin."

Paris's smirk disappears. "That was before you betrayed me," he says. "You tried to help my dad escape and then you tried to help him put me away. Even if you didn't fuck him, you still betrayed me. You're just a shithead now, Rose. A shithead like my dad, like all the other people in this fucking world who've looked down on me and made my life hell over the years. And that makes you ugly."

Paris's expression lets me know he's hoping I'm upset by this news, that he wants me to be devastated he no longer thinks I'm beautiful. Well, I'm not. I'm more concerned with the fact he's blaming the world for all his supposed troubles in life. I can get blaming his dad but what did the rest of the world have to do with it? Did he always get picked last for tag on the playground? Did he not get a date for high school prom? Or did he feel the other kids should've worshipped him for his supposed greatness and instead saw him for the monster he was?

The anger flares within me. Goddammit, I don't care what Paris does to me next, I'm going to make him really hurt. Even if the only thing I can do is use my words, I'm going to let him know what having hell for a life is really like.

"Well, you need to have a relationship with someone first to betray them, Paris," I reply. "And you and I were never a couple, were we?"

His face falls and he looks at me in terror. I smile. First attack a success. "Yeah, your dad told me," I continue. "He told me all about how you were just a student with a freak crush on his teacher. He even checked with me before I lost my memory. I told him you and I hadn't said two words to each other while you were in my class!"

"Shut up," Paris growls through clenched teeth.

I lob my next attack. "Yeah and your dad also reminded me of my fiancé. Mark Eskin. You called him ME in that murder journal of yours? You made him out to be my stalker and you were the understanding boyfriend who would do anything for the love of his life. Only that wasn't true, was it? Mark was the boyfriend and you were the stalker. How much of what Mark did in that journal was actually you?"

"I said shut up."

"We were nothing, Paris. And I doubt we ever would be. You're just a loser who's hot for his teacher and can't get with a girl no matter how much he tries—!"

"I said shut up!" Paris slams his fist into the soil, making the platform shake. His eyes are wild, his hair tousled and sweat beads on his forehead. Paris stands, breathing like a snarling beast and when he speaks his voice is a low, angry hiss.

"Yeah, we weren't a couple. But I wanted us to be! And I had it all planned out, too! I was going to take you home with me and use *the Record* so you'd forget about that Eskin loser and see what a great guy I am! I even wrote that journal so we could have a real story together. It would've been a real romance, not just something created on the spot! But that bastard...he tried to stop me. And then he knocked you into his car mirror—that was his fault! I didn't lie about that! Mark Eskin was the reason you nearly died!"

"But he wouldn't have ever done that if you hadn't tried to take me away from him," I counter. I bet it was an accident to begin with, assuming Paris isn't still lying about how I got hurt. And I'm not going to let up on him because of it.

"Yeah, but he did do it!" Paris roars. "And then I had to do another spell to save your life! It was easy enough to do. All I needed was some flowers, an animal to sacrifice and an incantation. Sure, it meant I couldn't use the original potion I was going to use but I was fine with that. I could still get you to love me. I knew that the moment you told me you couldn't remember anything. It was like God was telling me I had another chance to make you love me. But then you—ah, fuck!"

Paris spins, runs at the wall and slams his fist into it. He slams it again and again before sinking to the floor. All I can see is the top of his head.

"Goddammit," he whines like a child bursting into tears. "Why doesn't anyone love me? Why won't women date me? If they just gave me a chance, instead of just hooking up with jerks. God fucking dammit!"

I stare at his shaking head with contempt. "It's not something we're doing, Paris," I reveal. He stops shivering and turns his head towards me. I let fly my next volley with all the satisfaction someone can feel over telling another person the plain and obvious truth. "It's because you're an evil little freak."

Paris screams and leaps onto the flower bed. He grabs for my throat, only for two roots to zoom out of the dirt and smack Paris's hand away. He pulls his hand back and stares at the two red welts forming on the back of his hand. Enraged he throws himself at me, punching and choking me as he screams obscenities at me. Two more roots fly out of the soil and attack Paris as my oxygen supply is cut off. They whip and scratch him, ripping his face into a red, bleeding, swollen mess. Despite all that, he doesn't let go of my neck until one of them misses his eye by half an inch. Backing away from the twisting roots until he's at the other end of the flower bed out of range of the still swaying roots. I suck in life giving air, my neck raw to the touch where his hand squeezed.

For a moment, neither of us speak. We sit there, panting from exertion and the emotional drain. The skin on my face and neck tingles and I know it's healing itself.

Finally, Paris breaks the silence. "You're just like Christy," he breathes.

"Christy?" I repeat, sure I've heard the name before. Yes, there was a passing reference to a Christy in Paris's journal.

"Yeah, Christy," he says. "Christy Bruin. Bitch made me think she liked me, then betrayed me. She and her shithead boyfriend Thomas and all their friends got together and...hurt me. She told me I was a freak and said I deserved it." Paris shivers as if cold. "That fucking tough-love camp my dad sent me to. I haven't been the same since."

"You poor thing," I reply without pity sarcasm dripping from every word.

"Don't patronize me!" Paris snarls "Do you know what it's like to be tied up and have a bottle shoved up your rectum? Do you know what it's like to have the girl you were sure loved you and wanted you as much as you loved and wanted her piss and shit into your mouth like a toilet? Do you know what it's like to have ten boys kick and spit on you and then have nine girls cover you in piss and shit? Do you? DO YOU?"

I look upon Paris with fresh eyes, horrified at the torture he must have endured. Suddenly all the references to violence combined with urine and feces in Paris's journal make a horrible kind of sense. What he just described, if it's true, was the most appalling thing that ever happened to him, worse than any abuse his dad put him through. And he got to revisit it every time he wrote in that journal, only he got to be the one inflicting horrors on his oppressors.

Paris sees how stunned I am and smiles wickedly. "I thought so," he says. "But in the end, I got even. You see, two years ago, after I moved out and got my own place, I tracked Christy and Thomas down. And then I met Christy's younger sister Ariel."

My ears perk up. Ariel. She was mentioned in *the Journal* too. I don't remember the exact wording but I think it was in the content of an ex-girlfriend.

"I told her all about what her dearly beloved sister and the kind and handsome husband whom she'd met at camp had done to me," Paris continues. "And you know what? She felt so sorry for me and saw what a nice guy I was, she fell in love with me. And together, we got revenge on Christy and Thomas." The smile grows wider. "Oh, we got such sweet revenge on them."

Paris's expression makes me shiver. Still, I sense he's leaving something out. I ask the one question I can think of.

"Where is Ariel now?"

Paris's smile fails, replaced by a sad, wistful look. "She died," he replies. "She died and there was nothing we could do about it."

I stop myself from asking, "Did you kill her?"

"We loved each other so much," he goes on, looking off into the distance. "We spent entire days in each other's company, so happy and full of love. She listened to my problems and made me feel better afterwards." His eyes refocus on me, "I married her, you know, had a secret ceremony in front of a lake and then we made love. We made love all the rest of the day and through the night. She was the happiest girl in the world and I was the happiest guy in the world. When she told me she'd never been happier, in her fifteen years on the Earth, than on that day, I just about melted."

I stare "Fifteen?" I blurt out in surprise.

Paris ignores me and swings his legs out of the flower bed. "I miss her every day, you know," he says with a small sigh. "She was the only person in the world since my mother died who understood and loved me." His eyes go hard once more before he adds, "But I won't be lonely soon. You'll see. And then you'll really regret not loving me."

Paris chuckles and leaves, closing the bedroom door behind him. A minute later I hear the RV's engine roar to life and the bedroom trembles. As the RV pulls out onto the road, my roots, which had just been hovering this whole time now that the threat to me has passed, slide back into my body. A moment later the four roots which had been feeding in the rich soil slide in as well. Today's feeding is over.

My head is buzzing; from everything Paris has told me, from all the things he hasn't told me and from what he meant when he said he won't be alone soon and I would regret not loving him.

But most of all, my head is buzzing from the revelation about Ariel, who helped Paris kill her sister and brother-in-law—there's no doubt in my mind they're both dead. Ariel who married Paris and then died, all at aged fifteen. What did Paris do to her? She couldn't have done all that he described of her own free will.

Paris said something about a spell in *the Record* that would've made me love him. Did he use that on Ariel? If so, I'm glad he didn't have a chance to use it on me. Even in my current situation, I'm still able to make my own choices. I don't have to worry about Paris making me do whatever he wants, like a puppet on strings. I can't imagine what that must have been like for Ariel, especially if she was aware of what she was doing, unable to stop herself from fulfilling Paris's every desire, including lecherous ones.

I watch the door and anger roils deep within me. Paris has destroyed so many lives; Mark's, Christy Bruin's, her husband Thomas's, her sister Ariel's and mine. Thoughts of Ariel make me the angriest. She had probably been the same age as my sister Maddy is now, full of hope, excitement and possibilities —all taken away by a psycho using a spell book and obsessed with revenge. If he had done that to Maddy? — I push the thought away and make a silent promise to the dead girl. *Just you wait, Ariel. I'll find Mr. Kuyper, we'll get back at him for all of us and when we do? He'll regret ever being born. Just you wait.*

With that I close my eyes and lay back, content to wait and plan. When Paris stops to sleep for the night. I'll strike.

I open my eyes briefly and glance out the window. From this angle, I can see its midday and bright outside. Satisfied I at least have a handle on what time of day it is, I close my eyes again and start counting the minutes until nightfall.

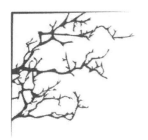

CHAPTER FOURTEEN

Several hours pass between Paris leaving me tied up in the bedroom and when he pulls the RV over for the night. During that time, I drift in and out of sleep, thinking of little else other than revenge. Even my dreams are of what I'll do when I'm free of him. By the time it gets dark, I've slept so much my body won't let me stay asleep anymore. So, I lay there, listening to the RV's engine roar and watching the streetlights through what little of the window I can see.

After God knows how many hours, Paris slows the RV and the road beneath us becomes bumpy and uneven. The streetlights disappear beyond the window and I catch outlines of trees outside. We're going off road. Are going to a campsite? Ohio has plenty of those, though they don't see much use during the winter. Assuming we're still in Ohio, that is.

Paris continues driving along for a few minutes before pulling to a stop. The engine turns off and the vibrations cease. I close my eyes and pretend to be asleep, sure he's going to check on me. Not ten seconds later, I hear Paris open the door. He mutters something that sounds like, "Bitch," and closes the door.

I open my eyes. Time to get to work.

I will my roots out from my neck, imagining them slipping under the plant ropes and breaking them apart. Sure enough, all eight slip out and under the bonds binding my arms to my sides. Together, they push outward and the bonds break with a snap. Two of my roots snake towards my wrists and make quick work of the ropes there.

I gasp loudly as the pressure that kept my wrists together for so many hours is released. It's so loud, for a second I'm sure Paris will come charging through the door to find out what I'm up to. But then I remember he said the bedroom is soundproof. I have nothing to worry about.

I wonder suddenly if Ariel was the one he tested the soundproof bedroom with. Not in the sense of loudly fucking her while wondering if anyone outside heard them—I won't call it making love like Paris did—but by using the gun to test the walls. It makes sense. The only person Paris could possibly trust to help him test bedroom in his RV would have to be someone whom he could control like a puppet. He must've made her stand outside the RV while he fired the gun. She would've come back inside after he fired off the gun to let him know she didn't hear a thing outside and then Paris would know he was fine to do whatever he wanted to whoever in this room.

My heart grows heavy just thinking about Ariel. I try imagining what she might've looked like. What I come up with though is a young girl in her early to mid-teens, with raven black hair cut into a stylish bob, eyes such a deep blue they look violet and a petite and lithe form made for dancing. I shudder. That's not Ariel, that's my sister, Maddy, as last I remember her. Imagining Maddy as Ariel disturbs me even more than imagining what Paris might've done to Ariel. I can't believe I pictured Maddy when I thought of Ariel. Especially Maddy.

I love all my siblings and I would claim in front of God Himself that I love them all equally. But the truth is, I love Maddy more than my other siblings combined. We're seven-and-a-half years apart and we're thick as thieves, as close as two sisters can be. I helped take care of her from the moment she came home, watched her first steps and heard her first words. I introduced her to ballet through library videos when she was four and watched as she got hooked and then trained to become a ballerina, even though our family couldn't afford lessons for her. When I did theater in junior high and high school, she was always my biggest fan in the crowd. In turn, when she performed her own original dances at school talent shows and started a YouTube channel when she was twelve, I supported her, made it to as many shows as I could and watched all her videos until homework made that impossible. I can't imagine doing all that for Brian or Hope, as much as I care for them.

Maddy. She must be so worried about me. My whole family must be but Maddy most of all. I bet she's crying her eyes out worrying about me. She used to always cry whenever I had to go back to school, a habit I hoped she'd outgrow eventually. If she saw me right now, what would she do? Would she cry, or—?

I shake my head and finish tearing the root-bonds apart before jumping out of the soil bed, simultaneously ordering my roots back into my body. Now is not the time to brood on my sister's tears. I'll bother about it when it happens. Right now, I have work to do.

I slide open the bedroom door and peep outside. Nothing but darkness. I let my vision adjust before tiptoeing into the living area. My first stop is the kitchen, where I open one of the drawers and withdraw a large kitchen knife, the kind a serial killer might use in a horror movie. Last time I hesitated to kill Paris, allowing the Oni to stop me. This time, I'll kill him before anything can interfere. And since Paris is probably keeping the gun close now that he's had it used against him, I'll have to settle for a knife. And hope he doesn't wake up before I do.

Or if he does wake up, that he's too slow to pull the gun out before I can stab him.

I take a step forward, then another. If I must guess, Paris is sleeping on the couch. If he is, then maybe I can sneak behind him and—

I hear a moaning and jump, covering my mouth before a scream can escape. My heart doing another samba on my ribcage, I look around the RV, sure I've been caught. But everything is still. There's no sign of Paris, or anyone else, for that matter.

What the hell was that?

I hear the moan again and jump a second time but now I can pinpoint its origin. It's coming from below me, in the RVs cargo hold.

I place the knife on the counter and kneel to the floor. Searching with my hands, I come across a groove in the floor. I trace my finger around the groove and discover what I expected to find: a trap door. I didn't see it when I first got on but I figure an expensive RV would have a trap door in the floor. Especially if the RV in question belongs to Paris Kuyper.

I unlatch the trapdoor and open it. I poke my head in and whisper, "Is anyone down here?"

From the dark, I hear a weak voice reply, "Ms. Taggert?"

I recognize the voice. "Mr. Kuyper!"

Mr. Kuyper moans. "Paris…" he croaks. He sounds so weak and out of it. I wonder if Paris beat him some more after our last escape attempt. Coupled with the accident I caused when I shot at the Oni, it's a wonder the man's alive. "He told me about what they did to him at the camp. He told me after he stuck me down here."

"I know, he told me too," I reply. I consider helping him out but who knows what state he's in? No, until I have a better idea of his health, it'd be better not to risk making it worse. "But don't worry, I'm going to take care of him now."

"He told me it once before," Mr. Kuyper clarifies. "Soon after he got back. But I didn't believe him. I thought he was making it up to shock us. He always held that camp against us."

I don't know how to respond to that. After all I've learned about this man and about his son, it's just one more example of how horrible this family is. So instead I tell him, "I'll be back in a minute. But first, I need to take care of Paris. Hang tight, okay?"

I close the trapdoor and stand up. Grabbing the knife, I tiptoe to the couch. As suspected, Paris is there, fast asleep with a thick blanket over him. He breathes softly, untroubled and unaware his long-overdue punishment for all the crimes he's committed is about to be visited upon him.

I raise the knife over his neck and start counting. Not because I'm hesitating but because I don't want there to be any doubt in my mind. This is going to happen, as soon as I reach three. One…two—

A hand the size of a trashcan lid shoots out of the dark and engulfs my hand and the knife, surrounding them in cold, clammy skin that has the texture of wet leather. At the same time, another hand closes around my mouth, preventing me from screaming, pushing me back against what feels like a hunk of cold rock. From behind me, I hear a voice like leaves scraping across concrete. "Shush."

Despite what the voice said, I scream into the massive hand. It's the Oni. It's finally caught me!

The Oni drags me back towards the bedroom. I try to resist but I'm frozen. Is it magic? No. No, it's fear. I'm frozen with fear.

As the Oni drags me past the kitchen area, the knife slips out of my hand, sails like some alien spaceship from a cheap science fiction movie out from within the Oni's fist and back into the drawer. When we cross the threshold into the bedroom, the door slides shut of its own accord.

The Oni stops. I look up at its face, seeing its horns and giant mouth. It gives me what I think is supposed to be a grin and then throws me onto the flower bed. I cry out, expecting my roots to fly out to defend me, like they should've the moment the Oni grabbed me. Instead they stay where they are. The Oni snaps its fingers. The ropes I just tore off me come to life, sliding around and tying me up again. I fight them but it's like trying to overcome a thousand tiny hands. In a few seconds they have me wrapped like a mummy again, unable to break them no matter how hard I try. If anything, they're stronger than when Paris tied me up in the first place.

The Oni lowers its head over mine. I freeze. "Don't go anywhere," it says, laughing. "Stay right here until morning. You'll get your chance at him. Don't worry about that. But for now, I need you to stay."

Somehow, I find the strength to speak. "And if I don't?"

"Then I'll have to make you stay." It places the tip of a long, pointed fingernail on the small of my back. I squeak as it applies pressure, all my courage dissipating in an instant. If I still needed to use the bathroom like normal people do, I'm sure I would've peed myself then and there. "And you do not want me to do that."

The Oni draws its finger back and shuffles backwards and through the wall like a ghost. When it is gone, I feel myself go weak and all my will to fight leaves me. I must stay here till morning, just like the Oni told me too, or it'll come back. And I can't fight it on my own. I don't think anyone can.

I lay there for a while, not thinking about anything except that I must stay put. After a while exhaustion permeates my body and I close my eyes. I'll do as the Oni wanted and sleep until morning. I'll try stopping Paris then—

Wait a damn minute.

I open my eyes. This is the third time I've witnessed the Oni. And except for the very first time in the greenhouse, every time it shows itself, it prevents me from escaping or stopping Paris. Why? Does it want me to stay with Paris for some reason? Is it protecting him?

And now that I think about it, when I had Paris's cell phone, the crow got into the greenhouse and prevented me from escaping as well. It played keep-away with the phone, first cutting down my time to make a phone call and then ending the call before the police could figure out where I was. And each time it gave the phone back, it vanished, like it had—

—like it had flown through the walls and out of sight. Like the Oni had.

I shiver again. For some reason, something's trying to make it impossible for me to fight Paris and the crow and the Oni are wrapped up in it somehow. But who or what is behind it? And why?

Well, the Oni said I had to stay here till morning. Maybe I'll get the answers to my questions then.

I close my eyes again, slip into sleep, praying to anyone who's listening that tomorrow goes much better than today or yesterday did.

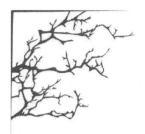

CHAPTER FIFTEEN

I must be dreaming, because I'm back at the family home in Marion. I'm standing in the living room, the most spacious and least cluttered room in our house. Our couch and Dad's easy chair line one wall, while a television, TV stand and rack of DVDs line the other. All around the room hang photos of the family at various dates and events.

At least, that's what the pictures should show but for some reason all the pictures have been replaced with drawings and photos of hourglasses. The symbolism hits me immediately: time is running out to stop Paris.

My eyes rove around the living room until they land on a figure a couple of feet away. It's Maddy, dressed in a loose-fitting purple tunic covered in sequins and the silhouettes of bulls painted on her cheeks with brown paint. She's standing next to a ballet barre, doing bending exercises, plies. She doesn't notice me as she practices.

"Maddy, what's going on?" I ask, hoping this is one of those helpful dreams where your subconscious helps you solve your problems like in books and on TV.

Maddy doesn't answer. Instead she does a pirouette and looks somewhere beyond me. For a moment, neither of us move or speak. Then Maddy opens her mouth and shouts, "W-Where am I?"

"Maddy?" I shriek, startled. Suddenly I'm not so sure this is one of those helpful dreams.

"Who are you?" Maddy continues, still looking through me.

"I'm a friend of your sister, Rose," I respond but it's not my voice. It's Paris's and he sounds like he's about to devour a delicious snack. "My name's Paris. It's a pleasure to finally meet you, Maddy. I've a feeling we're going to get along great."

"No," I cry in my own voice. A wave of fear hits me and a terrible thought enters my mind: what if Paris is here? What if he's somewhere in the house, hiding in the dark and waiting to strike, like some real-life boogeyman? What if he's after Maddy to get to me?

The idea fills me with anger. "Don't you dare touch her, Paris!" I shout. "Don't you dare fucking touch her!"

Classical music fills the air, a piece I've heard somewhere which gives me the chills, though I can't place the music. As the music plays, Maddy dances to it.

"Leave me alone!" she shouts.

I narrow my eyes. I know my sister's dance style, her abilities and something is off. Her style is graceful and weightless, like she's flying across water with her feet. But now her dancing is wild, jerky, spastic, as if she's not deciding her own steps. But worse than her dancing are her eyes; they're blank and glassy, like there's no life in them.

Abruptly she starts spinning, around and around like a top, kicking one leg out every turn while the other keeps her upright and spinning. The tunic flares out from her, the sequins on it flashing like starlight. Underneath is a pristine white leotard and as she turns a red stain appears above her stomach and spreads outward. From her lips, blood dribbles out and falls onto her chin.

"Maddy!" I scream, rushing to her. But no matter how fast I run, she stays far away, like I'm on an invisible treadmill moving too fast for me. I don't care, Maddy's in trouble and Paris is coming, he's coming for us both.

Maddy's screaming, begging for help, telling someone to stay away from her. Who is she telling to stay away? Paris or me?

Her screams reach a crescendo pitch with the music. I recall the name of the piece, it's The Rite of Spring, the one about the sacrifice of a virgin to the God of Spring. Maddy's playing the role of the young maiden, dancing until she dies of exhaustion. No. No Maddy! Don't dance to death! Please don't dance to death! I couldn't stand it if you did!

I call out her name, tears flowing down my eyes. Why can't I get to her?

Suddenly there's bright flash and I close my eyes. When I open them again, Maddy's covered in flames, still spinning like a top even as the flames consume her screaming in terror and unimaginable pain.

I awake with a jerk, panting as if I've run a marathon. I look around me, Maddy's screams echoing in my ears. I'm back in the RV's bedroom, still lying on my stomach as when the Oni tossed me on the soil bed. I search the room with my eyes, heart pounding but everything is normal. Well, as normal as my situation can get. But at least there's no pictures of hourglasses and my sister isn't burning to death right in front of me. No, it's just completely normal.

But Maddy's screams aren't going away. They're getting louder and clearer. And they seem to be coming from the main area of the RV.

"No, let me go! No! Help me!"

That's not the remnants of a dream. That's my sister. My sister's here on the RV. With Paris.

"Maddy!"

I don't even think, I just do. I send my roots out and they slice my bonds to pieces. I jump to my feet and run into the main living quarters, throwing aside the door as Maddy's screams are cut off.

I'm greeted by a scene out of my own personal horror movie. Maddy's backed against the dinette table, while Paris looms over her, close enough that at first, I think he's kissing her. Then my eyes register a glint off glass. Paris is holding a half-full glass of a blue, milky substance to Maddy's lips with one hand, while the other pinches her nose closed with two fingers. They both look towards me as I run in and I can't tell who's more shocked I'm there, Paris or Maddy.

Paris lifts the glass from Maddy's mouth and glares balefully at me and at my roots, out and primed to attack. "So, you got free, huh?"

"Rose!" Maddy coughs, blue milk lining her upper lip. "Is that you?"

I don't answer either of them as a high-pitched whistling grabs my attention. To my left, a tea kettle sitting on a hotplate is hurling steam from its spout. Two mugs sit beside it, the tabs of tea bags hanging over the rims. I rush at the kettle sensing an opportunity. Paris moves to stop me, dropping the glass of blue milk and reaching for me with his now-free hands.

One of my roots whips out and wraps around the kettle's handle. Paris brakes and tries to backtrack but it's too late: my roots lifts the kettle off the hotplate and tosses it at him, hitting him right in the face. Water spills out the spout and the loosened lid. Paris screams and falls to the ground as the hot metal and boiling water scalds his face, drenches his clothes and leaves him writhing in pain as a cloud of steam flies up around him. The kettle bounces off the ground and spins into a corner with a metallic scrape, steam filtering up from its open top.

I wish I could take some satisfaction in finally having some revenge against Paris and all he's done to me but there's no time. I jump over him and the steaming puddles on the ground, grab Maddy by the hand and, before she can start asking questions, yell at her to run. We fly to the front of the RV and down the stairs, crashing through the door into bright light and terrible cold.

My eyes quickly adjust, I see a great forest and the ground littered with fallen leaves and twigs. At least two or three miles off in the distance I see the gleam of cars on a highway. It's so cold out. How long can I run until I succumb to the cold?

From the RV Paris lets out a shrill scream, startling Maddy and me. No time to deliberate or worry. I turn to Maddy and shout "C'mon!" and pull her downhill toward the distant highway. At the same time, I command my roots back into me, sure that if I leave them out, my body heat will leave faster.

At first Maddy stumbles behind me, dazed from what just occurred in the RV, she quickly shakes it off and sprints besides me, matching me stride for stride. Pretty soon she pulls ahead of me, her dancer's body able to run faster than my plant one. We run as if the Devil were behind us. In a way, he is.

After several minutes of nonstop running though, we start to pant and I'm hit by a wave of dizziness. I'm not sure which of us slows first but eventually we both pause and bend over, hands on knees as we gasp for air. My oxygen levels return to normal but the dizziness doesn't go away and now I can't feel my hands and neck. Oh, why did Paris have to try and kidnap me in the middle of fucking winter? Why couldn't he wait till summer when I wouldn't have to worry about the weather destroying my freaky body?

"I-I need a rest," Maddy manages. "I can't run anymore."

I nod and look around. Underneath a tree I spot a hollow space like a miniature pit or cavern, with enough room between the roots for two young women to slip through. I point it out to Maddy and we race to the tree. She wiggles in between two thick roots and I follow her after making sure Paris isn't following us.

The space underneath the tree is tight but we manage to squeeze in and sit somewhat comfortably. Between the walls and my sister, it's a little warmer down here and I feel my body recover a tiny bit. Not much, just enough that I won't faint and die.

For a minute, neither of us says anything. We just sit there and allow the adrenaline to seep out. When I'm somewhere close to calm, I glance at Maddy. She looks at me, tears gushing from her eyes. To my surprise, I'm on the verge of tears as well. I didn't realize how much I missed my little sister until now. Or am I just glad that whatever scheme Paris was using her for didn't work out? I'm not sure I care either way.

We cry out each other's names and throw our arms around each other, tears spilling out our eyes and down each other's cheeks. I bury my head in her hair and kiss her right above the ear. God, I'm so glad she's okay. How did Paris even get her here? By my estimate, we should be over the state line out of Ohio by now, with Marion far in our taillights.

I pull back and take a good look at my sister. She's taller than she is in my last memory of her, maybe around five-five, and I can make out a bit more of the woman she will become than when she was thirteen, though that sweet, innocent face I've always loved is still there. She's still my buddy Maddy. She's wearing a light blue sweater, white pants and sneakers.

"Maddy," I fuss, "are you okay? What happened to you? How did you get here?"

She gazes at me with wide eyes. "I-I'm not sure," she says. "One minute I'm at home, in my room and getting ready for school. I got my shoes on and then...I thought I saw something in my bedroom mirror, I don't know what and then—I'm not sure what happened after that. I felt a hand on my shoulder but it wasn't a hand. I can't explain it. It felt like a hand, like the pressure of a hand but without any of the skin or bones or whatever. Anyway, it grabbed my shoulder, I looked up and I was on that RV and that guy was there."

"Paris."

"Yeah, him. He said he knew you and that we were going to get along great. But I didn't like him. He scared me. He reminded me of the ogre under the bridge, like in the book Mom used to read to us, the one who tries to eat the goats. And then he made me drink that stuff! It was gross. It was too sweet and left a weird taste in my mouth. And then you showed up and...Rose, what happened to you? Why are you green? You disappeared after the graduation party and then Mark...Mark was found dead and—"

Maddy's voice trails off, staring at my face as a fresh wave of tears threatens to overtake me. Mark's death was never far from my thoughts but hearing Maddy utter his name and remind me he's gone forever brings back the grief back in full force. I manage to get myself under control again and Maddy continues.

"Anyway, a lot of people were thinking the worst. There was blood on the side mirror of Mark's car and nobody has seen you since that night. The whole family was freaking out! Hope and Brian took time off work to look for you and Mom and Dad were talking about moving down to Columbus to help out and so I could still attend the Trainee Program."

"Wait, what was that last part?" Something's trying to emerge from the grey fog in my memory and Maddy's the one who triggered it.

She gives me a funny look. "The Trainee Program?" she repeats. "I'm moving from Marion at the end of the school year so I can train with BalletMet? I was going to stay at your apartment to save on rent?"

A fleet of memories rocket out of the grey fog like fireworks and I suddenly understand what Maddy's talking about. That's right, I think, she was going to live with me for a while. She was going to make her dreams come true.

My family could never afford ballet lessons but that never stopped Maddy. From the age of four, when she first saw Nutcracker on a library DVD, she watched every video of ballet she could get her hands on. She imitated their moves, mastered them and performed them on the carpet of our living room. As soon as she could read, she devoured every book the library had on ballet and dancing and when we got Internet used it to continue her studies as well.

By age eight she was performing learned and original routines at church and school talent shows as well as in our house. By twelve she started a YouTube channel with money earned by babysitting, which allowed her to earn a little extra money from ad revenue for tutus, leotards and shoes.

And then last year, Maddy took the huge step of auditioning for the Trainee Program at BalletMet, Columbus's premier ballet company. The program would involve a full year of training and lectures, with the opportunity to audition for the company cast. A tense couple of months had followed before she'd heard back. Not only had she been accepted but she'd been given full scholarship to attend the program.

Finally, her career as a professional dancer, something she'd always dreamed of, was beginning. And we were all ecstatic for her. Mom and Dad were even going to let her stay with me while she trained, as I lived not too far by bus from BalletMet's studio and it would be cheaper than renting a brand-new place near the studio that could cost several thousand dollars in rent. Mark and I were even discussing moving into a house together earlier than we'd planned, one with a spare bedroom for Maddie to stay in.

If all had gone as planned, she would've come down in June, a month before the Summer Intensive began.

All of this comes back to me in the space of a second, leaving me dazed. "Oh yeah, the move," I reply. "Sorry, I forgot." It's the truth.

Maddy's still giving me an odd look. "Rose, what happened to you?" she asks. "It's not just your hair or skin. Something else is weird about you. What's going on?"

I heave a deep sigh. Time to blow her mind. I give her a brief rundown of what Paris has done to me. I emphasize that Paris is the one who killed Mark, that he's killed others and plans on killing me and his father, still trapped on the RV and dealing with God only knows what sort of injuries. I leave out that Paris has been violent with me. I don't want to go into that yet. The last thing I need is Maddy fussing over me like she did after Andy Claycraft slapped me. Especially not now.

When I'm done filling her in, Maddy scrutinizes at me as if I've grown horns, which might be the only thing that could possibly make me look any weirder.

"A magic book?" Maddy says. "I'd say that's crazy, I mean, look where we are." She gestures at the hole we're hiding in. "So, what do we do now?"

"Well, I—wait." I catch something out of the corner of my eye and turn to get a better look. Beyond the roots and several yards away, someone or something, is moving through the trees. I squint my eyes. Is that Paris? Why does his outline seem so shaky? Like a desert mirage.

Paris moves in our direction and that's when I notice that he isn't solid, instead he's made up of what looks like hundreds or even thousands of tiny pieces of forest floor, leaves and sticks and stones, swirling around in a miniature twister to make his body. As he gets closer, I realize he isn't walking or running towards us but floating. The tips of his toes hover six inches above the ground making him look like some sort of weird CGI ghost out of a summer horror film, only real.

That's not Paris, I think. *That's another spell from the Record.* But what does this one do, besides making Paris scarier than he already is?

Behind me, Maddy whispers, "That's what I saw in my mirror. Right before I felt a hand on my shoulder and ended up on that RV!"

I place a hand over Maddy's mouth as the Paris-thing gets closer. I don't know what Maddy's revelation means but I know that whatever this spell does, it's not anything good for us. We scoot deeper into the hole, hiding in the shadows. Outside the tree, the Paris-thing makes a left and flies towards a hollowed-out log. It disappears into the log for a few seconds, emerges and flies towards the sky.

It's looking for us. What'll it do if it finds us? It's solid, so I guess it can harm us. Wait, Maddy said that she saw the Paris-thing, or something like this one, in her room before she felt a hand on her shoulder and ended up on the RV. Does that mean—?

Suddenly, Maddy cries out and curls herself into a ball. I look away from the Paris-thing to Maddy. Her face was screwed up in pain and terror, just like in my nightmare.

"Maddy?" I whisper. And then, a louder and more urgent, "Maddy? What's wrong?"

"R-Rose," she stammers, tearing up again, "something's wrong. I feel like someone's pouring ice water on my brain!"

"Maddy!" I grab her by the shoulders and turn her towards me. All worry about the Paris-thing disappears from my mind. Desperate, I shake her shoulders but that doesn't do anything. Maddy looks up at me, her face wet.

And then her face twists, going from agony and terror to malicious glee. I feel my soul chill just seeing it on Maddy's face. In the back of my head, a voice whispers, *you've seen this face before on Paris.*

Maddy jumps on me and pushes me to the other side of the hole. Laughing maniacally, she reaches for my neck, her fingers curled into talons.

"Maddy!" I shout as I throw my arms up and grab her hands. "What are you doing?"

My roots fly out, interpreting my sister as a threat. I tell them to back off with my mind and they stop in midair before slinking back inside me. Maddy doesn't notice them at all though, too intent on choking me.

Something strikes me in the stomach, sending a flare of pain throughout my abdomen. I buckle, glimpse Maddy's knee burying itself in my solar plexus. She laughs again, her voice high and shrill.

"I'm going to kill you, you bitch!" she screams. "This is what you get for betraying Paris! You hurt the man I love!"

I stare at Maddy, my insides freezing with a chill that has nothing to do with the winter air. Did she just say Paris is the man she loves.?

I hear a slithering sound from outside the tree and glance to one of the bigger gaps in the roots on my left. The Paris-thing is there, looking at us with eyes made from thousands of shifting pieces of forest detritus, grinning like it's viewing an amusing cell phone video. It slips through the gap and places its hands on Maddy and my arms.

There's a tug at the base of my spine and the hole under the tree disappears, replaced by shiny surfaces and mahogany cabinets and warmth that can only come from a heater. I'm back in the RV. No, we're back in the RV, both Maddy and I, we're sitting on the floor and Maddy's still trying to kill me!

What happens next happens so fast, I can barely process it: a foot slams into the back of my head, sending me rolling into a cabinet door; Maddy jumps off me and delivers a kick to my butt, shouting "Take that!" as she does; my roots fly out, unable to resist the instinct to protect me; and then someone grabs four of the roots and uses them to drag me towards the refrigerator. The person opens the fridge door, throws me into the shelves inside and slams the door into my back. And then they do it again. And again. And again, over and over and over, sending waves of overwhelming pain throughout my body. By the time they finally stop slamming the door into me, I'm one throbbing tangle of angry nerves and close to blacking out.

The door opens and I fall to the floor. My attacker closes the door gently and says, "I see it's going to take a lot more than ropes and isolation to keep you bound up."

Paris towers over me, buck-naked except for his glasses. Most of his face, chest and limbs are covered in a greenish paste that seems to be alive and moving, like millions of tiny worms moving through a green swamp. In an instant of clarity, I understand the places with the green paste are where the boiling water and the kettle burned him and the green paste is a magic healing ointment.

Paris leers at me, a triumphant smile on his face. But what scares me more than his smile is what happens next: Maddy takes three balletic skips and throws herself at Paris. He catches her and they wrap their arms around each other. "I love you, Paris," Maddy confesses. And then she and Paris lean in towards each other and kiss.

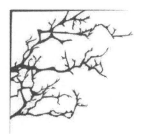

CHAPTER SIXTEEN

I watch, horrorstruck and sick, as Maddy passionately kisses Paris, who glances at me and flashes me a self-satisfied sneer before sticking his tongue in Maddy's mouth. Maddy makes ecstatic noises, pushing her own tongue into Paris's mouth. Between his legs, his dick hardens and rises to attention.

I try to stand but I'm in too much pain. My body's already healing itself, sealing cuts and knitting broken bones back together but it's taking all my energy to stay conscious after the beating I've endured. Even my roots, twisted and bent and torn in places, can only slide back into my body, like terrified dogs slinking into their dens. Instead of moving, I talk.

"Don't you dare touch her," I rasp. "You filthy bastard."

Paris unglues his mouth from Maddy and looks at me with annoyance. "What are you going to do about it, shithead?" he taunts. "She's mine now." He lets her go and bends down so we're eye to eye. Naked and with his dick pointed like a missile from his pelvis, it looks like he's about to rape me. I shiver. "You know, if you'd loved me like you should, this wouldn't happen," he states in a low voice. "Now you and my dad are going to be punished, just like that shithead bitch Christy and that shithead asshole Thomas were."

"And you made Ariel your slave too." Terrible realization dawns on me. This is what the cop shows call an MO. Paris is recreating his revenge on Christy Bruin and Thomas Washington with his father and me and he's punishing me further by making Maddy his love-slave, just like he did with Ariel. All because Christy and I wouldn't love him like he wanted to be loved.

Paris frowns at me. "Ariel was my wife," he says. "She loved me and I loved her. I just had to show her what an awesome guy I am. I deserve to be loved."

Maddy bends down and wraps her arms around Paris's neck. She kisses his cheek, avoiding the areas covered in green paste. Paris takes her hand in his and smiles, his face one of utter bliss. I want to throw up.

"Is that what you call giving people that potion?" I ask, thinking of the blue, milky stuff Paris forced down Maddy's throat when I ran out of the bedroom earlier. "Showing them how awesome you are?"

Paris's frown reappears. "You know, I'm tired of you talking," he declares, standing up and walking away from Maddy. She looks forlornly after him as he goes to the front of the RV, then flashes me a look full of hate. I've never seen Maddy look at me like that before. Maybe angry once or twice after an argument but never hateful. It shocks me and at the same time breaks my heart. Even though I know she's being controlled, it hurts to think that any part of her could hold a grudge against me.

From the glove compartment, Paris pulls *the Record*. Opening it and skimming through the pages before stopping at the one he needs. His lips move and I can make out barely audible muttering as he returns to the kitchen area, where he pulls out a mortar and pestle and several brown paper bags from one of the cabinets. Each bag has its contents written on it in marker with big capital letters. BAMBOO-LEAF OAK SAP, BUNA LEAVES, CHERRY TREE SEEDS, HUNTSMAN SPIDER VENOM. Paris adds ingredients to the mortar and grinds it with the pestle. Maddy dance-walks to watch, her eyes wide like it's the most fascinating thing in the world. Then he speaks in the language he used before when reciting spells, Middle Japanese, I think. A strange light flashes from the mortar, as purple steam rises from the concoction. Paris grins and reaches into another cabinet. When he pulls his hand out, he's holding a medical syringe, the kind used to deliver vaccinations. My heart skips a beat, resuming at a quick-tempo dubstep.

"I know I said I couldn't use magic on you," he says, filling the needle with purple liquid before turning to face me. "But the book actually says most magics not all magics. I wonder if this one will work on you. I hope it does, because tying you up doesn't work, a barrier around the bed would be too weak and I really don't want to go out and buy police-grade handcuffs. That'd be an inconvenience."

Paris bends down, holding the needle right in front of my face. I try to move away, sweat already breaking out on my forehead but my body is still too weak. Paris's smirk grows wider. "Yeah, you're afraid of needles. Which is why I'm not making you drink this. A needle is way more fun."

Before I can let out a scream, he sticks the needle into my neck and pushes the plunger down with his thumb. Cold liquid enters my veins a second before the pain arrives. I expect my roots to jump out and defend me, instead they rattle. When the syringe is empty, Paris pulls the needle out. As the potion moves through me, leaving its cold touch wherever it goes, I open my mouth to ask what he put in me.

Except my mouth doesn't move. No matter how many signals my brain sends, my lower jaw refuses to swing open. It's frozen in place. I tell my arm and hand to check my jaw but they refuse to move, as does my other arm and hand. A chill that has nothing to do with the potion Paris stuck in me rushes up my spine as I grasp what he's done.

I'm paralyzed. Paris has paralyzed me.

Something must be showing on my face, because Paris's savage smile grows so wide I'm sure the top of his head will be separated from the bottom. "Good," he says. "That'll keep you from causing me any more trouble."

Maddy claps as if a stage musician has shown off an amazing trick. "That was great, Paris!" she coos. She looks at me with contempt and I go colder. I've never seen Maddy look at anyone with contempt before, let alone me. "Now what should we do with her?"

Paris grins. "Help me bring her into the bedroom," he orders.

Paris grabs me by the armpits and Maddy grabs my feet. They lift me up, my head lolling forward against my chest. They carry me into the bedroom and onto the soil bed. The moment my skin touches the soil, two roots at the back of my neck, somehow immune to the paralysis, dig into the dirt. I'd forgotten that I hadn't put my roots down yet today. I guess they were holding back while Maddy and I were running away.

"Now what do we do with her?" Maddy repeats.

Paris smiles and encircles her from behind. She leans against him, a dreamy look on her face. His dick, which went flaccid while he was making the paralysis potion, hardens again. "Well," he says, kissing her on the cheek, "I figured we'd take what she fears most and torture her with it."

I blanch. No, he's not going to rape her now, is he? Not now, not in front of me! If he did that, if he raped my sister in front of me, while she has no choice but to take it and think she wants him, while I'm unable to help her, I don't think my mind will be able to take it. I'll go crazy and accept my own death, bite through my own tongue, gouge out my eyes so I won't have to see any more. Suicide would be preferable to that.

"Oh no, I don't mean make love to her," Paris says to me, as if reading my mind. "I'm not going to do that just yet."

Maddy looks at Paris, her expression hurt. "But I want you to make love to me!" she pouts. One hand reaches out and grabs his dick, which hardens further in her grip. "I want to give all of myself to you! I love you!"

Despite the paralysis, I nearly puke.

"In time, babe," Paris assures her, breathing hard and wearing a rueful moue as he extricates himself from Maddy. "When I cement our revenge against her. Until then, I've got something almost as good."

He steps out of the bedroom and we hear him rummaging in the kitchen. While he's gone, Maddy glowers at me with contempt again. "You hurt my Paris," she asserts. "I can't forgive you for that. You're no longer my sister. You're dead to me. And I'm going to enjoy every moment I hurt you with him."

She spits in my direction and my heart breaks again.

Paris returns, thankfully wearing a pair of boxers and a white undershirt with yellow pit stains and holding a box under an arm.

"You know, after you caused me to drive off the road," he says, "you were out for more than a day. I used that time to get a few things, as well as scope out Maddy so I could bring her here this morning." Before I can process this new information, Paris tugs the lid off the box and pulls out a long, shiny needle. My eyes grow wide in their sockets. A scream builds in my throat. I'm sure if I still needed to urinate, I'd be wetting my pants now.

"It wasn't easy getting acupuncture needles in Marion," Paris remarks, handing the needle to Maddy and grabbing one for himself. "Not many places sell them to just anyone on the street. But I think it'll be worth the trouble, Rose. You agree, right?"

Paris and Maddy climb into the soil bed, holding the needles like weapons. I let out a scream, muffled by my closed mouth, well before the needles plunge into my skin.

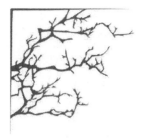

CHAPTER SEVENTEEN

The door slams open and someone flicks on the lights. I groan, open my eyes and say groggily, "What's going on?" It takes me a moment to realize that's the first time I've spoken in days. I can move again. They've never let me go a moment without the paralytic potion, not since Paris first dosed me. Why the change?

I blink several times and Maddy comes into focus, standing in the doorway and looking at me as if I'm lower than a worm. "Get up," she scoffs. "It's time to go."

Slowly, my limbs as heavy as lead, I pull myself into a sitting position and look Maddy up and down. Today she's wearing a slinky, sleeveless sea-green dress that reveals way too much skin and matching high heels. Picked out for her by Paris, no doubt: since he put her under his control, Paris has had Maddy dress up in a different outfit every day. The first day it was a sexy maid costume; the second was short shorts and a tube top; and the third was a black nightie with a very short skirt. I know Paris is dressing her up this way to torture me as well as for his own lascivious pleasure. He gets a thrill seeing me see my sister dressed like that, just like he gets a thrill from paralyzing me with potion every day and then torturing me after a long day of driving, Maddy at his side fawning over him and helping him torture me.

I thought being alone in Paris's home was bad but these past couple of days have been the worst of my life that I can remember. Not even Mark's death can compare to the horror of having my own sister help this psychopath stick me with needles or cut me with knives or smash my joints with hammers and steak mallets every day, treating him like a god and me like trash and then going to the couch in the main living area to noisily make out before going to sleep.

The making-out part is worse than the needles, because every night, I'm sure Paris is going to rape her, even though he said he'd wait till he had his revenge and neither of us will be able to stop him. And every time Paris goes to sleep without violating

Maddy, I feel only slight relief, because I know tomorrow, he's going to do the same thing and maybe tomorrow he won't be able to control himself. And if that happens, all will be lost. Paris will have won and I'll be better off dead.

"Maddy," I croak, my voice hoarse from disuse.

"I said get up," she snaps. "Paris says it's time to go."

"Maddy, listen to me," I plead. I know I won't get through to her, still, I must try. I couldn't bear it if I didn't try. "Paris is not a good person. He's a monster and he's controlling you. You don't love him and he doesn't love you. You're just a fantasy to him!"

Maddy runs forward and slaps me so hard, I'm thrown against the wall of the soil bed. My roots fly out to hit her back but she dodges and skips out of range. She's really taking after him, I think, my cheek stinging.

With an effort I pull myself up again and will my roots back inside me. When I look at Maddy, she's staring at me with such intense hatred, I fear being burned by it.

"Paris is a victim," Maddy asserts, her voice dripping with venom. "He told me all about how the world has treated him like shit since his mother died. His dad, his classmates, the people at that camp, you." She places extra emphasis on the word *you*. "Especially you. I mean, he loved you! He saved your life! And you betrayed him. It's all I can do to comfort him!"

"He stalked me," I point out, knowing what I'm going to get for it and hardly caring. "He killed Mark and then turned me into a plant-creature so he could control me and turn me into his fantasy girl. But I saw him for what he is, so he cast a spell on you to spite me."

Even though I'm prepared for the blows and raise my arms, Maddy still manages to land another slap. She follows it up with a ballet spin-kick into my ribs, sending me back onto the wall. My roots fly out defensively until I will them back into my body. No matter what state she's in, no matter how many times she strikes me, I can't bring myself to hurt her.

"You'll get your just desserts soon," Maddy promises. "Paris has arranged for it. Now get out here. We can't keep him waiting."

Maddy storms out of the bedroom. I slowly get back to my feet, my belly throbbing in time with my heartbeat. I lift my shirt and look where Maddy kicked me. What I see causes me to shudder: there's a big, purple bruise forming over my ribs, as well as dozens of tiny dots lining my tummy and chest.

Dots?

I check again. Those aren't dots. They're the remains of being pricked every evening by Paris and Maddy, red and half-healed. But how is that possible? My wounds are supposed to heal as soon as they're made.

I flash back to the past couple of nights and realize something. I stopped being afraid of the acupuncture needles after the second night. I'd been pricked so many times, I just grew used to the needles and stopped caring. If I remember the one psychology class I took in undergrad correctly, that's called operant conditioning. But while I stopped being afraid, the pain never ceased. In fact, it only increased every night, as Paris and Maddy escalated their torture to get the same reactions out of me. I wonder if that did something to my healing ability, weakened it somehow. Plausible, considering how many times my bones were broken and healed and broken again.

I inspect the wounds again and notice that among the red dots, a few are black and necrotic. Perhaps I'm a bit closer to Paris killing me again than any of us know.

My train of thought is broken as I detect Maddy's familiar light step coming down the length of the RV. I rush to the door before she can enter and beat me for keeping them here. Maddy stops at the edge of the kitchen as I emerge turning around with a loud "Hmph!" and shouts, "Paris, she's up and ready to go."

I look beyond Maddy and see Paris. With him is Mr. Kuyper. With all that happened with Maddy, he'd been banished from my mind until now. I wince at the state he's in. His bruises have yellowed and some of his wounds have turned an ugly shade of infection green. Our eyes lock and a silent message passes between us, an acknowledgment that one way or another, this is all going to end soon. And it will likely end with the both of us dead.

Paris sneers at me. "Glad you could finally join us, Rose," he says. Then to Maddy, "Grab the knife."

"Yes Paris," Maddy responds, sounding a little like a robot. She strides to a drawer and pulls out a large kitchen knife, possibly the same one I pulled a million years ago on my second night in the RV. To my shock, she raises the knife and places it at her neck.

"Maddy, what are you doing?" I shout.

"Just a precaution," Paris explains, moving to Maddy's side and wrapping his arms around her from behind. "You two might attack me or try to run away. So Maddy's going to make sure you two don't do anything stupid. The moment you do..." He laughs and kisses her head. "You get the idea."

We do and my hands ball into fists. I open my mouth to speak but Mr. Kuyper beats me to the punch. "You sick bastard, Paris," he says. "You told me you loved that girl. And here you are, putting her life in danger just to save yours."

Paris frowns at his father. "I do love Maddy," he says, kissing the side of her neck not blocked by a knife. Maddy gasps with pleasure and my stomach roils. "She cares for me like no one else does. But you two need to behave. Maddy's making sure you do. Even a bastard like you won't risk the life of an innocent girl to save your own damn hide."

"I'm happy to do this," Maddy reveals. "I'd do anything for Paris."

Paris smiles. "I know you would, baby," he says, licking her neck. Maddy giggles, her jugular bobbing horribly close to the tip of the knife. I watch the distance between her neck and the knife grow and shrink with every movement, too terrified to be disgusted.

With his dominance asserted, Paris heads to the door. A rush of cold air fills the RV as he slides it open. Everyone but Paris shivers. "Come on," he calls, stepping outside. "If either of you stay behind, you know what will happen."

Mr. Kuyper and I exchange another glance, then turn to Maddy, still holding the knife to her neck. We step outside, the ends of our lives and our alliance coming much too soon.

I stare at the world around us in wonder. The RV is surrounded by a sea of snow tinged blue from the grey cloud cover over our heads. Rising from the sea are long, brown structures with pointed roofs covered in snow falling in waves from above. Beyond them I can make out a forest populated by firs reaching up to the sky and beyond them the tops of snow-capped mountains.

The chill that rushes through my body almost makes me faint. It's happening faster than usual. I must really be sick if the cold is affecting me already. I grab my chest and shiver, looking behind me as Maddy steps off the RV. She's still wearing that slinky sea-green dress with nothing over it. She shivers too but doesn't complain about the chill or ask Paris if he has a coat.

And he says he loves her, I muse, still able to muster a little bit of anger. Only enough to get her into sexy outfits and nothing practical, apparently.

I glance over at Paris. He seems unaffected by the cold and it's at least twenty degrees colder than when he forced me outside onto the balcony to punish me my first morning with him. Instead, he's looking at the buildings with a mix of emotions I can't read.

"W-Where are we?" I shout above the wind.

"Brading Youth Rehabilitation Center," Paris answers. "A year-round facility for children whose rich parents want some undesired trait or another worked out of them. Well, it used to be in operation year-round, even in weather worse than this. But then the body of a former patient was found and word got back to civilization. And then years of suppressed abuse made its way into the public consciousness." Paris turns to his father and adds, "My story might have come out too, if a certain someone hadn't threatened to put me in the nut hatch if I came forward and brought shame to the family name."

Mr. Kuyper doesn't respond but the moment Paris looks away, I hear him mumble, "I was just thinking of your best interests."

"This was the place where I finally understood how much the world hates me," Paris continues. He points at a building rising out of the snow. "That there is the cabin where I slept every night, with only a thin blanket to combat twenty-degree nights. And it was on one of the coldest nights that winter that the other kids tied me up, used me as a punching bag and toilet and then left me outside to brave the cold." He closes his eyes, as if reliving the experience. "I have no idea how I survived that night but since then, I've never needed more than a sweatshirt to get by in cold temperatures. The only good thing that ever came out of me attending to this damned place."

Maddy steps awkwardly through the snow to Paris's side and takes his free hand with hers. He squeezes it and I realize as psychotic as he is, all he's really looking for is some sort of comfort from the painful life he's lived. That's why he could go from wild, raging beast to a crying child in an adult's body at the drop of a pin. Under very different circumstances, I might feel sorry for him.

But all I need to see is Paris glance at my sister with a mix of pride, possessiveness and lust and any pity in me is extinguished.

Paris trudges toward the cabin he pointed to, pulling Maddy along beside him. Maddy looks back at Mr. Kuyper and me, the knife still clutched in her hands and we follow reluctantly. We make our way slowly through the frozen landscape, our feet making three-foot-deep holes in the snow. By the time we reach the cabin, everyone's legs are slick and wet and Paris is the only one who isn't on the verge of fainting. Even Maddy's knife-wielding arm is barely able to stay up, something I note uneasily.

Paris pushes open the door, the one remaining hinge screaming loudly and we enter the cabin. He then says something in Middle Japanese and suddenly the cabin is lit by brilliant lights. I hold a hand to my face, momentarily blinded. When my eyes adjust, I spot three trees in the center of the cabin: a yew, a beech and an orange tree, their trunks breaking through the floor and their branches reaching towards the roof. Somehow, despite it being winter and there being no holes in the ceiling, all three trees have their leaves and the one on the right, the orange tree has fruit hanging from its branches, each fruit giving off light bright enough to put any lamp to shame.

Mr. Kuyper inhales. "My God, what is this?"

I glance at him. He's gawking at the trees. Knowing I probably won't like what I see, I follow his gaze.

I gasp as I lock on to what Mr. Kuyper's staring at. The center tree, the beech, has something wrapped around its trunk. No, that's not right; it's more like the tree is wrapped around it. Something as white as the tree's bark, with holes and gaps through which small branches sprout, something I know from sight.

"Oh wow," says Maddy in a voice filled with awe. "Did you do that, Paris?"

"I did," he confirms. "That was Christy. And now she's a sign to all of what happens when you go too far with me."

A sense of dread fills me. Pairs said the skeleton was Christy. As in Christy Bruin, the girl who betrayed him with her boyfriend and all the other kids at the camp? That's her rib cage and toothless skull, the beech's trunk rising from the skull's gaping jaws. By the foot of the tree, bones from her arms and fingers litter the ground, resembling some terrible offering to a twisted tree spirit.

"My God," I whisper. Then a little louder, "What did you do to her?"

Paris lets out a maniacal laugh loud enough to shake the building's rafters. The rest of us jump as Paris gazes at the beech tree and Christy's remains with a wistful smile. "I put her out of her misery. You see, by that time Thomas had been torturing her at my command for three days straight. Add that her sister and I were in love and the realization that her current circumstances were her own fault and she was begging me for her death. So, I granted it to her." He laughs again. "Of course, I made sure it was as painful as possible. The tree entered her digestive system through one end and grew out the other. Painful doesn't begin to describe it. It was something to see."

"You monster!" I shout, seething. I can't help it, I'm so angry and upset. Whatever she did to Paris, Christy Bruin didn't deserve what happened to her, not by a long shot.

Paris glares at me. He points at the beech tree and says, "Go break off a few branches from the beech and build it into a pyre. Maddy's getting cold."

I open my mouth to let Paris know what he can do with the branches from the beech tree but my protest is stilled by the sight of the knife quivering in Maddy's hand and I stride to the beech tree, somehow able to stand despite the cold in my bones. Behind me I hear Mr. Kuyper following, though, he's having more trouble walking straight than I am. Our feet make the boards underneath our feet creak and whine, filling the cabin with uncomfortable echoes.

As we reach the trees, I stop. The yew tree and the orange tree. I've seen them before. I do a double take to make sure and features in the trees jump out at me: whorls and depressions like faces, bumps like breasts, branches like arms raised into the air. It's the yew and orange trees from the greenhouse of Paris's home, the ones that disappeared when we left Paris's home and were replaced by a palm tree. What the hell are they doing here? How are they here?

"Hurry up!" Paris shouts. I jump and help Mr. Kuyper pull branches off the beech tree. We take several branches back to Paris and Maddy and arrange them into a pyramid shape. The whole time, we glare at Paris and watch Maddy in case she interprets something we do as resistance or an escape attempt. From under his sweatshirt, Paris pulls out *the Forest God's Record* and opens it to a certain page. He recites a spell and the beech branches burst into flame. Maddy lets go of Paris's hand and kneels in front of the fire. Paris kneels beside her and places *the Record* on the floor. We aren't invited to get closer to the warm fire, nor do we try. Still, the heat of the flame reaches and warms my body. I'll live a little while longer.

"Happy, babe?" Paris asks.

"Oh, very much," replies Maddy.

"When did you do this?" Mr. Kuyper asks. We all look at him, standing beside me and swaying on his feet but somehow embodying the size of a giant again, more resembling the man he was on the night I woke up in the greenhouse and he argued with his son.

"When did I do what?" Paris asks.

"When did you do this to that woman?" Mr. Kuyper gestures at the beech tree and Christy's remains. "When the hell did you have time to kidnap a woman and do this to her?"

Paris regards his father for a second before answering, "Remember that summer I told you I was going hiking through the Appalachian Mountains and I'd be doing it without technology, so I'd be totally off the grid?"

Mr. Kuyper's eyes grow wide. Paris chuckles.

"Yeah, while you thought I was hiking and being your definition of manly, for once, I was here," he gloats, "getting my revenge. Didn't you ever ask yourself why my muscle definition never changed after that summer? And I didn't kidnap Christy Bruin, Dad. I first met her sister Ariel and we fell in love. Then she helped me lure them here and...well, you know." He laughs, glancing at the trees. "Boy, that was a good summer. The best I've ever had, really."

"You're sick," says Mr. Kuyper.

Paris's smile disappears and he glares at his father. "I was taking care of business, as you'd call it," he growls, rising to his feet. "You always say a real man takes care of business. You also say that a man doesn't take shit from anyone and if he does, he should find a way to salvage his dignity so that he comes out on top, at the end." Screaming now, he circles around the fire and finishes with, "All my life, I've tried to be like the man you want me to be! I can't be him one hundred percent, though I've fucking tried! I did that for you, dammit! I did that for you!"

"Don't lie to me." Mr. Kuyper's tone is calm and even, yet it thunders through the confines of the cabin. "You never cared about me, not since you started seeing me as your enemy. And all this?" He gestures at the trees. "You did this for your own sick pleasure. You're the farthest thing from a man I've ever seen. Rose said it best: you're a fucking monster."

It's like having a front-row seat to a volcano erupting: Paris seems to grow with anger, his hands balled into fists and his face going pink. Then he lets out a guttural scream and throws his father to the ground. I see a brief flash of an incomprehensible smile on Mr. Kuyper's face before Paris lets his fists fly. Maddy watches from behind the fire and cheers Paris on, shaking her knife-less fist in the air. I watch as well, wanting to help but afraid of what Maddy might do if I did. Around Mr. Kuyper's head, blood starts to pool.

Suddenly there's a flap of wings from above my head. I look up and a familiar form flies towards the trees. The crow lands by the orange tree and morphs into the Oni.

I watch on, uncomprehending but for once unafraid. The Oni gives an approximation of a smile and jerks its thumb at the trees. The orange and yew trees' forms waver and reform into two familiar people, a dark-skinned man with a face tattoo and a blonde-haired teenager. The two figures from the greenhouse who looked like they were in pain.

And then a connection clicks in my brain. Thomas Washington and Ariel Bruin. They became the yew tree and the orange tree. So that's what happened to them. That's why Paris isn't with Ariel anymore and why he became obsessed with me. After a while they became trees and Paris had to search for someone new to desire.

The Oni points at something behind me. I follow its finger. *The Forest God's Record* is sitting there on the ground, just a few feet away from where Maddy's sitting and far from where Paris is still punching his father's face in.

I look back at the Oni. It nods at me, as if giving permission and then gives a guttural laugh.

I look back at *the Record* before turning to my sister. "Maddy."

She looks up, annoyed at my interruption of her entertainment. "What?"

"I'm not about to attack Paris. And I'm not about to run."

Before she can process what I mean, I run around the burning fire, scoop up the book and sprint back to where I was standing a moment ago. "Hey Paris!" I shout, a note of triumph in my voice.

Paris stops punching his father's body and glances around. He sees I have *the Record* and his face falls.

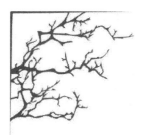

CHAPTER EIGHTEEN

Paris stands up slowly. Beneath him, Mr. Kuyper's chest rises and falls, still alive despite the latest beating. How much can one man with a normal human body endure?

"Rose," Pairs says. His voice is calm but I sense the emotion behind it; terror and anger threaten to burst loose. "Give me back *the Record*. Right now."

I sneer at him. That's the closest I've ever heard Paris beg. After all he's put me through, it's satisfying to see me get under his skin. Instead of handing it back to him, I hold the book over the fire. All I have to do is uncurl my fingers and it'll fall. The heat from the fire's flames is intense and my skin feels raw even from a couple feet above the flames. I ignore the pain as Paris blanches, I've got him right where I want him.

"Rose," he says louder, the fear detectable in his voice. "Give me that book. Now!"

"No."

Paris's eyes go wide, blinks and stares at me, as if he's the one who's been slapped. I haven't said no to him since I asked him if we could slow down our relationship. His mouth opens and closes several times before he responds. And when he does, it's only a pitiful "What?"

"I said no."

He seethes. "Do you know what you're doing?" he asks. Something small and round drops from his hand, which becomes long and green the moment it hits the ground. One end of the green thing stretches out toward Mr. Kuyper, while the other end divides into eight arms reaching outward. By the time the end stretching for Mr. Kuyper worms its way to his leg, it's now three feet long and starting to thicken. I watch, mesmerized, as it races up his pant leg, growing and twisting underneath the fabric. When it reaches his waist, Mr. Kuyper screams in agony, the first time I've heard him react to pain. At the same time the eight arms, as thick as extension cords, break through the floorboards and into the ground below. The end inside Mr. Kuyper's pants—inside Mr. Kuyper—lifts him into the air. Blood seeps down his legs and stains the thing extending itself inside him red. No, not the thing: the trunk. A tree trunk. Paris is giving Mr. Kuyper the same sort of treatment he gave Christy Bruin.

My arm shakes and I look away, barely able to keep an eye on Paris when I know what's happening behind him. Mr. Kuyper's screams continue for several minutes before abruptly being cut off. When I look again, there's a white beech trunk rising out of his mouth and branches covered in blood poke out of his chest. Even though its victim is dead, the tree continues to grow, branches dividing and reaching for the ceiling while the roots become thick as bodybuilder arms and covered in bark.

Paris is still glowering at me, his eyes flicking to the book every few seconds. "Give me *the Record*," he growls. "Now! Or I'll do the same to you!"

"No." My voice breaks, I clear my throat and repeat myself. "No!"

"Then Maddy will have to die."

I glance at Maddy. She's looking at Paris, her face like a puppy willing to do anything for praise. Instead of terror though, my reaction is incredulity. Unbelievable. This poor excuse for a human being is telling the girl he was showering with promises of love that she'll have to die for him and the spell still makes her think of him as some fucking mistreated messiah who's worth dying for. I look back at Paris and respond in my firmest voice, "The moment she so much as scratches her neck, *the Record* burns."

Paris screws his face up like he's having an internal debate. Ten seconds pass. "Maddy," he says, "throw that knife away."

Maddy lowers the knife and throws it into a far corner, giving me a dirty look as she does.

"Fine, I did what you asked," says Paris. "Now give me back *the Record*."

"No."

His eyes narrow. "No?"

"No. We're not done here yet."

Paris's face creases with anger, making him look like a wild beast. "What else do you want?"

"I want you to lift the spell on Maddy. I want you to make me a human again. And then I want you to let us go and stay here while we take the RV. Maybe then you'll get your book back."

Panic crosses Paris's face. "I can't do that."

"Can't or won't?" I ask.

"I can't!"

"How do I know you're telling the truth, Paris? You've lied to me most of the time we've known each other!" My fury is funneling through me like a tornado. "You might be lying now, you freaky bastard! You shithead!"

"I swear, I can't!" he insists, flinching as I call him by his favorite insult. "Most of those spells can't be reversed! That includes the ones on you and on Maddy. You're both going to stay that way for the rest of your lives!"

The tornado inside me breaks free. "So Maddy's going to stay your love-slave until you get tired of her and turn her into a tree?" I shout. "Like you did with Ariel and Thomas!"

"No!" Paris cries, desperate. "No, I didn't do that to Ariel! I loved her. It was a side effect of the potion! It turns those who drink it into trees after a few months. That's what happened to Ariel and Thomas, I swear!"

I stare at him, incredulous. "You gave that to them knowing they were going to turn into trees?"

"No!" he cries. "The book just said those who drank the potion would follow me until they became stiff as trees. That's literally what it says! I thought that meant when they become skeletons or something! I didn't know that meant they'd become trees! Please believe me. Do you really think I want to keep having to look for someone to love me every couple of months?"

I don't believe him. Perhaps he's serious about not having to look for multiple lovers but I'm sure he's lying about the other stuff. One of the times I looked through the Record, I remember seeing a creepy illustration of people turning into trees. How do I know that doesn't refer to the potion Paris used?

And he used it on my sister, knowing what it will do to her! That bastard! Pulsing with rage, I uncurl my index finger from the cover.

"No!" Paris shouts. "Please! I modified the potion from the Record! Maddy won't turn into a tree!"

"Is that true?"

The voice asking is high-pitched, quavering and isn't mine. It's Maddy's. We both turn to her and for once, she looks worried for someone other than Paris.

"Paris," she says, "am I really going to turn into a tree? You're not going to let that happen, are you?"

"Of course not!" he assures her. "Darling, I tested the modified potion on rats and stray cats! I found how to keep them from turning into bushes and flowers! It took some time but I figured out the right combination of ingredients! That's the potion I gave you, I swear. You and I are going to stay together forever!"

Maddy's face lights up with relief.

"Don't believe him!" I yell. Maddy's eyes go to me and I see the hope die in them. Well, too bad Maddy, because your older sister found a flaw in what Paris just said and it's a big one, too. And it might save you and stop you from doing something stupid.

"I'm a sociologist, remember?" I remind them. "That's a kind of scientist. And I know for a fact what works during animal trials won't necessarily work on human trials. You could still turn into a tree, Maddy. And all because he used a potion on you to get back at me."

Maddy is on the verge of tears. She turns to Paris, who looks like he's close to tears himself. "That's not true, is it?" she asks, though I'm not sure if she means turning into a tree, the spell he cast on her, or both.

"It's true," I confirm anyway. "He killed Mark just to get to me and use the same potion on me that he used on you. But when he nearly got me killed, he used a different spell on me. The results are right here before you." I gesture at myself with my free hand. "Only doing that made the potion useless on me. And when I realized how unlovable he was, he retaliated by kidnapping you and making you drink the potion so you would have no choice but to love him. You remember that, don't you? You told me you were at home when Paris whisked you away and onto his RV."

"Shut up!" Paris shouts. Maddy's looking at the both of us with a mixture of terror and confusion on her face. His face, meanwhile, is more terrified than angry now. Is he worried that I'm breaking his control on her? Is that even possible for me to do?

"You know that something's messed up about your relationship, Maddy," I remind her. "Think about it. What about him made you fall for him in the first place? Was it something he said? Was it how he treated you after you met him?" I remember what Maddy said right before Paris took control of her—I feel like someone's pouring ice water on my brain!—and add, "Or is it because there's something in your head telling you to love him and it's too powerful to disobey?"

Maddy eyes widen and tear up as I wait for her answer. "I—" she stammers. "I-I just—!"

"Maddy, don't listen to her!" Paris roars. "She's trying to trick you! You know you love me! You knew it the moment you saw me and I told you about all the awful things I've had to endure. You remember, right? All that made you fall for me."

Maddy looks at Paris and says in the smallest voice, "But you only told me about your life after I fell for you. And after I attacked Rose because...because that's what you wanted me to do."

Maddy grabs her head and screams, as if she's being assaulted by the worst migraine ever suffered in human history. Her knees buckle and she falls to the floor, curling into a ball and sobbing while holding her head.

Paris gapes at Maddy in terror. Then he turns to me and his terror is replaced with rage, the same rage I saw in the greenhouse after he threw the flowerpot at Mr. Kuyper's head. "You're doing this!" he screams. "You're taking her away from me!"

He sprints at me, arms outstretched and fingers curled into claws. I see him coming and I do the only thing I can think of: I drop *the Record* into the fire.

"No!" Paris screeches. He bends and leaps to catch the book in midair but he's too late. The Record, the true source of his power, falls into the burning pile of sticks, sending up a stream of sparks. Paris screams in rage and sorrow as he sails over the fire, crashing to the floor and rolling to a stop against the wall. He stands, spins around and rushes at me like a football player. "Yooooou biiiiiitch!" he shrieks.

Paris grabs me by my midsection and tackles me to the ground. I cry out as we tumble to the ground. Locked in a crazy embrace, we roll away from the fire, until I end up on my back with Paris straddling me, legs pinning my sides and hands on my shoulders.

"I'm going to kill you, you fucking bitch!" he yells. "You shithead bitch! You've ruined everything!" Taking one hand off my shoulder, he punches my head, my skull vibrating from the impact. I struggle to keep myself conscious as he shouts in my face, tears mixed with spittle landing like raindrops on my face as he draws his arm back for another punch.

"You've ruined everything," he repeats, sobbing. "I'll fix you, you fucking bitch. I'll break every bone in your body! I'll stick barbed wire up your cunt! I'll use your body as my toilet! I'll make every second so unbearable, you'll beg me to kill you!"

I gaze defiantly up at him. "Just shut up already," I answer back.

And then, after keeping them back for so long, I release my roots. They zoom out of my neck faster than they've ever gone before, all reaching for Paris. Four wrap around his wrists and pull his hands off me, while the other four twist around his neck and pull him forward, making Paris look like he's doing an awkward bow over me. The roots around his neck tighten their grips and Paris's eyes bulge out of his skull.

I regard him coolly as he gasps and struggles against my roots. He's never been in a position like this before with me. Every time before, he's been prepared to fight me and grab my roots, to make sure I was the one who got the beating. This time though, he wasn't prepared and I'm taking full advantage of it.

Paris's lips turn blue. From them, I hear him manage to utter one single, strained word. "Rose."

"Shithead," I reply. Two of my roots unwrap from his wrists and plunge into his eyes, their sharp tips drilling his eyeballs into jelly.

Paris lets loose a horrifying, banshee-like scream. I pull the two roots from his eyes and command the other six to push him away from me. They obey, throwing Paris back onto his feet. He totters blindly away from me and towards the fire he made, his hands over what remained of his devastated eyeballs as he moans and screams. With the help of my roots, I push myself off the ground. I let him stumble around for a minute, enjoying every minute of it, before I dash toward him and shove him into the fire.

Paris falls face-first into the flames, his head upsetting and breaking the pile of sticks underneath. He screams and shakes like he's having a seizure, the fire licking his face and hair. Before he can lift himself out of the flames, I jump on his back, pushing him down again and grab the back of his head. I thrust it deeper into the fire, ignoring the urge to bring my hand back as the heat sears my skin.

Paris continues to scream and flail beneath me for what feels like forever. Then his movements slow and weaken and his screams die. His body twitches a few times and then goes still.

I wait a moment before I pull my hand back, stand up and retreat a few paces. Paris doesn't move.

Ten seconds pass. Then twenty. Then thirty. When he doesn't move, I tilt my head back and scream in triumph, my roots flying outward like a lion's mane, swaying to the sound of my voice.

I killed Paris.

I stopped him from hurting anyone ever again.

I won.

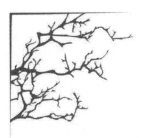

CHAPTER NINETEEN

I stand over Paris's body, motionless as a statue allowing the events of the past few minutes sink in. Paris is dead. He's finally dead. Mark has been avenged, as has Christy and Ariel Bruin, Thomas Washington and Mr. Kuyper and Maddy and I—

Maddy! I almost forgot about her! I run around the fire to her prone figure, still curled into a ball, my roots retreating into me as I kneel beside her. She's not crying like she's in pain anymore. That must be a good sign, right?

"Maddy," I whisper, giving her a shake with the hand that doesn't look like a lobster's claw. "You alright? Maddy!"

I shake her harder. She slumps onto her back, her limbs unfurling like the lifeless appendages of a dummy. Her eyes are blank and glassy. Not a sound escapes her.

"Oh my God, Maddy!" Panic fills me like gas as I shake her again and call out her name. She doesn't respond, her head lolling against the floorboards, as lifeless as a doll.

Lifeless. Oh my God, she isn't—?

I check her pulse, detect a steady, weak drumbeat underneath the skin of her neck. Good, she's alive. But then, why isn't she moving? Because Paris is dead? Or did this happen because I tried to break through his mind control over her?

"Help us!" I hear two voices whisper behind me and spin around. Thomas Washington and Ariel Bruin are standing where the yew and orange trees were, their arms still lifted towards the sky. Their eyes plead with me.

"Please, help us!" Their lips are moving but the sound that comes out doesn't match their lip movements. It reminds me of YouTube videos where the audio is just a half second ahead of the video, creating a jarring, disorienting effect.

Thomas and Ariel implore me again to help them. Somehow, I manage to find my voice. "What do you want me to do?"

"Burn us!" Thomas implores, his voice a quiet rasp. "Destroy us! We're stuck here as trees until we're destroyed. Burning us would destroy us."

"Ever since we became trees, we've been freed of Paris's mind control," Ariel explains. "But we've been left with all the memories of what he's done to us. What he made us do." She shudders, as if reliving all the horrible things Paris forced her to do. Just thinking about it makes me want to shudder too. "Please release us from this Hell. We want to be free. We want to see Christy again. We want to be at peace."

I glance at Maddy, who's still as catatonic as before. Then to Thomas and Christy I ask, "But what if burning you ends up hurting you?"

"It'll be worth the pain," Thomas assures me. "We've been in pain every second we've stood as trees. Fire can't be any worse."

"Please save us!" Ariel cries, desperation in her voice.

"Um—just one second," I say and turn back to Maddy. "Don't go anywhere, okay?"

I stand up and trudge towards the door we entered through. "I'll be back in a minute, okay?" I call behind me as I step out into the ocean of snow.

The snowstorm has died down and the outside world is as still as a painting. Even so, it's fucking freezing and I nearly collapse several times as I make the trek back to the RV. Once I get back on, the warm air greets me like an old lover, encircling me and bringing me back to life. I don't stay long enough to enjoy it, though. Instead I move to the kitchen and start looking through the drawers for something flammable. Sure enough, I find a jug of lighter fluid under the sink. I smile, though it's tinged with sadness. I'm saving them by killing them. And I know these deaths will affect me more than Paris's death ever could.

Only by sheer strength of will do I make it back to the cabin without falling or fainting. Maddy's still lying motionless like a doll and I consider checking on her again. No, I can check on her in a minute. She doesn't need me as badly right now.

I lift a branch sticking out from the fire, the heat from the lit end igniting a fresh wave of pain from my burnt hand. I hiss but don't drop the branch as I make my way over to the three trees, wishing the cold had done more to numb my hand.

Ariel and Thomas urge me to hurry. I ignore them as best I can and pour lighter fluid at their feet and over the roots of the beech tree between them. When all three trees are doused, I set them alight with the branch. They catch quickly and I watch as the flames travel up Ariel and Thomas's bodies. They don't scream, even as their bodies turn black and their hair catches fire. Instead, I hear a soft "Thanks," before they are entirely consumed. A moment later they are trees again, trees that no longer keep living people trapped in them. At least, I hope they don't.

I watch for a little while longer before turning around and heading towards Mr. Kuyper, enjoying the heat that is filling the cabin. It's becoming easier to move now that it's warmer in here and my hand doesn't hurt as much now either. Thank God for finally sending me something good, I guess.

When I reach Mr. Kuyper, I force myself to look at him. The white tree trunk is covered in blood, as are many of the lower branches. Even his previously white shirt is the color of wine and his cheeks, ripped down the center to accommodate the tree passing between them, look like some grotesque zombie's mouth. My stomach churns but I look anyway. No matter what hand he had in making Paris the monster he was, he didn't deserve to end up like this. Nor did Christy Bruin, or Thomas and Ariel, no matter what they did or didn't do to Paris. Not in a million years.

I don't know if the lighter fluid will light the tree with all that blood, so instead I douse Mr. Kuyper's body and clothes. I set him alight and watch as the flames engulf him.

"You're such a kind young woman, Rose. I like that about you."

I jump and spin around. The Oni is standing a few feet behind me, watching Mr. Kuyper burn with a contemplative look on its face. I'd forgotten it had been here. The Oni regards the burning corpse for a moment longer before looking down at me. As it lowers its head, its body becomes smaller and feminine; its head becomes rounder; its hair turns bright pink; and its tiger loincloth becomes a form-fitting dress with a plunging neckline. I stare as the Oni becomes a pale, horned version of me, with deep red eyes and a smile which is both inviting and wicked. Oni-Rose examines itself—herself—and says, "Not bad, if I do say so myself." To me, she asks, "Do you know who I am, Rose?"

I gulp, the familiar terror I held for this creature back in full force. "No, I don't."

Oni-Rose rolls her eyes. "You mean it's not obvious? I mean, you just threw my book into the fire a few minutes ago." She glances behind her to the small fire Mr. Kuyper and I built before returning her attention to me.

My eyes widen in their sockets as my brain makes the intended connections. "You're the Forest God."

The Forest God claps as if I'm a small child performing a cute dance for her parents. "Very good! You win the grand prize!"

A million questions buzz in my head. But Maddy lying just beyond the God's shoulder, still unmoving, pushes them out of my head, leaving only one thing behind.

"Please help us."

"Hmm?" The Forest God cocks her—its--head to the side. "What was that, sweetie?"

"Please help us!" I beg, dropping to my knees. "Please! You're a god, right? That's your book! You can undo the spells in it, can't you? You can release her from Paris's spell and make me normal again, can't you?"

The Forest God bursts out laughing. "Oh honey, I can't do that for you."

Despite my terror and desperation, my anger smolders back to life. "Can't or won't?" I ask for the second time that night.

"A bit of both, really," the Forest God replies. "You see, I'm not that kind of god. In fact, I'm the furthest thing from it."

The God's words bounce around in my head, not making any sense. What does it mean, it's the furthest thing from that kind of god?

And then I remember something Paris said after we first met. But there are also demons, ghosts, ancestor spirits, they can be gods too and some of those could become so awesome, worship was the only way to keep them from laying waste to the world... I look up into the God's face and see confirmation in its face. Confirmation and horrible glee.

"You know, I love you Humans," it muses, stroking my cheek with its pale, cold hand. "You're so much fun! All I must do is present an opportunity to you and so many amazing things happen! Murders, wars, kidnappings, rapes...and buildings on fire!"

The god raises its arms and the flames on all the trees explode upward in great gouts, setting fire to the remaining branches and leaves. The cabin fills with smoke, light and heat. I scream and cover my head with my arms, my skin sizzling from the sudden change in temperature.

"And you know what the best part is?"

I lower my arms as the Forest God walks away from me to the original fire, tiny in comparison to the infernos now raging around us. It reaches into the flames and pulls out *the Record*, its hand unharmed as is the book.

"The best part," the Forest God continues, brushing ash from the cover, "is that you Humans never fail to take an opportunity when presented with one and you never fail to surprise me with the results once you do. Doesn't matter if you're Japanese nobles trying to get in good with the new shogun, Dutch traders hoping to make a profit off an insular country, or a lonely, angry American boy who simply desires control and someone to tell him he's wonderful. In the end, you'll take the bait and give me the greatest show on Earth. And it never gets old."

I stare at the god as it saunters back to me, holding the book in front of it and gazing at it like a loving parent. Suddenly everything it has done, the way it appeared to me as a crow and then as the Oni, makes perfect sense. Each time, it was to make sure I didn't escape from Paris and cut its fun short. Even showing me those illusions of Ariel and Thomas and the trees they turned into in the greenhouse makes sense now: it was trying to scare me, to get a rise out of me the way a kid does when he sneaks up on a classmate and shouts "Boo!" And showing me that Paris had dropped the book? Simply a way to make the last five minutes of the game more exciting.

The Forest God sneers down at me and says, "I can hear the gears turning in your head, Rose. And guess what? The fun isn't over yet."

"What do you mean?"

"It's simple." It looks back at Maddy lying senseless where I left her. "I'm going to give you two choices: I can either turn you back into a normal girl and make all the damage Paris dealt you disappear, or I can undo the spell on your sister and keep her from turning into a tree."

"Save Maddy," I answer without hesitation. I've already lost Mark. If I lose Maddy, then even if I regain my human body and a normal life, I could never forgive myself. In fact, I'm not sure there'd be anything worth living for if I lost her so I could live.

"Alright, I'll save her," says the Forest God. "You just have to do one thing for me."

And then it plops *the Record* in my hands.

I stare at the book, its cover feeling all gross and alive and wrong in my hands. I consider the God, astounded and dismayed. "You want me to use this book?"

It nods. "But you have to do something big," it says. "Something truly spectacular. I want the fun to never stop and I won't settle for a small show after watching Paris try and find a soulmate for over a year now.

"So, what do you say?" it asks. Before I can reply, the Forest God changes and grows, becoming a mass of tentacles and arms, hundreds of eyes and mouths, glowing orbs whizzing around the room like electrons around the universe's most disgusting nucleus. It's so vast and terrifying, my mind threatens to break just looking at it.

The Forest God regards me and its many mouths grin hungrily. "So, what do you say, Rose?" it asks, a thousand voices speaking in unison. "Do we have a deal?"

CHAPTER TWENTY

The Greater Columbus Convention Center has always looked to me like an architect couldn't decide between having an artsy building or a utilitarian building, so they threw them together to get a splash. The result is a large, colorful building of glass and steel and brick occupying an entire city block. I've never been inside before, at least not that I remember, so I have no idea if that mash-up of style extends to the interior decorating.

At this point, I doubt I'll ever find out.

Even on a day like this with temperatures barely above freezing, or perhaps because of it, the convention center has a constant flow of people walking in and out of its doors. Some of them have signs but I'm too far away to read what they say. Perhaps it's some sort of political event.

I stand across the street in front of the Greek Orthodox Church, watching the crowds entering and exiting the center to make sure there's enough people inside. The Forest God said whatever I did, it had to be big and I'm running out of time. I've spent too much time driving back to and then through Columbus, a city I'm familiar and comfortable with, to find the right spot for something big. I could've gone back to Marion and done something there but I have too many good memories of that place to really do any damage to it. Likewise, I considered doing something on campus but Ohio State also has too many memories for me. That, and on a Saturday outside of football season in the middle of winter, campus is too sparsely populated to make a good target.

The God wants death in addition to destruction and panic. That's why it must be the Convention Center. It's the only place that works, the only place the God can derive its fun. Nowhere else will do.

"You sure you don't want me to change you back instead?" I sense the God's presence like a giant, living heater in the cold, winter air. "Those needle wounds on your tummy look pretty nasty."

I don't answer or even look behind me. I know the half-healed wounds left by Paris's acupuncture needles haven't healed properly and are now infected. I know that my body has been growing steadily weaker over the past week since leaving the camp and Paris's body at the camp. Even now, with the God keeping my body warm enough to operate in the cold air, I'm barely able to stand without swaying.

But I don't take the God's bait, just like I haven't taken the bait the other times it's asked. Yes, I'm sorely tempted to be normal again. Even without Mark, I'm sure I could find some meaning in my life. I could throw myself into work or adopt some pets. Hell, I could volunteer or mentor, I'm sure I'd find meaning doing that.

But one look at Maddy, standing beside me staring into space and my resolve is hardened. She hasn't spoken a word since I killed Paris and the most she'll move on her own is to open or close her eyes when she wakes and falls asleep. I've had to drag her, pose her in chairs, feed her with a spoon and even change adult diapers I stole in the town nearest the camp, so she didn't soil herself while we've been on the road. I even dragged her off the RV, which I left illegally parked on a nearby residential street and across several blocks here to this spot. Nobody passed us on the streets and I have no idea if anyone noticed us from their cars or homes, or what they thought of us if they did. I don't care if they did think. All that matters is getting Maddy back.

I open *the Record* and find the page I earmarked. Just like Paris said, even though the book is written with Japanese characters, my brain translates the spell's effect into English and the incantation into an easy-to-recite transliteration. Is that something anyone can do with this book, or just for those whom the God picks to wield its awful power? I hope I never find out.

"You'll keep your promise?" I ask the God, going over the spell one more time in my head.

"The moment you cast the spell, she'll be back to her old self again," it promises..

"And she won't turn into a tree?"

"Of course."

I hesitate and ask the question on my mind. "How long would she last with Paris's modified recipe? Do you know?"

A pause. "Maybe a month longer. Like you said, what works on animals doesn't always work on humans. And what worked on the animals only gave them a couple more months anyway. I'm sure that boy could've found a way to keep someone in that state forever, if he'd had the time and enough girls to test it on. But you decided he was better off dead, so I guess we'll never know."

Enough girls. It talks about people's lives so casually, as if discussing the weather. That thought makes me shiver, even though the air around me is warm like late spring. Or is that me? I never checked if I have a fever but given the many infections I've picked up by now, it's more than a possibility. And it would explain why I feel so woozy.

I glance at the incantation again and pull out the flower I'd stolen from the flower shop in Indianapolis, a red and gold tiger lily with the stem cut just below the petals. I recite the incantation, annunciating each syllable so I don't stumble over the words and mess up. As I recite, the tiger-lily begins to glow in my hand. When the spell is finished, it rises out of my hand, spinning like some small, colorful flying saucer. It flies across the street, over the heads of the convention-goers and into an open door. I'll know in a few minutes if what I've done is successful. Will I come to regret it, if I live? I hope not. After all, I did this for—

"Maddy!" I close *the Record* and grab her shoulders as she moans, the first sound she's uttered in nearly a week. At the same time, the God's presence vanishes, leaving me aware of how bitterly cold it is. I shiver but otherwise ignore it as Maddy blinks and the light returns to her eyes. Tears well in my eyes. She's back. My little sister's back.

"R-Rose?" she says, confused. She takes a step towards me, nearly falls, regains her balance and looks around her. Through my tears, I see the shock on her face give way to realization, followed by more shock. Finally, she turns to me and I see tears in her eyes too.

"Rose?" she says again. "I-I remember what Paris made me do to you. I'm so, so sorry. I didn't mean any of it. I—!"

I hug her to me. "All is forgiven," I assure her. "All is forgiven."

Maddy buries her head in my shoulder and we cry in each other's arms for a minute. I wish I could stay with her. But I need to stay here to make sure the spell is successful. I have this nagging suspicion if I don't, the Forest God may go back on its word and return Maddy to that catatonic state and this time it won't be reversible.

And I need her to do something for me as well.

I shove *the Record* into Maddy's arms. She stares at it, recognizes it and recoils in horror, holding it out at arm's length. "Rose, why are you giving me this?"

"Maddy, I need you to take it!" I say.

She stares at me as if I've morphed from green to purple. "What?"

"Take it!" I demand, pointing westward with my arm. "Keep going that way till you hit the Scioto River and throw that book in there so nobody can ever use it again! Then you must go to police headquarters on Marconi Boulevard. Tell them who you are and that you've been missing for over a week now. They'll take care of you until I meet you there."

"But what will you be doing?" she asks, tears filling her eyes again.

I consider my words carefully before answering. "I'm making sure our family is done with this nightmare forever."

I hug her again. We stay in that hug for too short a time and eventually I pull away from her. When I do, Maddy struggles but eventually I manage to separate her from me. She holds onto the book, squeezing it close to her chest like a beloved keepsake.

"Maddy, I need you to do something else for me," I add as something else occurs to me.

Maddy nods her head. "Anything."

I inhale deeply, knowing what I'm about to impart to her is the most cliched thing I could say in this moment but it must be said.

"Don't stop dancing, Maddy," I instruct her. "Don't stop trying to achieve your dreams and trying to find your own happiness. And know this: no matter what happens, I love you and I'm always with you."

"You make it sound like you're about to die," Maddy replies. "Why can't you go with me?"

I don't dare answer that. Instead I tell her I love her again. She says it back and starts running west towards the Scioto. I follow her with my eyes until she's halfway down the block before turning to face the Convention Center once more. As I do, my feet trip over each other and I stagger towards the edge of the sidewalk. I look up from the curb to the Convention Center and see the first wave of people running out, some of them with blood on them, everyone screaming in terror.

I hope this is the last time *the Record*'s used. I pray it is. I pray that Maddy throws it into the river and puts an end to the Forest God's reign of terror.

I doubt it will, though. I'm sure the Forest God will make sure its book finds a new owner and the cycle of chaos will start over again.

Still I pray, because that's all I can do now.

The street is very close now, it's coming to meet me. And across it—is that Mark? Yes, it is! He's here! He's waving to me, urging me to join him. I'm on my way Mark, I'm coming my love! I'll be there before the black at the edges of my vision can take me. I'll be right there!

Truly happy for the first time in I don't know how long, I step into traffic.

A horn blasts to my left.

***

I run and run until I'm at the end of the block, the book held against my chest. When I get to the intersection though, I stop. I can't leave like this; I can't leave my sister to face this alone. We'll see whatever's about to happen together—because of course something is going to happen, she was using this damned book, wasn't she—and then we'll rid the world of *the Record* together. We'll go home together. We'll go home Mom and Dad, Brian and Hope and I will find some way to help her, to make sure Rose is able to live a happy life despite her condition.

I owe her that much. She's my hero and my favorite sister. She saved my life, even though I tortured her. Doesn't matter if I was under that monster's control when I did it, I still did it and I feel horrible just thinking about it.

So, I'll help her face whatever she's about to face. And I'll make sure she never regrets saving my life and fighting Paris for as long as she did.

I turn around and look for Rose. I see her careen into the road. A city bus blares its horn at her, moving too fast to stop in time. I gasp and close my eyes, unable to watch. I hear the bus's tires screech.

Thank you for reading Rose by Rami Ungar.
If you have enjoyed this book, would you please leave a review?

Would you like to know when the next book is published at Castrum Press?
Sign up here: www.castrum.com/subscribe

ABOUT THE AUTHOR

RAMI UNGAR KNEW HE WANTED to be a writer from the age of five, when he first became exposed to the world of Harry Potter and wanted to create imaginative worlds like Harry's. As a tween, he fell in love with the works of Anne Rice and Stephen King and, as he was getting too old to sneak up on people and shout "Boo!' (not that that ever stopped him), he decided to merge his two loves and become a horror writer.

Today, Rami lives and writes in Columbus, Ohio. He has self-published three novels and one collection of short stories, and his stories have appeared in other publications. Rose is his first novel with Castrum Press.

When he's not writing your nightmares or coming up with them, he's enjoying the latest horror novel or movie, anime and manga, ballet, or collecting anything that catches his fancy and giving you the impression that he may not be entirely human.

BOOKS BY CASTRUM PRESS

SCIENCE FICTION & FANTASY SERIES

The Saiph Series by PP Corcoran
The K'Tai War Series by PP Corcoran
The Formist Series by Mathew Williams
The Deep Wide Black Series by JCH Rigby
The Feral Space Series by James Worrad
Arc of the Sky Series by LMR Clarke

STANDALONE NOVELS

Horror/Thriller
Rose by Rami Ungar

ANTHOLOGIES

The Empire at War: British Military Science Fiction
Future Days Anthology
Alien Days Anthology

More at: www.castrumpress.com/scifi-fantasy-books

THE SCALPEL

By James Worrad

SWIRL'S LIFE IS NOT GOING TO PLAN. Exiled by her alien masters to the scuzziest part of the galaxy for crimes she did not commit, the once promising combat agent is reduced to peddling drugs aboard a mile-long space slum. If there is an upside, Swirl is sure her sister isn't part of it. Regrettably, the frivolous Sparkle shares Swirl's brain and body. Nevertheless, when the sisters are attacked, they learn to cease bickering and flee for their lives.

Hargie's life never really had a plan. One of the bubblefolk, a race of faster-than-light addicted lowlifes, Hargie jumps from star to star, bar to bar, forever outrunning a past best forgotten. When Swirl buys a ride on his ship, Hargie tries to see the enigmatic woman as just another job, one he can abandon when the time comes.

Melid's life is but a cog in an immense machine. Empathically bonded to her own kind, she feels naught for the rest of humanity. The merciless Melid is ordered to hunt down a mysterious woman before she can return to her even more mysterious home world.

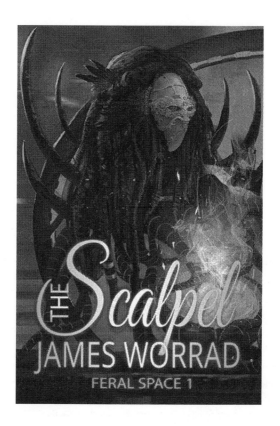

Following is an excerpt of The Scalpel Copyright © 2018 by James Worrad

1. RIG

ONE

SWIRL TOOK A COMPACTION BARREL OUT of the crate and fitted it to the pistol grip.

"You should take one," she said to Lyreko over her shoulder. "Idiot."

His laughter rattled against the storeroom's gunmetal walls.

"Funny thats," he said. "Funny the missy calling everyone feral be the first to lift a gun."

"*Because* you're all feral."

"Meet-up's slap-middle of the Strip, tune?" She felt his breath upon the back of her neck. "Say the rig-pigs stop you with that gun? You explains thats?"

"A risk, granted." She checked the pistol over. "But we should be acting. Vartigans have us *reacting*. Reacting in an open space with no weapons. They're ex-soldiers, Lyreko. Bred soldiers. You're neither."

"Think I can't handle?"

"I know you can't, sweet."

Lyreko's arm drifted around her waist, his chest resting against her shoulder blades. Solid, warm.

"Okay, takes it," he whispered. "Pigs never check anyhow. But I've lived the rig life twelve year, and no one fucks on the Strip. Respect. Respect only a cramp fuckin' life provide." He parted her chin-length dreadlocks and brushed his lips against her neck. She shivered, relaxed, watched his pale fingers surround the darkness of her fist. Their tips caressed the gun as much as her own skin. "Vartigans just wanna deal, you tune?"

"Deal? They've kidnapped our pusher."

"Ever known a kidnap that wasn't?"

She turned around in his arms and faced him, brushed her lips against his.

"Lyreko," she said. "I've had... intimations."

"The Delighted Ones?" The tanned patch of skin around his left eye was a calm pool within a frown. Dermal reconstruction: you got what you paid for.

Swirl nodded. She gripped the pistol tighter, barrel pointed at the floor, safety on. "It may well be nothing to do with this meeting. But these..."

"Intimations."

"They point toward something *now*. I can't tell you anymore."

Lyreko stepped away from her. "Then you don't needs a gun." His expression was blank as ammo.

She dropped her pistol into the crate behind her, never taking her eyes off Lyreko. "Love your business face."

"This? My *belief* face, girl. Cuter."

Lyreko smiled, stroked her chin and walked out of the storeroom. The door closed behind him.

:He's disgusting: Sparkle sent.

"Shut up," Swirl replied to the warmth rising in her mind. "If you don't like me and him, you can always go to the villa, Sparkle."

:The anthropologist in me can't stop watching,: Sparkle sent. *:You better not be falling for that feral.:*

"He's a comfort," Swirl said. "An ally. Nothing more."

:I'll concede he helps. But whenever he's around, you hog the driving seat.:

"You could take pleasure in him too," Swirl said. "I wouldn't mind." A joke, of course.

:Words can't express...:

Swirl had ceased listening. She gazed at her palm. No arguing with the matter: the skin blemish there had become even more defined, more undeniable since last night. Two arrowhead shapes with a dash between them: the Divine Eye.

Their symbol. *Them.* Could they be watching now?

Swirl shivered. Three years since leaving Harmonic space, two years of it upon this rig-ship, and she'd never known the like. She'd never expected to know the like her whole life. Divine attention. The Delighted Ones.

She knew Sparkle gazed at the blemish through their shared eyes, too. Knew her to be just as frightened.

"Sparks," Swirl said. "You're getting cranky in there. Why don't you be ascendent when we hit the Strip? I can always step in if things get involved."

:Thanks, Swirly-girl.: Sparkle sent. *:I mean it. I'd really like that.:*

"What are sisters for?"

*

"What's with the beast?" Hargie Stukes asked.

142

The barkeep looked at him and frowned. Not at the question--Hargie wasn't so drunk he was seeing things--but that his only customer had spoken. Just that kind of bar.

"That?" the barkeep said. He nodded at the backstreet taxidermy job leering from between the snacks and contraceptive serums on the high shelf behind him. Piebald and canine, the stuffed beast was a muscled thing. Its fangs were bared, though a couple had long since fallen out. A short life spent belly-to-ground, no doubt, snarling at every passing crotch. "That's a Jaqruzzil."

"Name's familiar," Hargie said.

"You've been drinking them for two hours," the barkeep said.

Hargie grimaced. He snatched up the bottle and scoured the ingredients list. No dog therein. Transpired *Jaqruzzil* was the brand name.

His last beer. Hargie hadn't a single rupee to piss on, or near-as-damn. Worse: two, maybe three hits of jumpjunk left in the cockpit. Two weeks his baby had sat on the landing pad and not a sniff of a job.

Was this it? Trail's end a-nearing? He'd seen his kind out of junk and all hope to get more. Street trash, shambling, their eyes red and dreaming of lost stars.

He shivered. He looked up to see the barkeep studying him.

Hargie pointed the bottle's lip at the stuffed animal. "Product placement, huh?"

"Local, actually," the barkeep said. "Local beer, local mutt. One named after the other."

"That so?"

"Walk to the edge of Import some time and look out: nothing but Jaqruzzils fighting and fucking," the barkeep said.

"Good to know *something* goes on around here," Hargie said. "Eh, big man? Ha."

The barkeep didn't smile.

Hargie did, soft and reassuring. Had to be careful as a traveller, as a bubbleman. Always remember locals everywhere thought their shithole world an Elysium.

Chances were he'd already done quite enough to piss this town off. He couldn't remember. He'd gone crazy these last two days, drunk himself atavistic. Faced with financial and narcotic ruin, he'd adopted the doctrine of the cornered animal. What else? He'd always been his own worst enemy. The enemy had won.

"You smoke?" Hargie said. He pulled out his pack and gestured toward the front door.

"It's all right," the barkeep said. "We can smoke here." He took a straight and lit it with his finger.

Hargie did likewise. Good ol' neuralware. "You're a scholar and a raj, sir."

"Story is," the barkeep said, "someone dumped a shipment of tiny dogs here long ago."

"What, like a big freighter?"

"No, man," the barkeep said. "This was like... two kay ago. Golden-olden shit. Wasn't any Freightways back then. Just..."

"Bubblemen," Hargie said.

"Yeah, guess. Anyway, the dogs' descendants adapted to the high gravity. Out beyond the spikes, I mean."

They could always tell, Hargie thought. Collar up, neck hidden, and still they knew. Hargie had the wide brown eyes of the old bubblefolk: tan skin, strands of their crimson in his brunette mess. Yet so did lots of other people. How'd they always tell?

He swigged. Maybe the slouchiness. Maybe that.

"Impressive," Hargie said. "Whole species born from a little bubble's hull."

"Guess inbreeding wasn't a problem here," the barkeep said.

"Guess not." Hargie hid his grin behind a sip of *Jaqruzzil*.

The front door hummed open and four guys stepped out of the night. The largest one, in some kind of peaked cap and navy uniform, had that camp strut tough men got when they meant to get tough. Hargie chugged down the last of his last beer.

"No one scrap-mouths Import," Uniform said. He strutted right up to Hargie's stool and slapped a gloved palm on the bar. Liquid splashed Hargie's cheek. "Hear me, Captain Fucko?"

King around here, then. Yet walk a mile, and no one there nor beyond gave a fuck, and that truth forever stung an asshole. He made examples of those passing through. Demur, and he was paid.

"I tune," Hargie said. "I'll keep it in mind, sir."

"Don't ratshit me," Uniform said.

His pals crowded around. Hargie sensed the barkeep move back.

"What say I buy you all a drink?" Maybe he could open a tab here. Stranger things had happened. Hargie turned to the barkeep. "One beer, please. Four straws."

The smallest tough laughed at that, then stopped himself. A positive sign.

"Fucking bubble-turd," Uniform said, and he yanked back Hargie's collar, exposing a chrome stud on either side of his neck. "We *heard* you. Saying shit about... about watching Jaqruzzil's hump being the only fun in town. Well, screw you! Outworlder motherfucker warp-jackal fuck."

Hargie looked at the barkeep. "This place bugged?"

"We're a Totalist town, little guy," the barkeep said. "No one tell you?"

Totalists. Their eyes recorded everything all the time, all of it shared on some local cloud. There existed as many reasons to totalise as there were Totalist communities but the general idea was to create some pioneering communitarian utopia. The flaw, as far as Hargie's philosophy went, was that everyone could see you whack off. A person's retinal cameras were their own business, damn it.

"And you had such honest eyes," Hargie told the barkeep. "Makes me weep." He turned back to Uniform. "I'm drunk," he told him. "I apologise profanely. Profusely. Ah, you tune what I mean."

"That Jaq comment's the least of it, dickhole," one of Uniform's guys said. "Town's been watching you two whole days."

"Oh," Hargie said.

"You pocketed stuff from the store," the shortest guy said. "My kid saw you."

"Old Annu," the fourth said, "found you, you... urinating against her generator."

"Think I remember that," Hargie said. "She got quite the show." He thought a moment, then looked at them all. "Uggh..."

"No one was impressed," Uniform said.

"Next time, use wide shot." Hargie smiled amiably.

No one smiled back.

"Smoosh," Hargie said, "I'll leave, tune?" He put on his lucky green hat with the flaps and the silver badge and got up from his stool, all five foot two of him. "Leavin'..."

"Exit denied, bubble-turd," Uniform said. Hargie saw his uniform was for some takeaway chain with a military image. "Import's got a certain punishment for shitscum like you."

"I see."

Hargie grabbed his empty beer bottle, screamed, and swung it down on the bar top. It bounced out of his hand.

The bar fell silent a moment.

"It's plastic, moron," Uniform said.

"Yeah," Hargie said. "Yeah."

"Grab him, boys."

Ten minutes later, Hargie stumbled in the cold smelly night in nothing but his underwear and his lucky hat with the flaps. Damn it, something in this planet's atmosphere reeked. His bare feet slapped tarmac.

"Guess where we're going?" Uniform asked, strutting ahead of Hargie and the cronies holding him.

The edge of town. Black out there, beyond the last lights. They were joking. They would just give him a roll, a kicking, and be done. He'd take it. He never let idiots embarrass him into calling the authorities.

"Gonna shoot me? That it?"

"You see a gun?" Uniform said.

"Fuckin' *wish* we'd have shot you!" the guy holding his right arm said.

Bad craziness, Hargie thought. No jape. These Totalists were simply perverts, sadists. Screw embarrassment: he logged onto the local memestream and alerted Import security. A window popped up at the bottom right corner of his vision: was his call regarding police or takeaway? The logo above the window showed a cartoon Jaqruzzil dressed like the uniformed guy.

"Nice try," Uniform told him. "All Import's watching this. Or will do. Think about that. While you *can*."

Hargie wouldn't pee himself. He wouldn't let them see him piss himself. He was surprised he still had some pride, some fight.

They walked past the last building at town's edge, into the broken ground that lay before the big spikes. Hargie could see two of those spikes just ahead: obelisks looming forty feet into the night sky, their blade-like silhouettes outlined by stars.

They stopped just before the spikes. Hargie's feet stung. They bled. Uniform pulled out a gun.

"Hey, now, wouldya look at this," Uniform said, waving the pistol. His pals stepped away from Hargie and laughed.

"No," Hargie said. "C'mon."

"Keep walking." Uniform nodded at the darkness beyond.

"You're screwing," Hargie said.

"I'm cleaning house, jackal. Move." He raised the gun to Hargie's throat.

Okay. Bad crazy, but okay. Hargie limped off toward the dark. He'd risk the dark, sit out there and run back in once these toughs got bored. They'd get bored.

His feet were agony; he couldn't see where he trod. He passed the line of spikes.

Something barked in the darkness. Hargie froze.

"Walk," Uniform called to him. Hargie wanted to scream at him to shut up. He began walking again, realised he walked like some primate: a loping gate. Everything heavy. Heavier...

"Boy got a weight on his shoulders," one of the guys shouted. Laughter all round.

Gravity. He was leaving the obelisks' dampening zone, entering the world's real-and-natural.

"Gravity won't kill you, little man!" Uniform called. "Just slow you down. The Jaqruzzils *love* that!"

Hargie dropped onto all fours. He didn't move. Fuck 'em. He wondered whether, secretly, he'd been grasping for something like this all along. Suicide on instalment.

"Shoot me!" he shouted. Whimpered. "Shoot!" It hurt his chest shouting that. *Sorry, Mother*, he thought. *Sorry, Father...*

"So endeth the lesson, bubble-turd!" Uniform shouted. "Goodnight!"

"Don't mess with the good guys!" shouted one of his pals. "Don't mess with Import town!" They whooped and laughed as they headed back.

A lesson. The whole town watching. All those good guys. Taught the villain the error of his ways. Probably watch it every holiday for the next twenty. Good guys dispensing homespun justice like some cutesy memestream drama. A plague on the galaxy, good guys, a plague.

Hargie turned around on all fours and crawled back, breathing hard, his muscles burning. A howl came. Somewhere behind. Closer.

He shuffled faster, tried not to think of the stuffed beast in the bar fang-deep in his ass and balls. Almost ran the last part, collapsing in the dust somewhere between the spikes and the lights of Import. They didn't come in here, he told himself, the gravity...

Breathing easier now, his world lighter. Remote from his body. He felt only one thing: a kinship with beasts.

He saw the silhouette of a figure gliding silently, silently, toward him. Too tall for a man, too slender. The silhouette grinned. White fangs.

Hallucinating of course. The drink, the fear. Had to be.

Damned galaxy, Hargie thought. *Everyone always seeing things their own way.*

The night blurred.

*

Swirl had to wonder at it. For all Sparkle's disgust at feral humanity, she seemed eternally at ease talking to them. Good at it, too. Better than Swirl, at any rate.

"Oh, I know all about having a penis," Sparkle was telling some stranger called Crowbone, and anyone else listening in the busy public cable-pod. "Don't explain the story for my sake."

The man's mouth, nestled in its beaded goatee, fell slack. He scratched his shaved head. "What?"

"We've a machine for it, back in the Harmonies," Sparkle said. "Takes days, mm-yes. Turns out I'm hung like a freighter's undercarriage when you switch my chromes. Who'd have thought?"

"You can't just *drop* that shit on a stranger, girl," the man said, curling up with laughter. "No way."

"Prefer I eased it in gentler?"

The man Crowbone cracked up at that. Even Lyreko beside her grinned, despite his obvious territorial posture.

Sparkle snatched a look at herself in one of the pod's windows, her reflection a translucent ghost against the black backdrop of deep space.

Being currently head-descendent--watching from the back seat, so to speak—Swirl's viewpoint was dictated by wherever Sparkle chose to point it. A lot of the time, that was Sparkle's nearest reflection. She'd been like that since they were kids. Swirl watched as Sparkle checked the two absurd pigtails she'd insisted on having their dreadlocks bunched into. Of late, Sparkle had been pushing to change the locks from their current ice blue to 'fun' pink. Not a chance.

"Gotta ask," Crowbone said, and Swirl could see it coming. "How's a dick rate compared to, you know..."

"Less hassle, less fun," Sparkle said.

"Figures," Crowbone said, almost melancholy. He looked to Lyreko. "Please tell me you knew about this. Please."

"Sure," Lyreko said, relaxing now that this other male had included him. "Smoosh with thats too. Means Swirl knows what to *do*, if you tune..." He stretched his arm around the back of Sparkle's seat. Sparkle took a breath and sat forwards, away from him.

The men picked up on it, Lyreko most of all. One of 'Swirl's' cold moods, he'd think. Again.

:*Appreciated, Sparkle,*: Swirl sent to her sister. Damn her.

Sparkle didn't reply, not even in their head. She stared at her reflection once more, as if she knew it irritated Swirl.

Forget her. Swirl made good use of their gen-altered irises instead: she could turn her full focus toward the edge of whatever Sparkle stared at--typically herself--with no adverse effects on either user's view.

She chose to take in the pair of mile-long chains far beyond the window, each running parallel with the cable pod and festooned with hundreds of spacecraft. Ingenious as it was crude, the 'rig': smaller ships tethering themselves to a main unit and donating their engines and computing power to the orbital journey around the Eucrow system, breaking off at their desired destinations. How like the feral worlds, making the best from what scraps they possessed. Swirl watched a tethered hauler discharge its old-fashioned thrusters against the black beyond, a single twitch in the rig's endless slouch.

"We're here," Lyreko said, standing up. "Let's dust."

The pod docked with the rig's core, and the door whirled open. Passengers poured out into the gunmetal terminus. Dock loaders, bubblefolk, a few rich kids from Luharna or Psiax. All hungry to squeeze whatever fun from the Strip. Sparkle's acquaintance, Crowbone, nodded and vanished into their mass.

Lyreko stopped beside a drinks 'n' hox machine. "Eyes up," he said to Sparkle. "This the place."

"No Vartigans," she said.

True enough. Those brutes weren't difficult to spot: white-skinned and blond, their faces tattooed so as to put some distance between themselves and their clone factory past.

"Using friends, maybes," Lyreko said, eyeing passersby.

Swirl felt Sparkle reach into her jacket.

:*I didn't bring the gun,*: Swirl sent to her, :*We get a situation where you wish I did, let me take over:*

"Obviously," Sparkle said.

"What?" Lyreko's eyes searched her.

"Nothing."

Lyreko frowned. "Just gots messaged," he said, staring into the mid-distance. "Sender unknown."

"What's it say?"

"Nothing." He looked at Sparkle. "Just a directional."

"Share it, then," Sparkle said.

Lyreko stared at nothing again, blinked.

Sparkle pulled a handheld out of her jacket and turned it on. Their shared brain's structure couldn't access the primitive neuralware feral humanity used. The sisters played it off as an allergy. Whenever they used their handheld in public, they got the most pitying looks.

The handheld's screen displayed a map of the Strip's length. An arrow flashed on the map at their current location, pointing north.

"This some ratshit," Lyreko said, suddenly uptight. "A trap. Our man's dead alreadys."

"Smoosh, tough guy," Sparkle said. "That's what you say, right? Smoosh? Keep it smoosh, prick. Fuck's sake..."

Lyreko side-eyed her. His pride chipped at, of course, but more than that. Swirl never swore. Sparkle always did. Lyreko knew nothing of Sparkle.

"Where's this arrow goin'?" Lyreko muttered. "Shit, they were meants to meet us *here*."

"Perhaps we need a little perspective," Sparkle said. :*You had better step in,*: Swirl felt her send. :*Five minutes*:

:*Of course,*: Swirl replied.

Their shared body tensed--that uneasy second where neither sister had possession--and then Swirl felt control return. She reached into her jacket and pulled out a silver cylinder. She flipped it open and shook a leaf into her palm: blue and transparent, its veins luminous with mauve serum. She tore it in half.

She placed half onto Lyreko's waiting tongue. "The Delighted Ones guide you," she said.

Swirl's eyes replied to Lyreko's fear--and, yes, weakness--with reassurance. Swirl was good at this. Sparkle exceeded her at making friends and fitting in, but it was Swirl who breathed ritual, who engendered reverence for the Hoidracs' narcotic gift, whomever she sold it to. She was more than just a supplier to her buyers here on the rig. She was a priestess, a hierophant of the access hatches.

Lyreko's face softened. "That's the shitsy," he said. "Right there."

No reverence, Lyreko, despite her work on him. Swirl swallowed the other half of the leaf, its surface smooth and tasteless. An act of solidarity: her tolerance for leaf, shaped from birth, exceeded such doses.

Swirl strode on, following Lyreko. She could picture his mental state well enough: the geometry of his own ego made manifest, blending into the tumult of all the heads around him. Mildly psychic, primitive societies might deem it.

:Forget something?:

Sighing, Swirl allowed Sparkle to ascend, felt her limbs succumb to her headsister.

"We're on a night out," Sparkle told Lyreko as they left the pod terminus. "Start acting like it, hmm?"

The Strip was a hexagonal tube half a mile in length. On each of its six planes--up, down, sides--heaved crowds of people making their way between shops, bars, and clubs. Music punched through the stink of fried carbohydrates that rose from stands, the fast food and faster tunes of a hundred human worlds. And everywhere movement, catcalls, laughter, parties of friends strutting along one plane then turning, strutting onto the next. Traffic was thickest at these points, as pedestrians manoeuvred into oncoming crowds at ninety-degree angles to themselves. A trail of searchlights floated in the air along the strips' lateral centre, held between the artificial gravities of all six planes.

A thousand enemies could lie in wait here inside the Strip, shrouded in neon, heat and bustle. *Caution*, Swirl thought, *always caution.*

"Party!" Sparkle yelled at everyone passing. "Raise this motherfucker, people!"

People whooped back.

"Little tourist girl," Lyreko said, trying a smile.

Sparkle didn't reply.

:Could you at least smile at him?: Swirl sent. :For me?:

Swirl felt their face make a sarcastic-feeling grin. Lyreko's frown confirmed it.

They walked on, turned right. Swirl felt the lurch as she crossed from one plane of the strip to the next, like climbing a step and suddenly the step 'wasn't there.

Lyreko halted. "Arrow says it's over there."

Things were quieter, moderately, at this end of the strip. Behind a rundown casino lay a derelict kiosk that once sold adrenoslurps. Behind the derelict kiosk that once sold adrenoslurps lay a thoroughfare no one passed through on account of the casino's trash. Under the casino's trash lay a manhole with the cover loosened.

"Bomb," Sparkle said. "I'm calling bomb."

"Varts ain't dumb," Lyreko replied. "It'd be slaughter."

"Yes," Sparkle said. "Because that doesn't sound like clone soldiers, huh?"

They stared at the manhole for some time.

Swirl received a message from Sparkle: :If you wanted to ascend right now, I'd be entirely happy with that, sister-my-love.:

She did so.

"Right," Swirl said to Lyreko. "You hang back."

"No way," Lyreko said. "Tag with you, all the way."

She smiled. "Thanks."

The pair of them sauntered toward the manhole. Swirl wondered whether blast victims ever saw it coming.

They shifted the manhole's cover to one side. Blackness below. Stale air. An aluminium ladder ran down a concrete wall into the gloom.

"Be just a 'con unit down there," Lyreko said. "Ten foots by ten. No tunnels or shit."

"Help me down," Swirl said.

"Swirl, I--"

"It'll be a corpse, Ly, a message," Swirl said. "If it were anything else, we'd know by now."

Lyreko nodded, looked around. "Make it quick."

Swirl clambered down the ladder. She almost stumbled over a box on the bare concrete floor. She switched on the light of her handheld, pointed it at her feet. Next to the box lay a body: their pusher. No visible wounds. She leant down, felt a pulse. A medicated slumber, most likely.

The box wasn't sealed. Gently, she pulled back the box's flaps and gazed inside.

A face gazed back, flat and eyeless. A stack of them: flayed, one atop another, real human faces. Bloodless and laminated, the top one reflected the handheld's light. Swirl recognised the DNA helix tattoo. Baron Jape, the Vartigans' leader.

:These Vartigans certainly know how to apologize,: Sparkle sent.

Swirl ignored her. A rolled-up note sat next to the faces. Ink and paper. An anachronism in feral space, though not at home...

"Swirl?" Lyreko said from the other side of the counter, "We smoosh?"

"Surprisingly so," Swirl said. "I think."

*

Hargie stumbled toward the landing pad, lucky hat flaps flapping and underwear rippling in the morning's breeze. Townsfolk grinned as he passed. No one said shit. No one looked surprised. Which figured, but only made his mood worse.

He tried to ignore them. He tried to ignore his stinging feet. Strange dreams he'd had, lying in the dust last night. He couldn't recall what. But they'd left him... uncomfortable.

He cheered up--almost--when he saw his bubbleship out on the pad. No graffiti on its orange-brown hull, at least: the townsfolk were clearly too virtuous for that. Lumpishly spherical and five storeys in height, *Princess Floofy* was as large as bubbleships dared to be.

And a bay chock-full of nothing, of course. Memories, maybe, which never filled a belly.

He stumbled into the shadow of *Princess*, the drop in sunlight causing him to shudder. It was then he noticed two silhouettes standing beneath the opposite side of the ship's underbelly.

Hargie stormed toward them, his face a grimace, his feet throbbing.

"One last visual, huh?" he said to the two figures. "Here you are." He gestured at his underwear. "Or a lecture, that it? Come on: drop that homespun A-bomb. Blow my mind."

The two men stared at him, their faces still as concrete. The closest seemed in late middle age, with grey in his slick hair and well-clipped beard, but there was a vitality in his bearing that bordered on incongruous. Tall, too, spindly. The square collar of his suit was of a fashion three decades in the grave.

The second, younger, was built like a frigate's shithouse, stocky and foreboding. He wore an orange t-jacket and fluorescent green shorts. That explained his grim face. Hargie wondered if the young man let some disinterested party dress him each morning.

"You're, er... not townsfolk, right?" Hargie said.

"No," the older man said.

Hargie laughed, whistled, made a show of a shrug. A job, maybe. Dared he dream? "I know what you gentlemen are thinking," he said. "Why's this lunatic dressed like a, a caveman?' Well—"

"No," the older man said.

"--since you're wondering I, er..."

"We wish to book passage to this system's orbital rig," the older man said.

A reprieve! Hargie shivered with elation, hid it in a shrug.

"Stukes." Hargie offered his hand to shake. "Hargopal Stukes. Hargie. This is my ship."

The older man regarded Hargie's hand. He smiled, nothing more. "A bubbleship," he said. Hargie couldn't place the accent. "A bubbleship."

"You know your star craft," Hargie said, nodding. *Congratulations*, he thought, *now see what you can do with these toy blocks.* Everyone knew bubbleships. Clearly some real dirt-huggers here, come adrift in a travelling man's world. Which, of course, would mean they wouldn't know a deal from a meal...

"I'll run you to the rig," Hargie said. "One lakh seventy. Usually it's two, but it's clear you respect the bubbletrade, so..."

"Could you travel full-speed?" the older man said. "What might you say to four lakh?"

"Carry your bags, sir?" Hargie said.

"We have everything. Could we leave now?"

"'Course." Hargie accessed his neuralware, and the gangway lowered from *Princess'* undercarriage.

"My name is Illik," the older man said. "This is my son, Doum. We're to meet my daughter."

Doum looked at Hargie, his expression blank as a rock.

Hargie smiled back regardless. "Family reunion, huh?" Doubtless a laugh riot. Creepy-doo-dee, these heads.

Short flight for tall money, Hargie told himself. *Lunch too*, his belly added. He could suffer coo-coo cargo for four hours. Came with the job. Hell, it *was* the job.

Hargie gestured at the gangplank, and Illik embarked.

Doum turned to Hargie. "This ship," he said, his accent his father's, rolled in gravel. "A name?"

"*Princess Floofy*, friend," Hargie said.

Doum looked at the hull. His frown softened to resolve.

"So be it." He made his way up the gangplank.

*

Swirl got up, threw on some clothes. Lyreko's place--their place--looked a mess again. A cramped mess. Always. Away from home, beyond the Harmonies' borders, out here in the great spaces of feral humanity, mess was the norm. An endless war. That fact was the clearest refutation--one that could be shoved in the faces of contrarians like Sparkle--against the insipid argument that life could ever be as good here as it was in within the Harmonies. Life was clean there. It had purpose.

She breathed out long. Lyreko's place. One primitive hatchway in and out. Dead end.

Mess was getting to Swirl and to her sister: clutter for Swirl to obsessively clean, filth for Sparkle to reel from but never do anything about. Trouble was, of late, both had ceased acting on their horror. They merely beheld it. It occurred to Swirl that neither of them had articulated this change to the other.

She washed her face in the sink, cleaned her pores with a dermshell, vibed her teeth. She thought of the faces in the box. The note.

The flayed Vartigan faces had proven a sort of handshake, the note accompanying them an invite. Three hours hence, they'd rendezvous with whoever had offered both: lot A574, out on the sunward chain's far end.

The matter ate at Swirl. Not the fact that parties unknown had chosen to flay her enemies' faces, nor that they now directed her to as remote a location as one could find on the rig--if anything, the former justified the latter--but that it coincided with the blemish, the symbol on her palm.

She studied it now under the basin's bleached light. The Divine Eye: clear as on a crest or monument. She had heard of this phenomenon, these sudden blemishes. She knew their ramifications.

Thus far in their reluctant travels as penal *flaneur*, Swirl and Sparkle (well, Swirl) had been a wandering pair of eyes exiled ever-outwards, desperately trying to find something that might spark forgiveness and a return home. The symbol proclaimed them an active tool, a hand for some purpose known only to the Hoidrac, the Delighted Ones.

But what? No amount of leaf ingestion offered any insight. Worse, she couldn't comadose on the stuff—couldn't drift into the limitless Geode--this far away from the Harmonies. Leaf's potency increased with proximity to home.

Swirl missed the Geode.

Lyreko stirred in bed. Their bed. His bed.

She didn't look at him. She wondered what Sparkle was doing. Asleep, most likely, or kicking back in the villa. Sparkle was spending a lot of time in the villa. She rarely let Swirl forget the fact.

"Morning, sunlight," Lyreko said, rising, sauntering close to where she stood at the basin. She felt his arm slide about her waist.

Swirl stared at the basin. She brushed away Lyreko's arm and stepped from him.

"This is not working," she said.

"What?" He squinted.

"Us. I'm no longer... comfortable."

She studied his limbs' movements, couldn't watch his face. They tensed with all that discomfort of intimacy abruptly denied, stirring then bringing themselves to heel.

"It *has* been fun," she told him. "But it's gone further than I'd like. Than it should have."

"No," Lyreko said. "Don't be freaking. Not todays."

"I'm sorry, Lyreko," Swirl said.

"This another mood," he said.

"What?"

"You flips all the time. Go cold, switch." He pointed a finger at his temple. "You be sunlight later."

"No." The forcefulness of it surprised even Swirl. "I won't. Not remotely."

His expression shifted, lightened. "Bitch," he said. "Can never tune who you are. Know that? Who the fucks are you?"

"Someone you're far too dull to comprehend."

She moved to step away, but Lyreko threw a palm against the mirror behind her, blocking her path. Swirl grabbed his arm and spun him around. She locked Lyreko's elbow, forcing him to his knees.

"Deep breaths," she told him. "Calm. We're allies, friends. But it's over."

Lyreko struggled and she pushed at his elbow. He groaned.

"Ask yourself what you'll do without me, Lyreko," she said. "Think you'll get your own leaf, hmm? Where would you even start?"

He ceased struggling.

"Smoosh," he said. "'Kay."

"Imagine your life *without* leaf," she said.

"*Okay.*"

"Now go," Swirl said. "Give me my space."

She let go. Lyreko leaped to his feet and spun to face her, fists clenched, red-faced save for the patch around his eye.

"Interesting," she murmured. "Let's see how that works for you."

He stared at her. Feral eyes. Then he stormed away, the hatch-door slamming behind him.

:Everything fine?: Sparkle sent.

"Listening in?" Swirl said.

:No,: Sparkle sent. *:I was on the beach and the sky began to grey.:*

"Oh," Swirl said. "Set off the adrenalin alarm, I see."

:Only a little,: Sparkle sent. *:But enough for me to venture out and risk a UFC.:*

"Sorry?"

:Unexpected Feral Cock.:

"Well, rejoice," Swirl said. "Your liberty is at hand."

:Pardon?:

"Lyreko and I are over." Swirl slumped down on the bed and tried to work a boot onto her right foot.

Sparkle was silent awhile. *:That's... unexpected,:* she said eventually.

"Is it? Is it really, Sparkle?"

:What are you insinuating?: Sparkle sent.

"What I'm *saying*, Sparkle, is any affection is doomed out here. Every time one of us picks up a toy, the other spits out her dummy and whines." Her damn boot refused to go on. 'We're cursed, living out here."

:I was happy for you.: Sparkle sent.

"No one's here," Swirl said. "May as well speak it."

"I was *happy* for you," Swirl felt her lips say. "In my way."

"Sparkle," Swirl said. "Why is it you're always the last one to realise you're miserable?"

"Because I take pompous questions like that in the spirit they weren't intended," Sparkle replied.

Swirl said nothing. She finally buckled the damn boot and set to work on the other.

"Swirl," she felt her lips say. "Let's be realistic here. And you know how much I abhor that, so you know I must be serious. We're never going to have an authentic love life out here in the feral spaces, and not because we're a Triune lost amid monominds. Ferals are simply not long-term prospects."

"We're not a Triune," Swirl said, pulling her dreadlocks into a ponytail. "Not anymore."

"Exactly. Even back home we'd be damaged goods. With Pearl tethered--"

"We do not talk about Pearl," Swirl said.

Swirl felt her lips readying to speak. Then they loosened.

"We do not talk about Pearl," they repeated eventually.

TWO

HARGIE SHUFFLED OUT OF THE DOCKING PIPE and onto the bay floor. The rig's scrubbed air filled his nostrils. Not an ideal night's sleep, that, lying in the gravel back on Import. A four-hour flight hadn't helped. Maybe he'd grab a couple of hours after lunch while his passengers got up to whatever nefarious pursuits awaited them. Clothes shopping, hopefully.

"So that was bubble travel," Illik said behind him.

"Afraid not, sir," Hargie said, smiling at the old man and his son. "Real bubble jump's for between systems. That was just sub-bub. G-wave."

"I'll get to experience it later, then, when we leave," Illik said.

"Leave for where?" Hargie said.

"Qur'bella sector," Illik said.

Hargie nearly had a coughing fit.

"Are you fine?" Illik asked. "You can take us, yes?"

"That's months away," Hargie said.

"You have other plans?"

Hargie shrugged. "Depends on the food court here..."

"My son and I pay assiduous professionals well." Illik studied Hargie's expression. "That would be you, Mr. Stukes."

"Right," Hargie said. "I mean, yeah, that's a given."

"Well?"

Hargie looked at the two men. The lakh would be useful. But weeks in a cramped bubbleship with Professor Strangenuts and his ogre child?

"Okay," Hargie said, "but I have to take someone along for the journey."

"Who?" Illik said.

"Anyone." Hargie cleared his throat. "What I mean is, to justify such a long journey--"

"No one," Doum growled.

"As my son says," Illik told Hargie.

"Six lakh," Hargie said.

"Twelve," Illik said.

"Erm. Okay." Illik was insane, clearly. "You drive a hard bargain. Pay me eight now, rest later." He'd take the eight and run.

"Mr. Stukes," Illik said, his face cracking to a grin, "we were rather hoping you'd come along. We've a fascinating business, my family. A business, yet a sort of game. Besides..." He placed a hand on Hargie's shoulder. "I wanted you to meet my daughter."

Father and son chuckled.

"Twelve lakh now," Illik said, "'twelve lakh later."

Hargie blinked. A man with twenty-four lo-los could quit the bubble game for a year. Kick back somewhere, let the jumpjunk pour out. And, well, this talk of a daughter, the knowing chuckles? Maybe generosity ran through the family. It had, well, been some time...

But why? What the fist-thrown-fuck was their game?

Hargie looked at the two men. In times like this, when uncertainty hovered, Hargopal Stukes fell back on the ancient bubblefolk philosophy of empathic rationalism. Empathic rationalism argued that, given the vastness of all things and the super-numerousness of human individuals therein, the overwhelming likelihood was that you and your worldview sat somewhere in the overall average, deep in the bell curve. You were nothing special. Statistically, then, the opinions and temperament of anyone you met would almost certainly resemble your own.

He didn't know if its logic stood up, not really--life had beaten him almost agnostic on the matter--but Hargie still lived and breathed, so...

So the question was why would *he* behave like Illik and Doum, if he *were* Illik and Doum? Well now... if Hargie were super-rich, he probably *would* throw credit around like confetti. Why ever not? And if he were pretending to be super-rich, it would be because he was either trying to rip someone off or make them look foolish, likely both.

Risk oft spewed reward. And he'd nothing else to do. That idiotic bubblefolk need to fill a hole. Bet high.

"Fifteen now, fifteen later," he said.

"Done," Illik said, and offered his thumb tip. Hargie pressed his own against it and let fifteen--fucking fifteen!--lakh into his neural account.

    *

Sat in the cable pod, chewing his last bite of noodlurrito, Hargie questioned his reasoning. Life had made him gullible by heritage, cynical by experience. He knew that. Arguably it was the manner of all bubblefolk. Looking at Illik and Doum--sat either side of him in the otherwise empty pod, dammit--he wondered if he'd become the very blueprint of his people's idiocies.

"Anthropology," Illik said out of nowhere. "That is our business here."

"Anthropology," Doum repeated. He studied the stars beyond the windows.

"Tell me, Mr. Stukes," Illik said, oddly chattier now. "Do you take an interest in the ways of other peoples?"

"Be dead if I didn't," Hargie said.

"Ha." Illik slapped his palm on Hargie's knee. "Mr. Stukes, today we encounter a mysterious people in possession of an enigmatic narcotic. My daughter walks with them, observes them."

"This a drug deal?" It made a kind of sense.

"For them, yes," Illik said, gazing at another cable-pod passing the window. The pod's four corner-cables had a strange stillness as it passed along them, unlike any on a world. "But for us this is..."

"Anthropology," Hargie finished.

"Yes, Mr. Stukes." He squeezed Hargie's knee and let go. Hargie wasn't cozy with this sudden leg tendency. "But you'll get your money, have no fear."

Doum grunted. A laugh? Yes: mockery. As if these men found wealth and barter a joke. Like Hargie was a dumb mutt and they kept feigning to toss a ball.

Their cable-pod approached the outermost ships of the rig's sunward chain now. The sun's edge rose over their hulls, dappling their supra-graphene features gold.

"The ship we're visiting," Hargie said to Illik. "Your daughter's, is it?"

"No," Illik replied. "Hers is elsewhere. The ship is rig-owned, confiscated from a bankrupt, I imagine. A public area."

Smoosh. The rig's equivalent of a dark alley, one with generous storage space for bubbleman corpses. Well, Hargie still had his neuralware. The rig's security was but a call and a cable journey away. If, y'know, they'd bother.

The ship lay ahead. A system corvette, a hundred yards long and a century old. No lights.

"Come," Illik said to his two companions. "Illumination awaits us."

The three of them stood before the cabin-pod's doors, Illik in the middle. The pod connected with the ship's docking unit, and the sudden inertia danced with the fear in Hargie's belly. The noodluritto, too.

The doors whirled open, and they stepped into a near-darkness. The air smelled of dust and sealed packaging. A tight cargo bay.

"Lights," Illik said.

The lights came on and two pistols stared at the three of them. They were in the hands of two shitscum, rig-gangers by the look of 'em. One man, one woman.

"Don't move," said the man, pale-skinned with a bad derma-job around his right eye that left it smoother and browner than the rest of him. "Gonna frisk."

"Feel free," Illik told him. "You'll find we are unarmed."

"Silence," said the woman. Short blue dreadlocks and skin dark as skin got.

The man worked them over like an octopus. His palms trembled.

"Smoosh, Sunlight," he told the woman once he'd finished. He strode back to her, trained his gun on Hargie and his clients once more.

"We were meant to wait for *you*," Illik told the gangers.

"Thought we'd come earlies," the man said. "Sorry if we're causing any, y'know, discomforts."

"Oh, you needn't have worried," Illik said. "We always see to our own comfort. Always. Hello, Zo."

"Hello... daddy."

The voice--female, amused--came from the darkness behind the gangers. The male ganger spun around in its direction, but not his comrade, the blue-haired woman. She grimaced, sure, but kept her piece on Illik. Impressive, Hargie had to admit.

A young woman stepped out of the dark. She wore some soft black body armour, and her hair was cut like the singer from Mute Elation: all shaved but for a black fringe and two short pigtails jutting upwards and outwards. She had two pistols trained on the two gangers.

It occurred to Hargie that the cable-pod doors were still open behind him. With the ganger-woman's pistol trained in his direction, it would be dopey to run, of course. But should everyone's attention be taken elsewhere--a gunfight, say--discretion was but a back-step and a button-prod away.

"Well," Illik said, "what a comfortable diorama this is."

"So," the male ganger said, "how cans we help you?"

"I was hoping my daughter's gift, the violent effort she went to, might assure you of our good faith," Illik said.

"The faces?" the male ganger said, his gun trained on the girl. "A food hamper would have cut it."

"Zo here has observed you a while," Illik continued. "It seems you are purveyors of a product we wish to procure. That is what you *do*, is it not?"

"Guess," the man said.

"Then you shall lower your pistols, Zo shall do likewise, and we can talk." Saying that, Illik nodded to Zo and the girl, quite casually, holstered her pistols. Too casually for Hargie's liking.

The male ganger nodded and holstered his gun.

The female ganger didn't.

"Who do you represent?" she asked Illik, her voice clipped, accent plummy. Hargie couldn't place it.

"We're a family business," Illik said.

"It's smoosh," the man-ganger said to the woman. "Stow your piece."

The woman ignored him. "I control the... 'product'," she told Illik with a vicious sneer. "I do not bless just anyone with it."

"We pay very well," Illik said. "Ask our bubbleman friend here."

All eyes fell on Hargie. He pulled out a cigarette and lit it.

"My advice?" he told the gangers. "Push for five. Settle for fifty."

The ganger-woman squinted at him. She returned her gaze to Illik.

"It's not the money," the ganger-woman told Illik. "It's the product itself. The gift which it bestows."

"A fascinating attitude," Illik said, and for the first time he sounded genuinely surprised. "If enigmatic. Where *are* you from?"

"That's my business," the ganger-woman said.

"The same place this 'leaf' comes from?" Illik said.

"Who's asking?"

"I would be fascinated to know," Illik said. "We've a sympathy for those who recognise money as a bauble and a weight. Credit merely paves a way, does it not? We feel your leaf could be important. It may have important work to do."

The woman kept her stance a while, either considering Illik's words or some inner counsel, then lowered her pistol. "Fine," she said. "But one condition."

"Name it," Illik said.

"I come with you," The woman said. "See your operation."

"That may be problematic," Illik said.

"Meeting over," she said.

"Fine," Illik said. He sighed; he smiled. "Fine."

"Sunlight?" the male ganger said to the woman. "You're leaving?"

The woman ignored him. "It's a deal," she told Illik.

"Wonderful," Illik said. "I believe there's a custom in moments like this..." He offered his hand out to shake. The woman took it, and reality exploded.

The room filled with what at first Hargie took to be light, intolerably bright blue light. But it consumed all detail, in all five senses. The taste of Hargie's cigarette vanished. The *idea* of tasting a cigarette remained, but the sense was gone. Same for everything else. Everything concept, essence. Hargie's body became abstract, more pure, more authentically *Hargie* than it had ever been, and yet physically not there at all. Everything a mirror: mirrors down to the very atom, reflecting and reflecting and reflecting beyond the horizon of awareness.

What was this? What in--

The male ganger had bloomed into an intricate star system of thought and feeling, one seized by a vast and sudden terror. What the fuck?

But that was as normal as this strange new crazy got. Illik and his two children weren't even *there*. They were voids, silhouettes of nothing. The blue light all around seemed to snap and prod and test their non-existence, a limitless beast furious at these three vacuums' affront.

And the woman, the ganger woman. She was a sort of... well, a *binary* system, a tree trunk rising into two boughs, branches and twigs intersecting in a complex matrix. And there, falling into the trunk, into the very depths of her, a sliver of Illik, a slice of his nothing-silhouette, somehow recognisably *him*.

An elongated figure, horned, appeared out of the haze. It had no eyes, no features save a fanged and grinning mouth. And yet it was the only thing that made any sense here, because Hargie had already met it, he just couldn't place where. The figure darted around the vacuum-people and the ganger-star-systems and rushed straight at Hargie.

Hargie felt the air punch out of him as he hit the cabin-pod's floor. Things were back as they were supposed to be. No more blue light. He could see and hear. He could feel pain.

Clambering, he brought himself back up on to his haunches. The light--the regular electric light--had gone out in the ship's cargo bay. His ass hurt. Had someone just pushed him into the cabin-pod?

Lightning sliced the darkness, followed by the familiar hammer-on-metal *tonk*, *tonk* of compaction rounds. Someone was pulling a trigger.

Hargie accessed his neuralware and commanded the pod doors to shut, requested to disembark. He leaped up onto the seating away from the door's shrinking metal iris. Something blue blurred through the dwindling gap, rolled along the cabin-pod's gangway and spun around, pointing a gun at the door. The ganger woman.

"Close the door," she told him.

"I was!" he said. "You slowed it!"

A round bounced off the closing metal, then the door sealed shut. The warm *clunk* sound was bourbon to Hargie's ears.

He turned to see a pistol muzzle trained on his head.

"Don't move," said the woman. She stood half a foot taller than him. "Don't say a thing."

He didn't even nod. Wisest course.

The cabin-pod disconnected and lurched away from the ship. The woman seemed ready for Hargie to use that lurch, but no way. He wasn't gonna do shit.

"Face-down on the floor," she said. "Slowly."

Hargie lowered himself onto the gangway floor, heard her stand up. A gun *behind* your head always felt worse. Just like Father...

"I'm not one of them," he blurted.

"I know that." She paused. "He said you were hired."

"I've kids," he lied. At least he assumed he lied. "Please, lady, imagine how they'd take it."

The woman shrieked.

Hargie flinched, but nothing happened. "Yeah," Hargie said, uncertain. "Something like that, I guess..."

His confusion subsided when a hand, mummified and steaming, fell in front of his face.

"Was still in my palm..." she muttered.

Illik's hand, then. They'd been shaking hands when it all went freak-o. Illik must have... well, exploded? Illik's burnt aroma filled Hargie's nostrils. He was too frightened to be sick.

"What happened just now?" Hargie asked the woman. "All that weird shit? That happened, right?"

"You're a bubbleman," she said.

"Yeah," Hargie said.

"So you've a ship?" she asked.

"Uh-huh."

"Get up and sit over there," she told him.

"Thank-you-sir. Lady." He did.

She sat too, on the seats facing his, gun still pointing. She inspected the palm of her other hand. "Listen," she said, "I want to get off this rig."

"Heading that way myself," Hargie said.

"I'll pay. Pay good. I'm merely pointing this gun for now."

"Call it a retainer," Hargie said.

"And don't neural security," she said. She winced. "There's a block-fi, localized, I got..." she sighed and muttered something like 'lyric oil' or 'leery-co'. She looked painfully sad.

"You hurt your hand," Hargie said.

The woman almost replied, but then the pod lurched to a standstill. It near-threw them out of their chairs. The woman sat back upright and trained the gun on him.

"See?" Hargie said with a smile. "Not a funny move on me." He just wanted out of the pod. He'd evade her later.

She sensed truth in his words, Hargie was sure. Leastways, she got up and went to see why the pod had stopped.

Hargie could have told her: the weirdos must have cut the power. But she'd figure that soon enough.

The woman stared out of the end window, back in the direction of the old corvette. She muttered something in a tongue not Anglurati.

"A problem?" he asked.

"It is a chase now," she said, still gazing out.

Hargie stood up and looked. He couldn't see anything unusual.

"What?" he said. "No other pods out there."

"They're on foot."

Hargie ambled to the window, a liberty the woman seemed too occupied to take offence at. It was then Hargie saw it: a black figure walking along the bottom left cable like a tightrope walker. No net save the endless void.

"They can't get in here," Hargie said.

"Not the plan," the woman said. "They've a gun."

"It'd bounce off the glass," Hargie said.

"Press a compaction muzzle hard against it, fire on full power and tell me again."

"Right," Hargie said. "Wouldn't that kill them too? Maybe?"

"Look at them, idiot," she said. "Do you think self-preservation their key skill?"

The figure was a little closer. The daughter. Hargie recognised the black bodysuit, now complete with helmet. Her progression wasn't fast--why should it be?--but it was the diligence that unnerved, the casual comfort.

"Surrender?" Hargie offered.

"Idiot," the woman said.

"No, really," Hargie said. "We just drop the gun and wave to her."

"Good idea," she said. "Let's wave with her dead father's burnt hand over there."

"Point taken."

The woman stomped away from the window and began to pace around the cabin-pod's interior, her head down. She was like a... well, *caged animal* wasn't the sort of imagery Hargie needed to contemplate right then.

The woman growled to herself. "Oh, fine then!" she barked at no one. "Why *ever* not!"

"Why what?" Hargie asked.

The woman ignored him. She appeared to freeze up a moment, rocking on her heels. Then she spun to face Hargie. She gave him the loveliest smile, a railgun shot through Hargie's heart. He wouldn't have thought her capable.

"Hey," she said. "Could you hold this a moment?"

She offered him her pistol. Confused, he took it.

"Thanks," she said. With that, she pulled a handheld from her jacket and started scanning the fixtures.

What was this? Hargie had the gun now.

He had to think this over.

Yes, empathic rationalism, the way of his forefathers. He looked out at Illik's daughter. If he were her, what would he do? Vengeance. Sheer bloody vengeance, no matter who got in the way. Like he was long meant to be doing, he thought.

He turned to face the woman, who now had her back to him, bent over, trying to dislodge a seat cushion.

Shoot her. Just shoot her. She wouldn't know. This was a him-or-her scene, bet your ball sack, Jack. He could... well, he could lift her body up to the window and Illik's daughter would know, and she and her brother would see Hargie was on the level, that he honoured their father or at least his money. Really, what choice was there?

He lifted the pistol and aimed. Then he positioned himself in a dramatic pose so that Illik's daughter--Zo, was it Zo? Lovely Zo--would see him shoot.

Wait. He might shoot through the hull. No. No, velocity too low. She'd already used it just now in the cargo bay, no problem.

Shoot her. Stop groping for excuses, shoot. Hargie aimed again. Cry later.

Wait. Why'd she pass him the gun, anyhow? Which was to say, if *Hargie* were *her*, why would he pass a damn gun? Good question. Well... well, there must be a lot of elements Hargie wasn't privy to. Elements that would make undeniable sense if Hargie were her. But what?

She trusted him, he realised. Trust.

Hargie lowered the pistol.

"What are you doing?" he asked her.

"This model of cable-pod," the woman explained, "is built in a certain system." She got the cushion off and threw it to one side. "There's a regular world there, and another where humans have fixed themselves to breathe 'dioxide. For that system's rigs, then, the life support needs to be a little more hands on. Mm-yes." She stood up and pointed at the seat with her good hand. "Could you shoot this off?"

He offered her the gun.

"Oh no, I'm useless with those things," she said.

Hargie didn't know what to say to that. He set his mind to the task. There was a lid on the white metal of the seat, with an inbuilt lock. Hargie braced, then fired. He fired again. The lock flew off.

"Thank you," said the woman, and she knelt down once more. She flipped open the lid and waved her handheld over the tiny processor inside. She ran a hack. Had to feel sorry for her, using a handheld in a neural age. Allergic to the 'ware. Shitty deal.

"Sit down," she told him.

The cable-pod began to roll forward. Hargie had expected to be thrown back in a sudden burst of momentum. No such. A tortoise-crawl.

"Engine damaged?" he said, sitting down.

"No," she replied, sitting next to him. "I've uncoupled our air supply. That's what's propelling the pod now."

"Clever. I think."

"Best to stop talking now," the woman told him. "Not much air."

Hargie opened his mouth. Then he closed it. The pair of them gazed out of the rear window. Illik's daughter wasn't out there on her tightrope anymore. Hargie looked quizzically at the woman.

"Whoosh," the woman said and she made a tiny Illik's daughter of her hand, cartwheeling off into a figurative eternity. Nasty.

The woman put her palm out and waited. Shrugging, Hargie gave back the gun. In return, the woman picked up Illik's scorched hand--her earlier squeamishness had vanished--and placed it in Hargie's jacket pocket. Hargie shuddered.

She smiled. "Analysis," she said.

An hour or so later, Hargie was surprised to find he still lived when the cable-pod docked with the rig's terminal zone. The pair of them lay on the floor by then, gasping for breath.

"Sparkuh..." the woman said as the doors whirled open and air rushed in.

"Whu..." Hargie said.

"Sparkle. Name's Sparkle. That's the name. Sparkle."

"Oh."

"Sparkle."

*

Sparkle had to hand it to that little slouching rodent of a man: he was a sort of artist. Somehow he'd manipulated the innards of his ship into a compelling abstract portrait of the feral mind. An installation piece in dust, gloom, and mechanical odour.

"Cockpit's through here," he told her, pointing to a bulkhead along the corridor. "But feel free to kick back in the lounge."

Sparkle had seen the lounge. It boasted a table, whose apparent sole function was displaying various planets' takeaway wrappers, and a large brown object that had recanted its sofa origins.

"Er..."

:Stay with him in the cockpit, idiot,: Swirl sent to Sparkle.

"I'll come see where it all happens," Sparkle told Hargie. "If it's all the same to you."

"You pay, you say," he replied. He looked at her a moment. "You're still paying, right?"

"Please, I'm not all pistol-whips and glares." She patted the pistol in her jacket pocket, if only to keep Swirl happy. In truth, she was surprised the man hadn't demanded it off her now they were aboard. "One lakh fifty. Another seven on reaching Calran."

"Appreciated," he said as he placed his thumb on her handheld and accepted the down payment.

###

Thank you for reading this excerpt of James Worrad's The Scalpel.
Would you like to complete the story?

Grab The Scalpel Here
Available on Kindle Unlimited

Made in the USA
Middletown, DE
09 April 2023

28299436R00099